TO KILL A WIFE

When Verna Hume is found strangled in her bedroom, Detective Inspector Peach is given the case by Superintendent Tucker who makes it clear he considers this an open and shut case, with the woman's husband clearly in the frame. DI Peach isn't convinced and once he meets the mild-mannered Martin Hume, he knows his reservations were justified. As a full-scale investigation gets under way, it soon becomes clear that Verna had a talent for inspiring hate in others and DI Peach finds himself dealing with not one—but six—murder suspects ...

TO KILL A WIFE

TO KILL A WIFE

by

J. M. Gregson

Gregson, J.M.
  To kill a wife.

© J.M. Gregson 1997 by J.M. Gregson

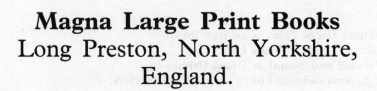

Magna Large Print Books
Long Preston, North Yorkshire,
England.

British Library Cataloguing in Publication Data.

Gregson, J.M.
　　To kill a wife.

A catalogue record for this book is
available from the British Library

ISBN 0-7505-1409-4

First published in Great Britain by Severn House Publishers
Ltd., 1999

Copyright © 1999 by J.M. Gregson

Published in Large Print 1999 by arrangement with Severn
House Publishers Ltd.

Magna Large Print is an imprint of
Library Magna Books Ltd.
Printed and bound in Great Britain by
T.J. International Ltd., Cornwall, PL28 8RW.

One

It was on a Wednesday evening that Martin Hume decided to kill his wife.

He sat alone in the comfortable, cheerless house. He had watched *A Question of Sport* with no great interest. The sitcom which followed seemed to him even more banal than usual. He had finished *The Times* crossword.

Murder came into his mind like an unexpected and welcome visitor, but it was not mere boredom which brought it there. He had often toyed with the thought of how Verna might die. She might have a heart attack at a moment of stress. Goodness knows, her life had enough stress: from her sexual excitements with others to her bizarre temper tantrums with him. She might succumb to a richly deserved skiing accident a thousand miles away from him. She might even walk obligingly under the proverbial bus. In his more baroque fantasies, she choked on her own vomit after one of her drinking bouts,

9

or fell backwards from a hotel balcony while taunting him, the lips which had been twisted in scorn rounding suddenly into a black hole of terror as she realised too late that she was dying.

But he knew in his heart that none of these things would come to pass. Convenient accidents were the stuff of fiction. Life just wasn't like that: not his life, anyway. Verna would go on filling it with misery; would no doubt outlive him.

Unless he took matters into his own hands. Murder. The thought sprang fully formed into his brain, clear and cold, as if he had walked under a waterfall. Within minutes, Martin could only wonder why he had never entertained the notion before.

Life was a fragile thing; there were reminders of that every day. Verna's wickedness might seem more than mortal, but even her life hung by but a slender thread. It just needed someone to cut that thread. This train of thought was so simple, so irrefutably logical that he should surely have followed it long ago.

He revolved his wife's death in his mind, picturing her corpse in a hundred different positions. Her expression in death was less varied: he saw her always with the same look of frozen surprise.

Time passes swiftly when one is enjoying oneself. Martin had repeated that old cliché among his few friends, often, as an irony. Now he found that over an hour had gone in a trice, as he explored the idea of making this thing happen. He could not remember when he had last enjoyed such simple, unalloyed pleasure as the thought of engineering Verna's death now afforded him.

While he allowed his mind to elaborate on this wonderful new idea, the television pictures flickered unseen before him and he was startled by the sound of Verna's key in the lock. He could scarcely believe it was five to eleven.

Martin feared for a moment that his resolve to kill her would show on his face. He need not have worried. She noticed nothing, and he wondered with a small, secret smile why he had feared her scrutiny. She never registered his emotions, did she? Unless he stood over her with a breadknife in his hand—one of the more vivid of the pictures he had painted for himself—she would never even suspect him.

He followed her into the kitchen,

11

watched her make coffee for herself and enjoyed rather than resented her failure to offer to make one for him. Her swift, graceful actions gave him pleasure now, as they had not done for months, even years. He could admire them dispassionately, as he might have enjoyed the silky movements of a leopard.

She reached up for the jar, and the loose dress fell away from her arm, leaving it as slim, brown and youthful as it had been when he had courted her thirteen years ago. She tossed the sleek black hair clear of the nape of her neck in that careless gesture he had once found so attractive. He caught the mingled scent of sweat and perfume from her armpits, imagined for an instant that he could catch upon her the scent of the man she had been with.

Verna's lie came right on cue, almost as if his thoughts had prompted it. 'Margaret sends her regards,' she said carelessly, stirring vigorously in the cup. 'I just wish she'd concentrated on her cards. Her bidding was as erratic as ever.'

Bridge was the usual excuse on Wednesdays. He wondered for a moment about the man who had been clasped by those slim brown arms tonight. How did he see

12

the woman who had given her husband so much pain? And what account, if any, did Verna give of that husband when she and her lover lay exhausted after copulation, staring at the ceiling of some room he would never see? That image gave him no pain now; he found that his own new secret had banished the last vestiges of those hot, hopeless jealousies which he had once striven so hard to control.

As Martin sat on the edge of the bed, Verna stood for a moment before him in her tiny, lace-edged pants, looking at herself over his head in the mirror, daring him to reach out and touch her. Then she peeled off the last of her clothes, stretched the limbs that in the subdued light of the bedroom were as lithe and unmarked as they had been when she was a bride, and climbed carefully into the space she had allotted to herself.

Husband and wife lay on the extreme edges of their king-size mattress, as far apart as if they had been in separate beds. They had not spoken since their brief exchanges in the kitchen half an hour earlier. Verna fell asleep quickly, as she always did. Martin lay on his back with his eyes closed, listening to her deep and regular breathing. Her easy, untroubled sleep had often seemed like another, unconscious, insult to his troubled soul. Henceforward, he decided, he would sleep in the room at the other end of the landing which he had always used after the worst of their rows.

But tonight he smiled in the darkness, listening to the quiet rhythms of his wife's sleep, hugging his secret like a comfort against his breast. Only he knew that Verna was going to die.

Two

The station dated from the prosperous days of Victorian railway mania. There had been six platforms once, and troop trains had carried Lancashire lads from here to the horrors of Gallipoli and the Somme, in the war to end all wars. The Great War that generation had always called it; it had produced not permanent peace but Hitler and his holocaust and another war. The platforms had dispatched Brunton men all over the globe, to a second catalogue of deaths.

The station was quieter these days. It had been given a new facade, an uneasy compromise with the urban development around it. But the ghosts of the past, of brave farewells and of raucously happy holiday week emptyings of the town, echoed still within its capacious interior. Martin Hume remembered waiting on the flagged platform for the Blackpool train as a small boy, before his father had bought their first car. The steam about which his father had spoken with such enthusiasm had gone by then, but the noise had still been deafening to his small ears as the monster roared into the station from the adjacent tunnel. Martin could recall even now how the grasp of his right hand had tightened nervously on his mother's gloved fingers, while his left clutched his bucket and spade, ready for the day of sun and sand which lay ahead.

The memories flooded back as he waited with only four other people in the high entrance hall, beneath a peeling sign over a long-disused Left Luggage Office. He looked through the archway to the day outside, checking that it was still fine for the three-minute walk back to his car. In the late morning of this April day, clouds scudded quickly across a bright blue sky, but rain was not far away. The remains of the last shower were still gathered in small puddles across the tarmac of the side road where the station lay.

The weather matched his mood. He always looked forward to the visits of his sister-in-law and her small son with a mixture of pleasure and apprehension. It was not because he had any fear of Sue, who was so different from her sister that she was a source of undiluted delight to him. His apprehension stemmed solely from the way experience told him that Verna would treat her sister and her nephew.

His disquiet dropped away as he saw Sue coming down the steps with Toby's small hand clasped carefully in hers. He saw her an instant before she saw him, and thus caught the small frown of concentration on her broad forehead which he found so attractive. When she spotted him, her face lit up with the open affection which made her at once so pretty and so vulnerable.

Sue was three years younger than her sister. He realised with a shock that she must now be thirty-two. She certainly did not look it. Part of her attraction to Martin

16

was the contrast in appearance between the sisters. Where Verna was willowy and dark, with shoulder-length black hair and eyes like charcoal, Sue was shorter, sturdy, with even a suggestion of plumpness. Her dark-blonde hair curled naturally and tightly, framing an active, open face. She had eyes of a remarkable blue; azure, he had heard it called, though he claimed no expertise in such things. There were freckles still faintly visible beneath her pale, smooth skin, and a tendency to blush, which she found embarrassing but he thought wholly becoming. Where Verna's face seemed designed to conceal and to hurt, Sue's was fashioned to reveal and to respond.

'What ho, Toby!' Martin called, and watched the small round face change from boredom to delight as swiftly as only a five-year-old's can.

'Can we go to the park?'

The child wasted no time on greetings. Long before he was installed in the car, Toby had established his priorities. The boy remembered his last visit and the fun they had had then. Martin felt absurdly flattered.

'Don't you go bothering Uncle Martin now,' said Sue, buckling the rear-seat safety

17

belt carefully around the small figure.

Toby's legs were so short that his sandals only reached to the edge of the seat; he twitched his toes experimentally, then shared a conspiratorial grin with Martin over the back of the driver's seat. With an infant's acuity, he was aware that the battle was already won: they were going to the park with the football. As the blue Mondeo moved away from the town and into the wallflowers and cherries of suburbia, the small boy sang tunelessly to himself.

Verna was waiting for them in the neat garden. She sized up the party unhurriedly as they left the car and came round the path to meet her. Then she said, 'You look well, Susan. Working life obviously suits you.' She always called her sister Susan, in defiance of her wishes and everyone else's practice, like an obstinate mother asserting her rights.

Sue said, 'I can manage the job at the office full time, now that Toby is at school.' She wondered why she was so certain that her sister's every comment was a veiled criticism, and why she had to rise to the bait and defend herself.

'I suppose it isn't too demanding,' said Verna dismissively. She turned her

18

attentions to Toby, visiting her most dazzling smile upon him. 'And how's the man of the house getting on? You get bigger every time I see you, young man. I shall have to hear all about that school, shan't I?'

Martin had thought of his wife as the Wicked Witch of the West as far as children were concerned; she had certainly been quite appalled at any suggestion that she should produce any of her own, even in the days when she had permitted him access to her precious body. Now, characteristically, she set out to charm her nephew. And succeeded.

She produced a jigsaw, the large pieces perfectly suited to the small chubby hands which her slim fingers guided over the mahogany of the little used dining-room table. Martin and Sue were left surveying the tops of the two bent heads, the tousled golden one so absorbed in its task, the dark one so conscious of the effect it was contriving, even as it uttered phrases of encouragement to the child who pressed against her side.

'Make us all a coffee, will you?' Verna said without looking up. It was a demand, not a request. And it could have been addressed to either of the observers.

Martin and Sue found themselves together in the kitchen, combining, without a word, upon the simple task allotted to them. They were too inhibited to speak, too aware of the ears beneath the black hair in the dining room beyond the open door, of the brain registering with an amused contempt their every action and reaction.

They were halfway through lunch before Verna mentioned the husband who had left her sister two years earlier. 'Do you hear much from Bernard?' she asked casually. She was helping herself to salad, shaking the olive oil carefully from the greenstuff, as though that and not her question was her main concern.

'I don't hear at all,' said Sue, a little too quickly, as if she had been waiting for the matter to be raised. 'And that suits me. I hope I never see him again!'

'Oh dear!' Verna shook her head with a small, secret smile. 'It's always so sad, I think, when a relationship which once promised so much leads to such bitterness. A pity it couldn't end in a more civilised way. But men's attentions stray so easily, once you allow them to do so.'

She was being the mother again to

Sue, thought Martin, and the worst, most insufferable kind of mother, who saw the departure of a man as wholly the fault of a wife who had not striven hard enough to keep him. He had never known the mother of these very different daughters: she had died when Verna was twelve and Sue was nine. He wondered what that long-dead woman would have thought of the way her elder daughter treated her husband, of the casual pieces of contempt Verna reserved for him, of her string of equally casual affairs.

Sue did not want to talk about Bernard. She found her hands creeping up the fabric of her loose dress and caressing her shoulders which had been so often bruised by her husband's drunken blows in the last months of their marriage. It was as if she needed to reassure herself, even at this distance, that the flesh was healed and unmarked. She had never told Verna about those blows, and she would not do so now. She said grimly, 'Bernard has got out of our lives. All I ask is that he stays out.'

'Well, you know best, Susan, I'm sure. It just seems such a pity.' Verna smiled. 'He was rather gorgeous, after all. And so well

21

endowed.' Verna smiled reminiscently, so that both her listeners were left wondering if she had extended her voracious sexual attentions to her brother-in-law at some time; it was exactly the speculation she had intended to plant. 'And it's always such a pity when children are involved. I'm sure Toby misses his father.'

At the sound of his name, the child's open face turned expectantly towards the aunt who had amused him so expertly before the meal, and Sue leant automatically towards him in protection. 'Toby was scarcely three when Bernard left. I'm sure he barely remembers him. And that's how I want it to stay.'

She put her arm protectively round the small body. The child, who understood nothing of the reasons, picked up the tension between two of the adults upon whom he depended; she felt the young muscles tightening.

Verna watched mother and son for a moment. Then she shrugged. 'It's a pity you feel so defensive about it, but it's understandable, I suppose.' Her gesture said that anyone with reasonable personal resources would have made a much better job of things.

Immediately after the meal, Martin took the insistent Toby to the spacious park which the burghers of the town had established a century earlier for the benefit of Brunton's hard-working citizens. He was apprehensive about leaving the sisters together, but his nephew was not to be denied. He trotted impatiently along the half mile to the broad expanse of grass beside the towering trees.

Toby's vigour and enthusiasm outstripped his skill, as was natural for a five-year-old, but his strength and balance had improved considerably in the six months since they had last been here. He managed to give the light plastic ball several resolute thumps with his right foot, though when Martin encouraged him to try to kick with his left foot, he fell into a hilarious heap without making contact. By the end of their session together, he was learning to time his kick on a moving ball, as Martin rolled it slowly towards him.

He was tiring now, flushed with excitement and effort, but when Martin announced that this was definitely the last one, the boy watched the ball with fierce concentration as it bobbled slowly towards him, then crashed it joyously past his uncle and into the corner of the goal they had set up between the two young oak trees. Adult and child were equally delighted.

Martin clutched the ball under one arm and stretched out the other to take charge of the small, hot hand. They made for the ice-cream stall and the two cones which were the perfect culmination of their half hour's exuberance. Then they walked past the lake with its ducks and swans, and Toby looked with the disdain of a practising footballer at the scene of which he had once been part, where infants threw bread at their parents' direction to the quacking hordes.

Toby chattered excitedly all the way back to the house, while his uncle grew silent, wondering what exchanges were taking place between the two very different women who awaited them there.

It was obvious that there had been enmity and high words. Verna's brow was creased, her dark eyes narrowed and trained upon the carpet. She roused herself at the sight of the boy, but the effort of will she had raised to charm him during the morning was beyond her now.

Toby was both excited and tired. He spilt his orange drink as he chattered about

24

their football in the park, and a blob of cream from his cake fell first onto his shirt and then to the carpet. Verna made a great show of cleaning the carpet vigorously with detergent and mop, a domestic activity which Martin could never recall her doing before.

She muttered to her sister about standards, and how she wouldn't have expected anything else. Martin saw Sue's white teeth pulling vigorously, almost viciously at her lower lip, and willed her not to respond. She did not: nor did she look at him. She had grown up with Verna, and seemed to realise that any searching for outside support would make things worse.

It was, on the surface, just a ridiculous family spat, and Martin tried without success to place it as no more than that. This aggression, this raw malice towards the child after her morning affection, was only the inconsistency he would have expected from his wife. But at that moment it seemed very important. He was pleased with the control Sue showed, just as he felt a small triumph in the annoyance her silence caused to Verna.

When the time came for the visitors to leave, Verna hugged the boy tightly against her for a moment in a caricature of affection, telling him he must come again soon. No one, not even Toby, believed that she meant it. She said the curtest of goodbyes to her sister, and did not even bother to issue any instructions to Martin as he went with them to the car.

Neither Martin nor Sue spoke for several minutes in the moving car, as if they feared that the woman they had left behind might somehow still hear them. Through the rear-view mirror of the Mondeo, Martin watched Toby's head nodding as his eyelids drooped; in two minutes, he was happily asleep in his harness.

The car moved carefully along the quiet suburban roads. Sue watched the hedges and the flowering crab apples dropping smoothly away behind them. Presently she said, 'I don't suppose she intends to hurt so much.'

It took Martin a long time to reply. Eventually, he said, 'You don't believe that.' This felt like a conversation taking place in slow motion.

'No, I don't suppose I do. Most of the pain she causes is carefully calculated.'

He wondered what exactly had passed between the two sisters when he was at the park with Toby. He had enough experience of his wife's malice to make a fair guess at the lines of battle.

The wide station approach was deserted on this bright Sunday afternoon. Though he had driven slowly, they had ten minutes yet before the train was due. Neither of them had been anxious to linger in that loveless house.

Martin drew the car to a stop with extreme care, watching the small innocent face in his mirror. Toby slept on, his head tilted forward, the fine childish hair dropping forward over his forehead.

Martin was aware of Sue looking at him from the seat beside him. He turned to look into the round, gentle face within its frame of golden curls. He expected to notice the faint freckling, which made her seem still so young; instead, he was conscious only of those remarkable bright-blue eyes. They seemed larger than he had ever seen them. Perhaps it was the moisture brimming at their margins which magnified the irises, affording them this remarkable dominance over the surrounding features of her face.

He made no conscious movement, yet he found himself kissing the broad, soft lips. And the lips welcomed him. Tremulous at first, they hardened a little in response. Sue's arms crept around his shoulders. He wanted to freeze the moment, the softness, the unspoken harmony. The tip of her tongue slipped gently, experimentally, between his lips, then rested for a moment against his teeth.

It was Sue who eventually withdrew, but scarcely more than an inch. Just far enough to say tremulously into his ear, 'We can't, Martin.'

He kissed her again, savouring once more that gentle, unforced response. It gave him confidence. He held her at arm's length, without letting her go.

The idea of killing Verna, which had so dominated his thoughts for the last four days, now seemed to have a context, an additional logic he had never entertained before. He felt a mastery which he thought Verna had long since destroyed returning to him.

Martin said simply, 'We can, Sue. There are ways of making things happen. Just trust me.'

Three

Verna Hume had grown familiar over the weeks with the Velux window in this roof. No sound came through the double-glazed rectangle above her as she lay on the bed, reinforcing the illusion she cherished that she existed here in a private and better world of her own.

Lines came back to her from a poem she had studied years ago at school for A level,

For love, all love of other sights controls,
And makes one little room, an everywhere.

John Donne it was, and a poem she thought she had long forgotten. The old boy knew a thing or two about sex and love. Well, this big attic room was now their world, hers and Hugh's, and they would make it spin to their command.

She looked again at that soundless glass skylight, the only indication of that other, harsher world outside this room and her love. Today the rectangle was blue. She liked that bright, uncomplicated colour, with its promise of the sun somewhere else in the sky outside. But she had enjoyed looking at the rectangle last time, too, when the rain had run in swift rivulets down the slope of the glass and the grey wall of cloud above had seemed to be almost caressing the roof of the building. She was aware that she would have been well pleased with the appearance of that small section of sky, whatever its colour. Love had that effect.

She recognised that what she felt for Hugh was love. It had begun like her other affairs, as a snatched interval of breathy physical gratification. Then pleasure had turned into passion, and passion into love. She had been surprised, and a little frightened. But love, even if you could never quite define the word, was what she felt. She was surely experienced enough to know her own reactions by now. She smiled, stretching her limbs luxuriously beneath the sheet, happy in that reflection.

The man who came through the heavy wooden door from the living room had fair hair and a nose that was just a little too prominent between his bright-blue eyes. He did not look at her but she liked that, taking the opportunity to watch his movements from between half-closed eyes.

He undressed discreetly at his side of the bed. Verna thought that it was a myth that men were less inhibited about these things than women. Hugh had been here when she undressed, but she had stepped out of her clothes without embarrassment, erect and firm, only just resisting the impulse to study her statuesque figure in the wardrobe's full-length mirror when she got to bra and pants. Janet Reger helped in these things, no doubt, but it was nice to know that what little she concealed was properly formed. It gave a certain confidence.

Hugh, on the other hand, sat on the edge of the bed and slid his boxer shorts discreetly over his invisible ankles. Verna slid an affectionate index finger down his naked back. 'Shy boy,' she teased, with that little throaty half-giggle which he found so exciting.

He stopped for a moment, enjoying her touch on his flesh, catching her mischievous eye in the mirror. 'I remember it being said

31

that a woman in just her stockings is very erotic, whereas a man in just his socks is always ludicrous. I take these axioms to heart, you see, even though I can't remember who says them.'

'Alan Plater,' she said, 'in a television play.' She was proud of her memory, and Hugh, unlike some men, didn't mind his women being clever. Woman, she corrected herself. He was only going to have one, in the future. They must talk about the future. But just now there were more urgent things in hand. Or almost in hand.

They were easy with each other beneath the single sheet. 'Shy boy's become big boy now!' she breathed into his ear, but it was less a joke than an acceleration of energy and joy. He took her violently, as she liked, and she shouted her pleasure at the friendly rectangle of blue above her, yelling the urgent four-letter imperatives at Hugh which excited them both; feeling his passion rise, exulting as it spilt uncontrollably within her.

She lay still for long minutes, feeling the two of them as one, unwilling to break the spell. Then she began to knead the large muscles beneath his shoulder blades.

Under these long smoothings of love, she felt his body stir, then slacken and relax still further. 'My love,' she whispered, in an exquisite lethargy. 'Oh, my love!'

It was Hugh who eventually broke the spell. 'I have to go, darling,' he said.

How lightly people used that word! And how glad Verna was still to hear it on Hugh's lips. 'Back to the wife you've hidden from me for all these weeks?' she asked, enjoying the teasing, testing her own confidence in him and finding it still secure, as she had known she would.

'Back to work, my girl,' he said with a grin, levering himself on to his hands above her and savouring her flushed face amid the spread of her long black hair on the pillow for a final moment. 'Got to earn a crust, you know.'

He shot quickly into the shower as she reached her hand towards his back. When he emerged from the dressing room, it was in collar and tie, with his blond hair carefully combed. She liked the contrast between this public, sharp-suited persona and the intimacy of the naked lover she had just enjoyed.

'He must be an important chap to drag you away from my charms so abruptly.'

33

'Wrong on two counts. My departure wasn't abrupt. And it isn't a man.' He grinned down at her, enjoying the little wrinkle of doubt which flickered across the smooth oval of her face. 'It's a woman. A rich widow, as a matter of fact. So I need to be at my smartest.' He checked his tie in the mirror, pretending not to study her reaction behind him.

'How rich? How old?'

He laughed. 'Very rich. And sixty-eight. She wants to know how to invest the ill-gotten gains of a husband who wrote himself into some hefty share option schemes but forgot about heart attacks.'

'She sounds as though she needs your services almost as much as I do.'

'She does. But not the same ones. She's refurbishing an office with new computers. Very expensive ones, I expect, when I've finished giving her the benefit of my expert advice.'

Verna sat up in the bed. 'I'll see you on Saturday, then. And we need to talk. To make some plans.'

'Sounds ominous.'

'It isn't. You know it isn't. But suddenly, with you, I'm happy to think about the future. I want to organise it.'

He looked up from the shoelace he was tying, serious for a moment. She loved him for that, too: the ability to recognise when things really mattered to her. 'I know. We'll find the time. It's just that there always seem to be more urgent things, when we're together.' He glanced for a moment at her calf, straying out from the sheet, and her bare shoulders, then into her dark, humorous eyes.

'I'm trying hard to blush, but I can't make it.' She reached her arms up to him, and they kissed briefly before he left.

She waited until the last note of his car engine died away, then showered and dressed unhurriedly. She liked being alone in Hugh's flat and the feeling of trust it left with her. The porter was in the hall when she stepped out of the lift. He said good afternoon politely, as she moved towards the high double doors and the street outside. Almost, she thought, as if I were already a wife here.

A cab purred obligingly alongside her before she had walked thirty yards but she ignored it, choosing instead the circuitous bus route. It would give her time to compose herself, time to become again that other person who lived out a half-life with Martin Hume.

As the green and cream bus moved ponderously along the side of the park, with its spring blossoms and fresh greens, she reflected on her relationship with Martin, a thing she had refused to contemplate for years. He thought her a slag. She knew that. And as far as he was concerned, he was right.

She often wondered why she treated him so badly. He asked for it, of course, but that was too easy an answer. For months she had had no feeling for him but contempt, but she now felt pity, a stirring of guilt within herself. They said that love lit up one's whole being, making one more generous towards others as well as the loved one. Perhaps it would be so. She would behave better to Martin in these last weeks of their relationship than she had for years.

She would even be able to give him the divorce she had refused so often. Maybe he would take up with that goody-two-shoes sister of hers. For the first time, she felt no impulse to destroy anything those two might have. It was true then: love was a benign influence, spreading its ambience outwards to a wider circle.

It was only as she walked the short distance from the bus to her home that a tiny anxiety pricked her. Hugh had avoided talking about their long-term future together. Again.

Four

Once he had decided that he was going to kill his wife, Martin Hume remained calm and relaxed in the months which followed.

Verna's steady stream of petty cruelties seemed unimportant, now that he could see an end to them. An end, moreover, which he would control. She would die when he determined she should. And where he chose. And how he chose. It was many years since he had felt so much in command of his own life and the course it was going to take.

His work improved. He had always been a competent accountant, but his employers had noticed a decline in imagination and commitment as his marriage tumbled into disaster. They had confined him of late

37

to routine clients, where the work was straightforward and the possibilities limited. Now he began to show a new confidence and a new interest, and his colleagues became aware of him again as a man, not a cypher; a man with his own views and preferences, rather than the unnoticed automaton he had become.

Martin began to go to the pub for lunch with his fellows, as he had not done for years. He indulged again in the office banter which had by-passed him for so long, enjoyed teasing and being teased. As he saw his revival remarked among the men and women around him, he was amused. But he was careful to keep the source of it concealed.

He hugged his secret to himself, treasuring it as a diamond beyond price. A dangerous diamond, of course: no one must even suspect why he was suddenly the Martin of old. But when he was sure of his privacy, when he was locked in the lavatory cubicle at work, or on one of his long, solitary walks, or on his own in Wycherly Croft, the detached house he had bought to house the family he had never had, he revelled in the knowledge of what he was going to do.

There was no hurry. It was important that what he was going to do was planned to the last detail. If anyone suspected he was guilty of his wife's murder, the whole point and the whole benefit would be lost to him. Not for him one of those untidy domestic killings, where pathetic people, driven beyond endurance, killed in a frenzy of temper or frustration and were immediately arrested. There had been times in the past when he had thought it might end like that. But the decision to take his destiny back into his own hands had given him a new strength and a new coolness.

He had several possibilities in mind. There were modern poisons which were virtually undetectable; he had found out a surprising amount about them in the reference library, taking care not to ask for assistance in case there should be questions after Verna's death. It seemed that actually obtaining the chemicals he wanted might be the stumbling block, but he was investigating that.

There was strangling, which he sometimes thought he would enjoy. When Verna's taunts were at their most cruel, he had often imagined taking that slim throat in his hands, the hands which had previously never threatened her with violence. There would be satisfaction in watching the horror spring into those glistening black pupils, as she realised, too late, the unthinkable thing that was happening to her.

The difficulty with that was that he would be the obvious suspect. Perhaps if he went away after he had killed her, then returned to 'discover' her body after several days, he could get away with it. He would wear gloves, of course. And he could arrange all the signs of a break in. Perhaps the neighbours would ring the police while he was still absent if they saw a broken window and milk accumulating at the door.

But that method was too inexact to appeal to his tidy mind. There was no knowing how long it would take for someone to notice that things were not as they should be in the quiet avenue where people kept themselves carefully to themselves. And he was not in the habit of going away on his own. It would look suspicious to the police, even if they could prove nothing. And the police did not let go easily when they had a murder suspect;

he had seen enough accounts of real and fictional crime during his lonely nights with the television to know that.

Asphyxiation was a promising method. You could kill a healthy woman in less than a minute by holding a pillow firmly against her face, without leaving too many signs behind. And if he took the body somewhere else afterwards, dumped it perhaps in one of the big disused gravel pits which were within ten miles of the house, it might not be found for months.

Perhaps the best method of all would be to contrive something which would appear to be an accident. A fall, perhaps. Or an electrical fault which would kill Verna in an instant, before she knew anything about what was happening to her. It wouldn't be easy for him to engineer, but it was worth thinking about. He had plenty of time to plan it.

And he was a man who enjoyed planning.

Thirty miles away in her village council house, the prospective victim's sister wondered about the changes she had noted in her brother-in-law.

Sue Thompson had too busy a life

41

for prolonged deliberations about the new elements which entered into it. She took Toby to school each day, then caught the bus into town to reach her desk in the office by quarter to ten. She was already doing more responsible work than the copy-typing for which she had been employed. She was trusted to draft letters, to deal with phone enquiries, even to take small decisions.

Had she not been tied to the responsibilities which attached to a small child, she might even have become a personal secretary to one of the partners when a vacancy had occurred in the previous month. But with the laws of discrimination as tricky as they were, it was not even safe for employers to discuss such possibilities with a worker. So the partners limited themselves to cautious hints that her work was satisfactory and that her temporary position might now be regarded as permanent.

Modest Sue was quite pleased to hear that. She and Toby were going to be all right.

And perhaps more than that. In the jerky, enigmatic phone calls, Martin Hume had taken to making to her, he had hinted at his concern for their welfare. 'Verna won't be around for ever,' he had said gnomically. Sue wondered if that meant that he had persuaded Verna to give him the divorce she had always so scornfully refused. But something she could not define held her back from asking for the details of what he meant. He seemed, after all, to be enjoying the air of mystery which accompanied his announcements.

Martin began to see her in the evenings when he knew Verna would be away. One memorable Wednesday, when Toby was on holiday from school, she took a precious day from her annual allocation of leave to be with Martin. They drove deep into the country and went on the river together in a rowing boat, with Sue sitting like an Edwardian lady on the wide seat at the rear with summer skirt spread wide. She smiled shyly at Martin as he leant far back and pulled smoothly on the oars. He rowed with a skill and rhythm she would never have expected in him.

Toby, leaning out with his mother's hand firmly grasping the belt of his small red shorts to feel the water racing through his widespread fingers, urged their oarsman excitedly on to greater efforts. Martin responded, lengthening his stroke still further, exulting in the release he felt in the physical effort. The boat moved faster and faster, its timbers creaking with his efforts, while the boy's shouts grew shriller and louder, until all three of them collapsed laughing into the centre of the old boat, watching the speeding banks gradually slowing to a lazy crawl beside them.

They had a cream tea at a place beside the river, quiet on this midweek afternoon. The sun shone obligingly and it was too early for wasps to be a nuisance. The two adults chatted contentedly, ever more at ease with each other, and Toby's happiness surrounded him like a tangible thing. A cloud of content seemed to rest like an aureole around the boy's tanned and laughing face. Sue took a picture of her son sitting on Martin's knee, with a blob of cream of which he was blissfully unaware decorating his freckled nose and his cotton sun hat sitting rakishly on the back of his small round head.

When they had returned the boat to its mooring, Martin walked hand in hand with Sue, while Toby skipped ahead of them on the path by the river, talking a little of his work, asking about hers, discussing the boy's school and his progress there, surprising her with how much he knew about these things. To any casual observer, they would have seemed a natural family. They felt so themselves on that golden afternoon.

Martin knew that he had fallen in love with the vivacious yellow-haired woman at his side. It felt like something he had been aware of for years, but which was only now being allowed to manifest itself. He was surprised by his own confidence, content not to rush things as he would have have wanted to do when he was younger, enjoying the slowly developing relationship. There was no need to hurry things along.

He wanted nothing sordid to taint what existed between him and Sue. It was good that he liked Toby so much. In time, there might be brothers and sisters for him. Single children could get spoilt, even with so sensible and loving a mother. But he did not talk about such things yet. That would have raised the question of Verna. And he particularly did not want to talk about that, even with Sue; especially with Sue.

For her part, Sue Thompson was happily

surprised. She had fended a few men off, and others had disappeared rapidly when they found she had a child to support. None of the departures had been regretted. The emotional bruises of her life with her husband and their eventual divorce were still with her, and she had thought herself content with her work and her life with Toby.

Now Martin, whom she had scarcely thought of for years, save as a fellow-sufferer at the hands of Verna, had suddenly emerged as a man who was not only kind but intelligent and attractive. The very unexpectedness of it was part of the charm and yes, she acknowledged it with wonder, the excitement. When the exhausted Toby had fallen happily asleep in his small bed upstairs, she and Martin kissed lingeringly in the untidy kitchen of her small council house. And, as this man who seemed so much in control held her against him, she was as surprised as she had been by everything else in this business to feel her affection developing into passion.

He did not go any further, and she almost regretted that. Perhaps he had been made cautious, as she had, by the batterings of an unhappy marriage. He held her at arm's length, and smiled that knowing, affectionate smile she had seen in him several times now. 'We'll be all right, you'll see, my love,' he said.

She thought of that 'my love', gentle and unforced, when Martin had gone and she sat bemused but happy in her shabby armchair. She wrapped herself contentedly in this new love, rejoicing in its contradictions. It was as comfortable and unthreatening as a well-loved garment. Yet—and this was what really surprised her—it was still exciting.

As if to remind her that life still held its threats, the phone shrilled in the narrow hall.

She knew the voice immediately. 'He's been with you, hasn't he?' Verna's harshness cut through her dreams like a razor.

'If you mean Martin, yes, he has. We've been on the river with Toby and—'

'I'm not interested in where you've been, Sister Susan.' Verna spat out the name like an obscenity. 'I wanted to know where the wanker had been, that's all. Playing happy families with soppy Susan and her sprog, that's where.'

The mention of Toby turned Sue's spine

to ice. 'Listen, if you think there's—'

'Don't bother. Do you think I care where the stupid bastard dips his wick?'

Sue realised her sister had been drinking. Her words were slurred, though her rage and malice came through clearly enough. Sue's mind raced. She tried again to stem the tide of invective. 'Look, Verna—'

'No. I won't look, little sister. Just you listen to me. I couldn't care less about the fucking wimp, but I'm not having him shagging my own sister! So take your tight little arse somewhere else.'

Verna banged the phone down, and Sue was left staring helplessly at the earpiece. She sat for a long time on the dining chair beside the phone, her euphoria permanently shattered. She must have been there for quarter of an hour or more; she felt that if she even stood up she would be physically sick. Eventually she made herself move, dragging herself heavily up the stairs to Toby's room.

She studied the innocence of the sleeping face, willing it to change her mood away from the black despair that had descended upon her with Verna's phone call. Toby slept with his thumb adjacent to his mouth, but not touching it. His fine hair, the colour of deep gold in the curtained room, fell on each side of the miniature, perfectly formed ear. The boy smiled gently, sleeping so quietly that the small breast scarcely rose and fell beneath the sheet.

The sight calmed Sue, but it could not dissipate the feeling of inadequacy Verna had, as usual, brought to her. She should have stood up for Martin; should have hurled back defiance at the virago who was spitting her hate from the other end of the line. Even a refusal to listen would have left her with a little dignity. Instead of which, she had been left shuddering with horror and distress, unable to stem the tide of malice. A tide that would no doubt be engulfing Martin by now.

She lay for hours in the darkness of her bedroom, her helplessness turning first to resentment and then to a hatred of her sister which was more powerful than anything she had felt in her life.

She wasn't going to give up Martin. Verna couldn't be allowed to go on ruining lives like this. Something would have to be done about her.

Five

In private moments, when she sought to excuse her conduct to herself, Verna Hume had often told herself that her marriage had foundered on the lack of constructive conflict. All good relationships had their spats. People shouted at each other, then made up, and got on with life. The making-up gave the relationship depth and understanding, leaving it stronger than it had been before. That was what the magazines said, and that was what she had chosen to believe.

But her sentimental resolution to be kinder to Martin, made in the contented aftermath of sex with Hugh, had not survived long. When he now stood up to her and fought his corner, she found it altogether less pleasurable than she had anticipated in the years of his docility.

Verna's automatic response to his opposition was to turn up the violence of her invective. 'Good screw, was she, my sweet little sister?'

'I wouldn't know, would I? We didn't hop into bed, you see, though I expect you would find that difficult to understand. But since you ask, I've no doubt she would be a considerably better partner in bed than you, Verna. That wouldn't be difficult.' Martin sat in the single armchair beside the dining table, pretending not to see her over the top of his *Times*, yet noting her every movement.

Verna cradled her beaker of black coffee in her slim hands, seeking feverishly for images which would infuriate him. 'Stroked her nice yellow hair, did you? In places more exciting than her head? Or is it not that bottled blonde in other areas?'

Martin almost sprang up to shut her filthy mouth. But he quickly gained control of himself. And with that control, he felt power surging through him, as if he had tested himself in a new situation and come through safely. 'She's an attractive woman. And gentle. You'd never think she was your sister.'

This coolness, this refusal to be hurt, this capacity to put her down so effortlessly, were all new to Verna, and she was disconcerted. 'Well, I told her what I thought of her last night on the phone.

And what I thought of you, too.' Verna laughed harshly, almost out of control.

'I expect you did. And I'm sure Sue knew just what to make of your opinion.' He walked over to the waste bin, opened the lid to put in the empty cereal packet and paused just long enough over the contents to let her know that he had registered the empty gin bottle on the top of the kitchen refuse, then sat down again.

'Well, sister Sue can have you, and welcome. I'd finished with you a long time ago.'

'And I with you, Verna.'

He spoke so quietly that she was for a brief moment stilled, even apprehensive. He made it sound very final, as if he had reached some decision. Verna felt for some reason threatened by him. She willed him to move, to reveal that she was disturbing him, but he sat with his eyes on his newspaper, a caricature of the suburban husband who is not available for breakfast conversation. His eyes were grey steel; he would not look at her directly, yet she knew that he was aware of her every movement.

Verna roused herself, usually contempt

came easy and unforced to her lips, but today she felt like an actress who had mistimed her opening lines and was struggling desperately for some sort of rhythm. 'Anyway, I couldn't care less where you put your greasy paws. I thought saucy Sue might have had a little more taste, but that's her funeral. I might even give you that divorce you've whined about for long.'

She waited for him to speak, for evidence of the eagerness she knew he must feel at the prospect. He looked at her briefly for an instant, then went back to his paper, a tiny smile lifting the corners of his mouth a fraction.

She ploughed on, floundering as she moved out of her depth in this unfamiliar water. 'It'll cost you, though. By God, it's going to cost you. You and that little church mouse sister of mine won't be living in luxury when I've finished with you, by God you won't!'

She stood still through a long pause, waiting for him to say money was of no consequence, as he had in the past when he had pleaded with her for a divorce.

Martin looked directly into her dark eyes for the first time, the grey steel of his irises seeming to cut laser-like through all her tawdry ambitions. He said, 'We shall see about that, Verna. In due course.'

Long after Martin had left the house on that Thursday morning, Verna was still disturbed by his attitude, and it was partly to reassure herself, to shut out the memory of her husband's face brimming with confidence, that she rang Hugh. She had rung him at work only once before, so he would surely know this was not a frivolous whim. They were closer than that now in any case, she told herself as she dialled the number.

The secretary's cool voice said, 'Mr Pearson's been in conference since he came in this morning. I'll just check whether he's free now, if you'd care to hold.'

She could just hear the woman's voice as she spoke into the intercom. 'It's a Mrs Verna Hume asking to speak to you personally, Mr Pearson. Do you want me to put her through?' Verna wondered if she had given that title as well as her name; she did not think so. She was already taking a dislike to that cool, detached voice. When she and Hugh were married, the woman had better watch out …

'Verna? What can I do for you?' Hugh's voice was suddenly loud in her ear. He came through well on the phone, she always thought, his voice not very distorted by the instrument. She could see him at his desk, his cuffs immaculate, his gold pen poised over the big leather-edged blotting pad.

'I've told Martin he's getting his divorce.'

'Really? How did he take it?'

There had been a tiny hesitation before he spoke, as if he had been searching for the correct reaction. And could her sensitive ear detect a trace of impatience in his tone?

'He was all right. He'll do what I say. Don't you worry about him.' She tried to force the confidence back into her voice.

'I wasn't. I've no intention of getting involved with poor old Martin.'

'No. No, that's right.' She was searching now for a reason why she had rung him. She could never admit that she needed reassurance. She said a little desperately, 'It's just that I'd like to get things under way, you see. Now that I've told him he can have his divorce. We need to give ourselves a timetable, so that we keep everything in control, make it happen the way we want it.'

'You're ringing to try to fix a date for us to set up house together?' This time he did not trouble to keep the surprise out of his voice.

'No. Of course not. I just thought you'd like to know that I'd told him. We aren't due to meet until Saturday, you see, and—'

'Yes, I see. I'm glad you've told him, of course I am. But this isn't really a time when I can talk, you know. I've got appointments lined up for the rest of the morning. Saturday will surely be soon enough to talk. And there's no need to rush things, is there? We must make sure we do what's right for us, as you say. I'll see you on Saturday night, as we arranged. There'll be plenty of time to talk then, darling.'

She was glad of that last word, even though it seemed to be stuck on as an afterthought, like a bribe offered to a wilful child. She hung up then picked up the notepad beside the phone and flung it furiously against the wall on the other side of the hall. She wished now that she had never thought of ringing him.

In his office, Hugh Pearson sat for a moment looking at the phone he had just put down. He walked across to the double-glazed window, watching the traffic passing oblivious below him for a full minute. Then he opened the door of his office and said, 'Debbie, if Mrs Hume rings again, better tell her that I'm out of the office.'

That afternoon, Verna journeyed to the Fylde coast. She sat with her back to the engine, looking glumly at the bright green May countryside as it raced away behind her. Things had not gone well so far that day. She must make sure that she got what she wanted out of the rest of it.

She could smell the sea when she came out of the station at Lytham St Annes, though she had gone half a mile in the taxi before she got her first glimpse of it. There was a stiff breeze, making the white horses dance on the bright blue corrugations of the estuary. 'The weather should hold for you over the weekend,' said the driver, assuming that like most of his other fares she was here to relax.

The raw new bungalows in the road near the top of the low cliff were too similar, each precisely laid out in its identical plot, cheerful but rather boxy. There was too much winter wind here for the ornamental trees which would have given individuality to flourish. But with its brilliant blue sky and clear sea air, it was nevertheless a pleasant spot. It was easy to see why her father had chosen to hide himself away in a place like this.

He came down the garden to meet her when he saw her paying off the taxi, grey-haired, stooping a little, smiling a nervous greeting to the daughter whose mother had so long been dead.

'Alice has got the kettle on,' he said. 'You'll be ready for your tea ...'

Neither of them volunteered anything more intimate than that. She noticed how he led her into the bungalow without once meeting her eye.

Her father had been married to the cheerful, buxom woman who waited inside the house for ten years now, but Alice Osborne was still a little in awe of her sophisticated stepdaughter. They did not kiss—Alice came forward and shook hands. They met as people in a similar relationship might have greeted each other fifty years earlier.

Alice had made a ham salad, and there were freshly baked scones and cakes on the table. 'You shouldn't have gone to all this trouble,' said Verna. She delivered the conventional line without embarrassment, knowing that she was acting a part here.

Neither of them laughed at her words. She meant what she said, anyway. There was no need for this woman, who was a stranger, to have taken such trouble. Verna would stay in this house no longer than was necessary to deliver her message.

They chatted conventionally over tea. Verna said the bungalow was looking nice and Alice blushed a little with pleasure.

'I do my best, but Derek doesn't allow me to spend much on carpets and furniture.' She looked at her husband affectionately and said, 'He's quite an old skinflint, you know, when it comes to spending. You'd never think he sold his business for any money at all, the way he goes on.'

This time, involuntarily, father and daughter did catch each other's eyes, but only for an instant, for each looked hastily away to the wide window and the distant view of the sea. Verna said, 'Well, he always was a cautious old thing. But he used to have the occasional headstrong moment, in the old days; you'd have been quite surprised by some of them.'

Alice laughed, trying not to feel that Verna was deliberately shutting her out from those years before she had known Derek. She was about to ask for examples of his impulsive moments when Derek said hastily, 'Well, we have to think of the future, you know. What with inflation and so forth. And people live for a long time, these days: you have to remember that.' He put out his hand towards his wife, was about to clasp it reassuringly over hers, then looked up at his daughter and decided against it.

'Yes, I suppose you have to think carefully about these things, especially when you're five years older than your wife.' Verna was amused to see both pairs of eyes trained now upon the table. It suited her to pretend sometimes that she resented her father's second marriage, though in fact she scarcely remembered her own mother. But it would be a useful confusion, if Alice ever wondered about the enmity between herself and Derek. He would never tell her the real source of it, she was sure of that.

They took their cups of tea into the little conservatory. From where Verna sat, in the best of the cane chairs, you could just see Blackpool tower six miles away to the north. Alice began to talk about Sue, whom they saw much more often than Verna. 'Toby is coming on beautifully,' she said. 'It's a pity he hasn't got a father, but Sue does wonderfully for him. He loves the beach, and we love having him down here.'

Verna felt the bitchiness she had subdued rising again within her. She said abruptly, 'I think Martin and I will be divorcing later this year.'

'Oh, I'm so sorry, dear,' said Alice conventionally. 'That's awful, Derek, isn't it? Of course, we knew everything wasn't as it should be between the two of you, but we hoped—'

'I must be on my way,' Verna interrupted. She stood up so decisively that the chair nearly fell over behind her. Suddenly, she had to be free of this woman, with her cloying, conventional niceness, her unaffected joy in simple pleasures, and her goodwill towards those around her.

Derek Osborne immediately insisted on driving her to the station. He had the car out of the garage and at the front door within two minutes. Alice thought unhappily that he seemed only too anxious to have this unpredictable daughter out of their lives again.

They said little on the short journey. She knew he was wondering why she had come, but she left the insertion of the dagger as late as possible, like a torturer enjoying his work. She didn't really need his money, she supposed. But she needed to make him suffer, to see his pain.

They were almost at the station when she said, 'We'll need to step up those useful little payments you make to me, Dad, when I'm divorced. I won't have Martin to draw on then, you see. Well, not to the same extent.'

She watched his fingers clenching the wheel, noting the tension with satisfaction, knowing that when his words came they would be powerless to sway her. He said hopelessly, 'I can't, Verna. You heard Alice back there. She already wonders why I haven't got more to spend on the house. Why we can't have the occasional holiday abroad, like other—'

'Your problem, not mine. You'll have to sort that one out for yourself. Father.' The last word was salt, expertly and precisely applied to the wound she had just opened. 'I'm just telling you I shall need some more, that's all. Twenty per cent. It's not negotiable. You'll find you can manage it.' She left him without a backward glance moving swiftly and gracefully despite the height of her heels. The holidaymakers streaming from the train which had just arrived turned their heads automatically to savour her dark elegance as she moved past them.

Her father stayed in the bay by the station entrance for a full minute, his forehead bent hopelessly against his knuckles on the top of the steering wheel. Then a taxi hooted impatiently behind him and brought him back from the darkness to the bright and blinding seaside light. He inched the car into the stream of traffic as carefully as a sick man.

Then Derek Osborne drove slowly back to the bright little bungalow, to the woman he loved and the agony he could never discuss with her.

Six

The neuro-surgery department in the Brunton Royal Hospital was one of its most respected departments. It was small but effective, and the man at the centre of it had a growing reputation among those best qualified to judge such things.

The reputation of the department stemmed, as in most cases, from its head. Two London hospitals and the Radcliffe in Oxford had already put out feelers to Richard Johnson, but he had so far proved surprisingly resistant to any move south. 'We've developed a good unit here,' he said. 'We're getting the equipment we need, and the work we're doing is as interesting as that in much bigger hospitals.'

Medics, especially distinguished men like Richard, never spoke publicly about the attractions of being king of one's own small kingdom, rather than one of a team of highly qualified surgeons. Richard was as near to being his own boss as was possible within the National Health Service, and would sometimes confess as much privately to his trusted friends. The managers of the hospital, conscious of the benefits brought by his reputation in a competitive world, had enough sense to allow their Mr Johnson the maximum degree of autonomy. With market forces being encouraged, Mr Johnson and his neuro-surgery unit were actually bringing in work from the surrounding areas.

Today was not one of Richard's operating days. He saw a succession of patients during the morning, reassuring some, explaining the treatment he thought necessary to others with polite consideration. His skills were not confined to the scalpel and the knife; he had considerable charm and understanding, and had not lost touch with the people he treated as his eminent reputation developed.

He had developed an empathy with the people of this ugly old cotton town where he had lived for the last ten years. All the people he saw that morning, the anxious and the relieved alike, came away impressed by his competence and sympathy, convinced that their destiny was in capable hands. It was a considerable feat.

As the end of the century approaches, old fears and prejudices are buried ever more deeply in the psyche of the average Briton. But they are not so deep that they will not surface surprisingly quickly under pressure. And Richard Johnson touched one of the most sensitive and embarrassing of social nerves. He was black.

He was used to the reaction of barely concealed panic when out-patients first saw him. He had long since disciplined himself against the irritation this had induced in him in his early days as a junior houseman. He enjoyed the gradual dissolution of tension and fear he saw in his patients as he examined them and talked to them about their symptoms and the treatment options available.

At this moment, he was reassuring an anxious mother of four about the results of her scan. 'There is cranial pressure, nothing more.' He smiled at the round white face with its fringe of greying hair. 'You were afraid of a brain tumour, weren't you, Mrs Pearce?'

'Well, there was a woman who lived two streets from us, you see, Doctor—er, Mister Johnson.' Even in her sea of worry, the woman had the English fear of getting a title wrong, the need to apologise for her anxieties about her health. 'She had the same symptoms as me, and she died in a few months.'

'No need to apologise for a bit of panic. As a matter of fact, we were quite ready to panic ourselves. When I first saw you and listened to what you said, I thought a tumour was certainly a possibilility. But now we know there's nothing to worry about.'

He showed her the scan results, picking out the area of the trouble with his slim silver ballpoint pen as he pointed to the printout on the wall, easing away the last of her anxiety, taking her patiently through what would happen next, the drugs they proposed to use, what she could do to alleviate the pain of her headaches.

He was always delighted when he had good news to relay. As he watched the woman gradually relax, first into relief and then into a rapture she could scarcely conceal, he reflected that this was a kind of indulgence for him. These were the easy cases, where he had good news to dispense; the real test came when he had to prepare his visitors for dangerous or critical surgery.

No system is proof against the public. His next patient did not turn up. Occasionally, seriously ill people with appointments were inconsiderate enough to die in the waiting period, and no one thought to inform the hospital. More usually, people simply forgot their appointments, or ignored them when they felt suddenly better.

Richard was left with a spare twenty minutes in a crowded schedule. It was to prove a fateful gap, for him and for others.

He rang his wife. He rang his lawyer. After a little uncharacteristic indecision, he rang a third number, from which there was no reply. It was surprising that a man who was so professionally calm and confident could be suddenly so full of personal insecurity. But confusion hit him often now, when he turned from his public to his private life.

He went on his round of the wards, first carefully taking the views of the ward sister about the post-operational progress of his patients, receiving the lift he always felt when the people lying in the beds were glad to see him, explaining to them what they must expect to feel, reserving until the last the pleasure of telling two of them that they could look forward to going home the next day.

In the short period he allowed himself for lunch, he shut the door of his office and wrote a letter. A reckless letter; its stark phrases seemed at first to have come from someone else. In the weeks to come, he was to wonder many times how he could have been so foolish and so desperate.

Seven

One man in his time plays many parts. The most profound of all students of human nature told us that a long time ago. Lest there be any hackles rising, let us be clear that he meant women too.

Verna Hume was a good example of this process in modern life. Behind her desk in the Osborne Employment Agency, she was the personification of the successful businesswoman. She took day-to-day decisions coolly but swiftly. Policy decisions were given more thought; she aired her views and listened to those of others, principally those of the woman who had worked alongside her to develop the business from its early, struggling days to its present five-branch affluence. The judgements they had made over the years had invariably been the correct ones.

She had been a secretary herself once, and an efficient one. She smiled at the thought of that gauche girl who had laboured to acquire the skills of shorthand, which were nowadays all but extinct among the girls who came to her in search of employment. But the young Verna had been a quick learner, even then.

She had realised that sheer black nylon stretched over young legs could often increase career prospects faster than mere efficiency. That a starched and apparently demure white blouse and a simple black skirt could be highly potent weapons in the sex war. And that 90 per cent of men were fools.

Moreover, Verna had realised by the age of twenty-one that there was more money to be made out of organising the labours of others than merely working for a boss. She had talked to the most intelligent and ambitious of the six girls who worked beside her in the typing pool, Barbara

Harris. They had done a little research, bided their time, saved for six months, and then simultaneously given in their notices, just as the holiday period approached.

In the early days, it was Barbara who was the more ruthless of the partners. When the directors of the insurance company had spluttered with irritation, appealed to their sense of loyalty, even, in desperation, offered them substantial inducements to stay, she had laughed in their faces. 'I'm afraid it's much too late for that,' she had said. 'You should have realised earlier what excellent workers we are.'

And within weeks, they were supplying temps to the very firm they had left in the lurch. It had a nice irony, which appealed to Verna and Barbara. And it was the beginning of a highly successful business. They often reminisced about the faces of the men they had surprised by their enterprise.

They supplied the temporary secretarial services which were much in demand in the town. They were careful to send only women who they knew were efficient —principally young married women who were only available for part-time work, because of the demands of their families.

Verna and Barbara took their commission and built a reputation for reliability.

Verna did most of the selling of their services. She had a way with men, a way of combining efficiency with a consciousness of her sexual attraction which Barbara was quite ready to acknowledge and admire. 'You can give them a price for the job and a hint that they might just be in bed with you by the end of the month without putting a word out of place!' she said, admiringly.

It was Barbara Harris who had seen the possibilities in vetting workers for employers who were too busy, too lazy, or simply too inefficient to sift job applications and make their own decisions about whom to employ. She and Verna were careful, and they knew better than anyone what to look for. As the numbers of the Lancashire unemployed rose steadily in the eighties, Barbara chose only the most efficient among those coming to them from schools and colleges, while Verna interviewed the experienced office workers moving into the town from Manchester and Liverpool.

In five years, Harris and Osborne (Verna insisted on using her maiden name as one more small insult to Martin rather than as any feminist assertion) was a flourishing concern, with a high standing. Workers came to them because they had a reputation for handling good jobs and securing good working conditions. Employers looked to them to help fill increasingly high-profile jobs. They were now head-hunters for junior executive posts in a variety of fields, no longer merely a secretarial agency.

Both Verna and Barbara enjoyed building up the business. They treated the workers who came to them well and understood their needs as well as the requirements of employers. When the business expanded, they used the best of them to staff their own new offices in neighbouring Lancashire towns. It was, as Barbara often remarked, almost a foolproof system. 'We observe the progress of people we place in responsible jobs, allow them to prove themselves at others' expense, and then offer them work with the agency.'

But no system is proof against human disaster. After eight years, Barbara Harris's husband died when the Mondeo in which he travelled the country was hit by a runaway lorry on a freezing night in North Yorkshire. She was much in love with him and devastated with grief. 'I don't think I can go on,' she said to Verna through her tears at the graveside.

'You can and you must,' Verna Hume replied firmly. She put her arms round her partner, feeling an access of pity which took her by surprise as Barbara's suddenly vulnerable shoulders heaved beneath her fingers with the pain of her loss.

She dismissed the feeling briskly before it could unnerve her. 'Pity it wasn't my Martin,' she said with a brittle little laugh. 'We could have spared him much more easily.'

There were other, less emotional repercussions of this untimely death. Three years earlier Barbara and her husband had moved into a large new detached house. That was in 1989, at the height of the property boom, when prices were astronomical but everyone thought a house was still a good investment. They had not insured against Michael Harris's death. 'It seemed so unlikely,' said a weeping Barbara.

Verna and Barbara had a crisis meeting a week after the funeral. This time Verna was ready with her plan. 'I'll buy you out. I can afford it, with the business doing so well. And when things have righted themselves, you can buy back in. It won't alter things. We'll just call you Chief Executive, instead of director, as far as the books and the taxman are concerned.'

In ordinary circumstances, Barbara would have been more cautious. In the trauma of her grief, it seemed a wonderful offer. 'We've come through a lot together, Verna. I won't forget this, believe me.'

It was a phrase she was later to remember.

Verna changed the company agreement, and in due course the name on the notepaper and over the office doors became simply 'Osborne' instead of 'Harris and Osborne'. Barbara thought that unnecessary, but she was glad of the lump sum of money to sort out her finances. And it made no difference to the development of the business: she worked as hard as ever as Chief Executive. In the four years which followed her husband's death in 1992, the firm opened two more branches. Verna, as proprietor, felt able to give a little less time to the business and rather more to her other concerns.

Of late, that had meant Hugh. Because she was in love for the first time in her life, she had indulged herself in the last few months, spending more time away from the business than ever before, leaving more and more to the very efficient staff they had installed over the years.

Now, on this bright Friday morning, it was time to assert herself, to demonstrate to herself as well as to Barbara that she was still the clear-sighted woman she had always been. She was closeted in her thickly carpeted office with her Chief Executive. She felt the old, familiar surge of excitement as she savoured the power she had and the urge to use it. The fact that she was using it this time on the person who had been her close friend for so many years seemed quite irrelevant.

Within minutes, Barbara Harris was white-faced and incredulous. 'But you said I could buy back into the company as soon as I was ready,' she said, hearing her voice rising towards shrillness. Even in her distress, her training made her wonder whether the girl at the desk in the adjoining room could catch her words through the wall.

'I don't recall any agreement of that kind,' said Verna calmly. She was ready for this exchange, as Barbara was not: she had rehearsed the scene in her mind many times over the last few years.

'But you must remember. You MUST! It was your suggestion. After Michael's funeral. You said—'

'I recall offering to help you. I recall providing money when you needed it, in return for your partnership in the business.'

'Yes. And you said I could buy back in whenever I was ready. You must remember that.'

Verna took her time, pretending to consider an idea which was new to her. Then she shook her head with an air of regret. 'No, I don't recall that, Barbara. I'm afraid you were mistaken in that idea. You were very upset at the time, of course.'

'I was, but I know what I know. It was your suggestion, or I wouldn't have considered it: I'd never have given up my share of the business for good. Not for anything. I'd have sold the house first.'

'Have you anything in writing about this?' Verna had difficulty in keeping a straight face as she delivered the question; they had often laughed together about the naivety of men in the firms they dealt with in not pinning everything down in official language. Now here she was turning the argument against her colleague.

For Barbara was still that: it was just that she could not own any of the business any more. She must be made to understand.

It was sinking in with Barbara that she was not going to get anywhere with this. She said sullenly, 'You know I haven't anything in writing. We've never needed that between us. But it was your idea in the first place.'

Verna furrowed her elegant brow, as if giving the matter serious thought. 'No. I'm afraid I don't remember any such arrangement. I'm sure I would if one had been made. And you know how I like to have things down on paper, whenever it's possible. It would be most unlike me to suggest an informal arrangement like that, I think you'll agree.'

It would. Barbara knew she was beaten, though she could hardly believe this treachery in her partner. Her employer. The bitter word drummed in her head and would not be dismissed. Her rage and frustration drove her to the assertions of moral right which she would normally have dismissed as irrelevant. 'But it's my business as much as yours. We started it together, and we've worked like slaves together.'

Verna shrugged her shoulders beneath the fine grey worsted of her jacket, listening to the desperate rising tone in Barbara Harris's words as much as to the argument. That note of near-hysteria signalled that the discussion was over. She was careful to keep her own tones perfectly modulated. 'That's how I think of it too, Barbara. I wouldn't dream of dispensing with your services.'

Verna paused, looking earnestly into the white, staring face opposite her, letting the audacious little threat sink into the ears beneath the now dishevelled chestnut hair. 'It's quite clear who owns the firm, but that's a straightforward business arrangement. Perhaps we could look at your terms as Chief Executive, if you're not satisfied with things.' She raised an inquisitive eyebrow at Barbara, her face full of sweet reason and concern.

Barbara Harris rose from her chair, her hands trembling a little despite her determination to control them. She left without a word or a backward glance, because she did not trust herself in either.

Verna Hume sat at her desk for quite a long time without moving, savouring the completeness of her victory. She was quite fond of Barbara, but these things had to be done. It was about power, she supposed, really, investigating her motives for the first time. And power was important.

What she failed to appreciate, and not for the first time, was that it is dangerous to leave people feeling desperate.

Verna went home early that day. She wanted to prepare her arguments carefully for her meeting with Hugh on Saturday. She might tell him about Barbara Harris, about how she had confirmed her complete control of Osborne Employment.

Then she went to her wardrobe to pick out what she would wear. She found she was still nervous about her appearance when she met him at the weekends; she rather enjoyed the adolescent anxiety she felt about how her lover would react to her.

And she was determined that on Saturday they would discuss their future. If he really was being evasive about their plans, as she sometimes suspected, it was important that she won him over and set his mind at rest. She was confident that she could do these things. She felt in control of herself and events around her after her meeting with Barbara.

When she got into the house, she found a message on the answerphone from her husband. Martin's dry, unemotional tones said, 'I haven't seen you for two days or I'd have told you. I'm going to be away for the weekend, at a conference on financial planning. The Radley Arms Hotel in Oxford, if you should need to contact me. No doubt you won't.'

Showing his independence again, was he? Well, she'd be rid of him in a few months. And he of her. She acknowledged, as she sometimes did when alone, what a bitch she'd been to Martin over the years. She must talk to him about the divorce, when he came back.

She felt again a little, unaccustomed surge of sympathy for poor old Martin.

Eight

Martin Hume enjoyed his weekend in Oxford.

The material provided by the organisers of the conference on financial planning was

81

not exacting for him. He was amused to see many of the younger conference members diligently writing down information which he had long accepted, and advice which seemed to him no more than common sense.

Martin realised that he had under-estimated himself. Now he had this new interest in his work, he found he was really rather good at it. When he began his new life with Sue Thompson and Toby, he would assert himself more within the firm, show what he was worth, and demand that he was rewarded appropriately. It was good to feel competent, even expert, in the work area of your life. For too many years, it had scarcely seemed to matter to him.

He even enjoyed the tour of Oxford which had been organised as a relief from the sessions on the course. They climbed Carfax Tower and saw the glory of the dreaming spires, on a day which had just enough heat haze to dim the view towards Cowley and the industrial part of the city, which made town visually so much less attractive than gown. Then they trooped through an ancient college, and gazed up like tourists at the high ceiling of the Sheldonian, while listening in awe to the guide's account of this last English stronghold of Latin speeches.

When the party's collective gaze was directed towards Balliol and the spot where Cranmer and the other martyrs had been burnt four and a half centuries earlier, his imagination was led to that other, less public, death which was to reframe his life. For a moment, he even considered arson as a means of disposing of Verna. If she could be trapped, or better still left unconscious, in a burning house, she would suffocate long before the flames got to her: he had no wish that she should suffer unduly. And the fire would destroy the evidence, with luck.

With luck. He did not like that phrase. The whole thing would be too chancy. Someone might intervene before his wife's death was achieved. And a fire would be far too difficult to organise if it was to appear that he was not in the area at the time. It would pinpoint the time of Verna's death, the very thing he had to disguise in order to leave himself in the clear. Regretfully, he gave up the idea. But even the elimination of certain methods was progress, he thought. He was beginning to get the details of this killing clear in his own mind.

When the rest of the party moved dutifully into the Oxford Story Centre to receive their illustrated potted history of the town and its fortunes through the centuries, Martin slipped away and sat for a while in the gardens of Pembroke College, watching the comings and goings of the busy young people who lived there. For the first time in ages, he wished that he had stayed on at school for another year, as his sixth form master had asked him to, and taken his chance of joining this privileged golden crew for three precious years at university.

If he had only opened up those horizons ... if he had only met Sue, not Verna, all those years ago ... Before the sweet conjectures of what might have been could turn bitter, he moved on, walking briskly down to Magdalen Bridge and thence into Christ Church Meadow. He walked swiftly by the Cherwell, his mind too busy to notice the ground he was covering as he began to make his plans.

When he eventually sat down, he found himself on a bench overlooking the Thames, watching the broad, slow sweep of the river, willing it to still his mind, which was racing too far ahead. It was delicious but premature, this blueprint of the life he would lead with Sue and Toby. There was one other piece of planning that was an essential preliminary.

He had to dispose of Verna.

But his excitement was justified, he thought. He had reached a further, almost a final, stage in the knowledge of how he was going to be rid of his wife.

He would book himself another weekend like this one. No, an extended course: four days, perhaps. The firm would be pleased enough to give him the extra couple of days, if he pointed out that he was giving up his weekend to further his knowledge. If he chose the right course, it might even be useful to him, in the career he planned to resurrect. Something with management studies grafted on to financial concerns. He was going to be a pillar of the firm, in due course.

He would even pay his own course fee, if necessary. But no, that would be a mistake. He mustn't appear to have been too eager to go on the course when the police came to examine his conduct at the time of Verna's death, as they undoubtedly would.

Martin felt a new surge of excitement at that thought. Not fear, just a thrill in the knowledge of the forces he was going to unleash and the importance of what he was planning to do.

Four days would be quite enough to confuse the issue; that was what he had gathered from his research. Apparently it was nothing like as easy to determine the time of death as some crime writers liked to suppose. And that applied even when bodies were discovered quite soon after death. After four days or more in normal house temperatures, it would surely be impossible for the police to pinpoint the exact time of Verna's murder. It was the first time he had used that word in his planning: a little *frisson* of exultation ran through the silent figure by the Thames.

He would have to decide whether or not to leave the central heating on in the house: everything would have to look as if Verna had been carrying on normally for the period when he was away. That kind of detail appealed to Martin. Retiring to his hotel room when most of the other course members adjourned to the bar that night, he even made some notes on paper.

There would be the milk order to

organise. If the man left their daily pint on the doorstep for four days, it might excite interest among their normally incurious neighbours, or even in the milkman himself. Perhaps they should cancel their order altogether, and buy from supermarkets. Verna would have done that long ago; it was only Martin's loyalty to old institutions which meant that they still had milk delivered. But they must cancel the delivery forthwith: it would merely excite suspicion to do it on the eve of Verna's death.

And he must give some thought to the contents of the fridge. A few frozen meals; some cheese, ham and tomatoes; perhaps a little sliced bread in its wrapper. There would be sell-by dates on some of these, but that wouldn't matter, if he bought carefully and late. It might be possible to indicate that Verna had died in the middle of a weekend she planned to spend at home.

And he would have to make it look as if her bed had been slept in. He did not know whether the police automatically investigated the area of a suspicious death with such thoroughness, or even whether they had the right to search through his property like that. He wished he had watched some of the television crime series more closely. But he could check it out. He would make sure that he gave proper attention to every detail of this business.

It was an hour after midnight when Martin concluded a series of thoughts of this kind. He found that he had covered both sides of an A5 sheet of paper with notes in his small, neat hand. He looked through them twice, mentally ticking off the eight areas of concern he had pinpointed. Then he tore the sheet into small pieces and flushed it down the lavatory in the en suite bathroom.

He was still awake at two, some time after the last rumblings of the hotel plumbing had signified that his fellow conference attenders were all abed. He had always had a good memory, and he was confident that he had committed his musings of the evening safely to it. He was aware, however, that the most important question of all had still to be answered.

Very soon now, he must decide exactly how he was going to kill Verna.

For most of Sunday, the conference kept Martin's mind fully occupied. He even volunteered to chair one of the small-group sessions on Inheritance Provision; it was a role he would never have consented to a few months earlier.

He was gratified, as well as a little surprised, to find that he enjoyed the experience. He took pleasure in guiding the discussion into the areas most likely to be useful, taking care not to speak too much himself, bringing out the expertise available in the more diffident members of the group. When the whole conference assembled again in its plenary session, his account of his group's findings and suggestions was the most precise and the most cogently presented of the three reports from the sub-groups.

By the end of the day, Martin was aware of the changes occurring in himself, he was rediscovering skills which he had almost forgotten he possessed. He realised that he was preparing himself for the more dominant role he proposed to adopt in the working life ahead of him. He was contemplating the future with optimism, even with eagerness. It was good to know that his heightened sense of life and its joys was going to extend into his work as well as his personal life.

He dwelt on these things as he drove the two hundred miles up the M40 and then the M6 towards Brunton. He did not hurry, but the traffic thinned as the evening wore on. After he had stopped for a leisurely coffee at Hilton Park service station, there were noticeably fewer lights racing towards him along the ribbon of the M6. For the first time in years, he moved back into Lancashire without feeling depression dropping upon him at the prospect of resuming his tortured married life.

It was almost midnight when he dropped down the long slope to the Ribble and left the motorway near Preston. Twelve minutes later, he skirted the high sycamores on the fringe of the park and turned the car into the tunnel of darkness which was a leafy cul-de-sac by day.

Suddenly, he was very tired after his successful weekend and the long drive back. But it was a pleasant fatigue, like those he remembered at the end of long Sunday hikes with his father in the summer days of his boyhood. He did not want to talk to Verna, even to see her, it would not be the right conclusion to this successful weekend. He willed her to be out of the house, as if already the mere effort of his newly positive mind would be sufficient to direct the woman from his path.

The notion seemed to work. He turned the car between the high gateposts of Wycherly Croft, his lights picking out the nameplate of the house, with the rather twee picture of a Pendle witch on a broomstick beneath it. There were no lights in the dark cliff of brick which loomed against the sky. Verna was out, then. He found it difficult to dismiss the absurd idea that it was his own determination which had expelled her. Probably that merely showed how tired he was.

He was anxious to isolate himself in his own room and shut the door against the wife who would soon be removed from his life. For the first time, now that her death was near, he feared that she might read something of his thoughts in his face. Tomorrow, all would be well and he would deceive her without effort. Tonight, he felt in desperate need of a long, refreshing sleep.

The house seemed even larger than usual, silhouetted as it was against the moonless sky. Its emptiness accentuated all sounds. Even his key as he inserted it into the lock seemed to him to rasp unnaturally loudly. When he pushed the door inwards, the wind rushed past his shoulders into the blackness beyond, crashing shut a door on the landing above. He started with fright, almost cried out at the thought of an intruder in the blackness ahead of him. Then he realised that it was no more than the draught he had admitted which had slammed the unseen door.

Hastily, he put on a light in the hall, noted the long mirror, the light fittings, the telephone with its white, unsullied notepad beside it. Everything just as he had left it. But why should he ever have expected anything else? Verna, whatever her darker vices, was a tidy woman.

He put lights on in the kitchen, the lounge, the dining room, his study, slipping his hand round the door of each room to the familiar switches, filling the place with light to flood away the foreboding which had fallen upon him with the darkness and the sound of the unseen door. Then he made himself a pot of tea, deciding that he would take it up to his room, knowing that Verna would not disturb him there if and when she returned.

He was aware as he came back into the

hall of a faint, sour smell that he could not identify. When he could not place the scent, he tried to shrug it away, as he went wearily towards the bed which seemed ever more desirable. But as he mounted the stairs, the odour became stronger. He turned on to the landing and tried the bathroom, but there was nothing unusual in there. He put the tray down in the room where he now slept and went along the corridor to the main bedroom he had relinquished to his wife.

He set his hand a little tentatively on the brass handle of the door which had slammed when he had entered the house, as if he still feared that there might be an intruder waiting within. But in truth it was the smell which made him move so reluctantly. It rolled upon him now like a tangible thing out of the darkness, as though only the shut door had held it back. It was when he switched on the light that he realised that it was the smell of death.

Verna lay sprawled upon the double bed, with one leg draped stiffly over the edge. Her shoe had fallen to the carpet beneath the slim foot. Her dark hair was spread all on one side across the pillow.

Her wide, dead eyes seemed to stare accusingly at Martin as he stood transfixed in the doorway, as if they knew now what he had planned for her.

Nine

It was a bright Tuesday morning when Detective Inspector Denis Charles Scott Peach, known universally as 'Percy' to his colleagues, parked his Mondeo and prepared to resume work after a Monday off.

He looked up at the blue sky and the high white clouds above him, then turned with distaste to the huge concrete slab which housed the new headquarters of the Brunton police force. The building seemed to soar away for ever, cutting out more and more of that splendid sky as he turned towards its entrance. 'This place is like a modern cathedral,' he mused. 'A cathedral erected to crime, the only millennium growth industry.'

Peach was not often subject to flights of fancy; he regarded them as weaknesses in a policeman. Retribution for this one was swift and uncomplicated. A pigeon, launching itself from the balustrade of the Victorian Town Hall which stood defiantly at the centre of municipal redevelopment, circled twice on motionless wings above the car park, wheeled a little lower, selected a target, and shat comprehensively upon the spotless windscreen of Percy's Mondeo.

Inspector Peach, finding his tongue in that moment as loose as the grey bird's bowels, vented his vocabulary on the heedless departing tail as it soared effortlessly beyond his vision. An omen for the week to come? Percy turned gloomily, stamped on the wide rubber mat to open the automatic doors, and moved into the world of work.

His interest was aroused despite himself as he went to look at the papers on his desk. For Percy Peach was a natural thief-taker, a CID man whose pulse and interest quickened instinctively with the scent of serious crime and the prospect of a hunt for the offenders.

On this particular Tuesday morning, there was not much in his in-tray to excite him. There had been the usual senseless violence outside a couple of the

95

town's pubs on Sunday evening. There were three drugs arrests for possession and one for dealing, but no hint that the big boys of this lucrative industry were in any danger. There were two domestic incidents, one of which looked as if it would end with a manslaughter charge, but both of them seemed too straightforward to interest Peach. There had been a building society hold-up while he was away yesterday, but only by a couple of amateurs, stupid and desperate unemployed youths with toy guns, who were already in custody.

It was a memo from the floor above which made Percy's dark eyebrows rise and brought an instinctive twist of contempt to the lips beneath his black moustache. The note asked him to see Chief Superintendent Tucker, Head of Brunton CID, as soon as he returned to his desk.

Percy crumpled the note in his squat, immaculately manicured fist and flung it accurately into the waste-paper bin with the swift underarm throw that had run out many an unwary batsman in his years in the Lancashire League. He stood for a moment looking out at the tight rows of terraced houses and the two mill chimneys

96

which were the last legacy of King Cotton's reign in the town; then he turned abruptly and marched resolutely through the door of his office.

He stuck his head round the door of the CID section and spotted Lucy Blake, who had been assigned to him as a detective sergeant three months earlier. Against the predictions of the CID room wiseacres, Lucy had formed an effective partnership with the bristling and bouncy DI Peach. 'I'm off to see Tommy Bloody Tucker,' he said. 'Send in the dogs if I'm not back in ten minutes.'

It was his way of letting her know that he was back in circulation after his day away from the coalface of crime. When Lucy Blake first arrived, he would never have dreamed of informing her about his movements or intentions; now it was automatic to him to treat her as part of his team. The most important part, in fact. The large group of chauvinists and the smaller one of feminists who had rubbed their hands at the prospect of this confrontation had both been disappointed, not to say mystified, by the working relationship the two officers had developed.

Human nature being what it is, the same people were now hinting at another kind of relationship between the two: baulked of one kind of gossip, they were eager to develop another. But not within earshot of the formidable Percy or his red-haired female detective sergeant: coppers, male or female, have more sense than that.

Peach's stocky form moved surprisingly fast on his short legs. He bounced up the stairs like a rubber ball and arrived quickly at the door marked 'Chief Superintendent Tucker, Head of CID'. He took a deep breath, banged the button on the right of the door jamb, and watched the bulbs light up beside 'Engaged', 'Wait' and 'Enter' in quick succession. Tucker was still staring at the buttons in front of him in a puzzled fashion when he found that Peach had arrived on silent feet in front of his desk.

'Sit down, Percy,' he said hastily, gesturing to the chair opposite him, as if helping in a selection from hundreds. He remembered why he had asked Peach to come here now. This was to be an opportunity to patronise him. Tucker determined to take his time over it; usually he was glad to get rid of this irritant to his domination as fast as possible.

'I suppose you were playing golf while we were all busy here yesterday?'

'That's right, sir. Felt I'd earned a break, after working all through Saturday. And of course, I wasn't worried about things here. Knowing you had your careful hands on the wheel, I mean.'

'Yes.' Hands-on management was definitely not Tucker's style. He delegated work swiftly; or as Percy was wont to put it, he passed on awkward tasks as quickly as if they were red-hot turds. The Head of CID stared at his DI suspiciously over the half-moon glasses he wore for paperwork, the only work he was happy with nowadays, as the nirvana of pensioned retirement with his roses increasingly beckoned. A chief superintendent, whether efficient or not, could normally rely on deference from those beneath him in the system; his exalted rank ensured that. But Percy Peach was a maverick, content to rely on his own aggressive competence as his safeguard.

Tucker was never quite sure when his DI was taking the piss. And he could never admit that he was not quite sure. 'Well, it rained on Saturday. We gave up our golf after thirteen holes.'

'Really, sir? Unlucky for some, eh? Beautiful day yesterday, sir. Played thirty-six holes, as a matter of fact. Really enjoyed it. And my golf's improving, now I've given up cricket and can concentrate on it. Of course, we had the course virtually to ourselves at the North Lancs.'

He dropped the name of the most prestigious local club into the conversation in the happy certainty that it would exasperate Tucker, who played on the much inferior course at Brunton Golf Club. Rumour had it that he had tried to join the North Lancs, but was too much of a hacker to meet the handicap requirements of that august institution. Peach's immediate acceptance when he applied there had infuriated his chief, and Tucker's annoyance was fuelled by the fact that though both of them were aware of it, he could never publicly reveal it.

He glared at Peach's determinedly innocent, round face. 'Yes. Well, I'm glad to hear you enjoyed yourself. Because we were busy solving crime here, while you were away on the golf course. Murder, in fact.'

'Really, sir? Well, no one is indispensable, as I've often told myself when I've

100

been tempted to overwork. Domestic, was it?'

He managed to imply that the only crime Tucker could solve was the most straightforward. Four fifths of killings were within families or close relationships; in these cases, there was usually only one obvious culprit, who often gave himself or herself up. Tucker, who had planned to deliver his information slowly while gloating over the success, found he was already being hurried. 'Yes, it was, as a matter of fact. Woman strangled by her husband. Chap called Martin Hume. Not much left for you to do, Percy. We've already brought him in.'

Peach noted that 'we'. It meant things.

'Went out and arrested him, yourself, did you, sir? Well, I've often told the rest of CID: "One of the things that I admire about Superintendent Tucker is that he's not afraid to get his hands dirty. You won't find him sitting behind a desk and letting other people do all the work when there's serious crime about. Keeps himself in touch." That's what I tell them, sir. I'm only sorry I wasn't here to see the master in—'

'DI Bancroft made the arrest, as a matter

of fact.' Tucker scowled across the desk at his voluble tormentor. 'On my orders. When I'd reviewed all the available facts in the case.'

'Yes, sir. Of course. DI Bancroft, eh. Nice efficient job it sounds.' Peach paused, looked down at the dark material of his trousers, and picked off a piece of thread which Tucker could have sworn did not exist. 'Confessed to the killing, has he, sir?'

'No. Not yet. He hadn't when I left here last night, anyway.' Tucker could not work out why a triumph was turning into a disaster. Peach had already succeeded in raising doubts even in his own mind, when he had been so confident yesterday. 'Well, you wouldn't expect him to, would you? He'll soon break down, when he's interrogated. That's your job, Percy. He won't hold out against Hard Man Peach. Thought we'd leave you something to do, you see. Few loose ends for you to tie up. Let old Percy feel involved, I thought to myself, don't want him feeling left out.'

Tucker attempted a beam of triumph, but it appeared on his uncertain features as a shaky leer. Peach regarded him steadily for a moment, watching the doubt creep back into the lined face with its fringe of crinkled grey hair. Then he said, keeping his voice carefully neutral, 'So we have a man arrested for the murder of his wife. Arrested but not so far charged. In the absence of conclusive evidence we need a confession, if we are to charge him within the hours left to us by the law.' He levered himself to his feet. 'Better go and get on with it, I suppose, sir.'

Tucker now felt that the case was anything but complete. That he might even have been precipitate in ordering the arrest of Martin Hume. That instead of smirking in the face of the egregious Peach with a *fait accompli*, he was after all dependent on that odious man to secure the conviction which had seemed to him so straightforward on the previous evening.

He called after Peach's broad back as it went through the doorway, 'It's a formality, you'll see. When the report comes in from forensic it'll be conclusive. But you'll probably have a confession from him by then.'

Peach stopped at the last words, then turned and confronted his chief from the door. 'If you say so, sir, then of course it's probably so. I have to admire your confidence—it's an example for those of us who are less certain about these things ... It's your decision, of course, but I wouldn't advise a press conference to announce the arrest, sir. Not just yet, perhaps.'

He went down the stairs treasuring the look of deflation which had collapsed Tucker's bright features. Was it too much to hope that this Martin Hume might not have killed his wife after all?

Ten

Sue Thompson's mind was reeling. When the news of the discovery of her sister's body had been brought to her, she had taken it surprisingly calmly. The uniformed WPC reported back to the CID section that there had been no great evidence of grief in the deceased woman's sister. But shock affects people in many different ways: her apparent callousness was not necessarily significant.

The moment which started the nightmare for Sue came when Martin Hume used his one phone call from Brunton police station to tell her that he had been arrested for Verna's murder. Martin followed this news with a little nervous laugh. And suddenly she could see him at the station, standing awkwardly over the phone with the little stoop she had come to love, flanked by burly policemen waiting impatiently to lock him in a cell.

For a moment she could not even draw breath, let alone speak. Perhaps he took her silence as doubt, for while her mind reeled and she felt, like a blind woman, for the chair behind her to sit down, she heard Martin saying, 'I didn't do it, you know. It will all be all right. I suppose they always think it might be the husband. Especially when he has as much reason to hate his wife as I had to hate Verna.'

She knew she must stop him, must prevent him from pouring out more words which those watchful men beside him would record and use against him. She tried to say, 'Of course you didn't. I know that.' But the words wouldn't come, and she faltered into some guttural sound that could never be any comfort to him.

Eventually, she managed to say, 'Will they let me see you?' But apparently they didn't want him to see anyone at that time, except the lawyer he was entitled to. And, as he said, she would have to get a babysitter for Toby. And he didn't want the boy to know anything about where he was. Or why he was there. 'I'll see you when they let me out.' He sounded as though he was in shock. All through the darkest hours of the night, Sue wondered if he had felt as confident about his release as he had tried to sound.

And now, in the brightness of the next day, Martin was still locked up, and the police were assembling God knew how strong a case against him. And Sue Thompson, who had hated her sister and was glad to know she was dead, felt that she too was being watched, that she must be careful of every movement she made if she was not to be arrested when they released Martin, as they surely must.

She did not go in to work on that Tuesday after the death. Her employers were full of sympathy for her in her loss; she was grateful for their understanding, and thankful that they did not appreciate the irony of it. She had told Toby that his Aunt Verna was dead, but nothing else. She was glad to have the boy out at school and the house to herself for a few hours. It was a chance to compose herself, to adjust to the dramatic events of the last twenty-four hours.

She did not realise quite how much she was still on edge until the phone shrilled in the hall behind her, startling her so much that she dropped the pewter tankard she had been cleaning to occupy herself. She watched it clatter noisily across the parquet floor before she picked up the phone. It was not the police station but her father in Lytham St Annes. Derek Osborne sounded strange: he had to give his name to his own daughter, because she did not at first recognise his voice. Then his tone changed and he said, 'So Verna's gone.'

It was a strange way for a father to put things, she thought. But she had not seen father and daughter together for years now, so she had no real means of knowing how close they had been. Derek and Alice Osborne never spoke to her of Verna, and were non-committal if Sue ever mentioned her. She had been happy to leave things like that, having no wish to confess to them either her own distrust of Verna or her developing relationship with Martin. Now she said simply, 'Yes. I'm sorry, Dad.' She wondered if her father knew that Martin had been arrested.

Derek Osborne, his voice still sounding strained at the other end of the line said, 'She had it coming to her.'

An even odder thing for a father to say. Yet Sue felt a bond strengthening with the words, which mirrored her own reaction. There was a pause; she could hear her father's uneven breathing as he strove to produce his next words. Several seconds passed. Then he blurted out, all in one breath, as if he wanted to deliver his message before he could be denied, 'She has to be identified. I said you might do it.'

Her mind reeled. She should have expected this, perhaps. Her first reaction was that she couldn't face it either. Perhaps that was a result of the feeling of guilt she was trying so hard to fight. She stuttered as far as a 'But, Dad—' and then the phone was taken over at the other end of the line.

'Your Dad's really upset,' said Alice Osborne's warm, concerned voice in her Geordie accent. 'I know it's too much to put on you, pet, but I honestly don't think he can face it. Not seeing her lying there dead, I mean. It's not fair to ask it of you,

I know, pet, but if you—'

'I'll do it. Tell Dad it's all right. It's only a formality anyway.'

She had not known she was going to say that. The words were out before she knew that her brain had made any decision. But she was younger and stronger than her father. He had sounded much older than sixty-nine when he had spoken to her on the phone just now. She would be all right; she was more resilient. And it was, at least, something to do. She realised now how much her limbs yearned for action.

It was only when she had agreed a time with the police and was on her way to the mortuary that she began to wonder if there were darker reasons why her father had not been able to face the task.

Percy Peach fulminated over the developing file on the death of Verna Hume.

'Even Tommy Bloody Tucker should have known about our police doctor!' he grumbled. 'That sour bugger gives out information as if it were gold cufflinks. You have to press him for it—squeeze the miserable bastard. There's not even a suggestion here of the time of death. I can just hear that stuffy devil saying, "You'll have to wait for the postmortem for details like that." And I can just see that moron Tucker accepting it meekly. Damn it, an informed guess from our doctor about the time of death might have put the husband right in the frame! Or right out of it.' Peach seemed to find the latter possibility the more attractive of the two.

Lucy Blake looked over his shoulder at the sparse facts as they flashed up on the computer. He tried and failed to ignore the light, attractive fragrance which hung about her. He was not sure whether it was a touch of perfume or merely expensive soap, but it was a vast improvement on the aura carried by his previous detective sergeant, Bert Collins, whom Peach had usually referred to as 'that long streak of discretion'. That lanky and swarthy professional had had many virtues, but fragrance had never been one of them.

Peach glared at the screen as if the instrument had actively offended him, then swivelled away in disgust to face his detective sergeant. 'Right,' he said. 'Tell me how far we've got with Tommy Tucker's little travesty of a case.'

'Not very,' said Lucy. She stood erect,

then bent her knees in the stage copper's hitching-up of her non-existent underpants; Percy found the move quite disturbing to his concentration. In a contrived basso profundo, DS Blake intoned, 'Police are proceeding with their inquiries. Superintendent Tucker last night revealed that a man had been detained and he was confident of an early announcement.'

Peach kicked a chair into place opposite him and nodded at the seat and then at Lucy Blake's attractively rounded backside. 'Park it, don't talk through it, Sergeant,' he said. 'Tell me who we can put in the frame to annoy Tucker.'

'You want suspects? Well, there's the husband, of course. Dangerous things, husbands, much better avoided. This one's an accountant. Martin Hume.'

'Did he do it?'

'Tommy Tucker thinks so. Mr Hume says he didn't.'

'Good. Let's hope he's right. I'll give him the chance to tell me why he didn't in a little while. By the way, where's Charlie Bancroft, the man who made this hasty arrest?'

'He's taken two days of his annual leave. Superintendent Tucker told him he needn't delay it. Our leader said the case was quite straightforward, and DI Bancroft could leave you to tie up the few remaining loose ends.' She kept her voice studiously neutral, trying to conceal her enjoyment as she quoted the phrases she had carefully committed to memory on the previous day.

Peach swore quietly, but without his usual vehement invention. Some instinct told him this was going to be one of Tommy Tucker's cock-ups, and he relished the prospect. Peach was a CID man through and through, a natural ferreter out of truths, and the truth was that he would have been quite miffed if a juicy murder had been tied up without his assistance. He leant forward, deadly earnest beneath his scorn. 'Who've we got as possibilities, Lucy?'

'Not too many, as yet. Immediate family: first the husband, obviously. Says he was away at a conference over the weekend when his wife died.'

'Where?'

'Oxford.'

'Best part of two hundred miles south. Not easy to nip back for a quick spot of homicide.' Peach smiled his satisfaction.

'There's a sister. And a father.'

'What about a mother? And a mother-in-law?' Percy had a neutral view on mothers, but a traditional view of mothers-in-law as sources of conflict. His opinions were affected by eight years' experience of a marriage which had ended in divorce.

Lucy shook her head. 'There's a step-mother. Verna Hume's mother died almost twenty years ago, apparently. Her father has been re-married for the last ten of those.'

'Happily?' Percy made it sound as though that would be most unnatural.

'No idea. They live in Lytham St Annes.'

'No guarantee of happiness, that. George Formby lived there at one time.'

Lucy, who had barely heard of the legendary ukelele player and never of his egregious wife Beryl, did not follow the argument but was totally unfazed by that. 'The sister is a younger one. Lives out beyond Clitheroe, I think. She's doing the formal identification of the corpse today.'

'What about people outside the family?'

'Verna Hume was a successful business-woman. Osborne Employment is her firm.

There's a Chief Executive who's been with her for years.' Lucy looked at her notebook. 'A Barbara Harris. She hasn't been interviewed.'

'She will be. Soon. Unless Martin Hume can convince me of his guilt.' Peach jutted his chin out as if it was Blake and not the man in charge of Brunton CID who was frustrating him. But she was used to that.

'I gather from what the husband said when he was brought in that there might be a few other men you might wish to see in due course.'

'A few?'

'Apparently.'

'Drawer-dropper, was she? Hmm.' At one time, he might have added, 'So she had it coming to her, did she?' but a few dust-ups with his detective sergeant had brought him discretion in these matters. Discretion was not a quality he rated highly or exercised much, so that was a kind of compliment to DS Blake. 'Any names?'

'Not yet. The scene-of-crime team is at the house now.'

'Anyone else? Burglars? Druggies? Rapists? Lancashire Rippers?'

'No one else as yet, sir. I haven't been directly involved myself, of course. I just had a chat with DI Bancroft before he disappeared on his leave.'

'Knowing we'd be left to pick up the pieces this morning, you mean. You did right, girl. And now you shall be involved, Cinders shall go to the ball, even though Baron Hardup Peach is now in charge of arrangements for it.' Percy sprang up and made for the door. 'We'll start with the husband. Poor miserable sod.'

Sue Thompson moved into the low modern red-brick building as though walking through a dream. She had never been in a mortuary before and had no idea what to expect. The fact that it was a trim, quiet place, with a carpeted reception area and comfortable chairs, made the task she had taken on seem more unreal.

She realised that she had never even looked at a dead body before. She had been too young when her own mother died to go into the funeral parlour with the adults to see the corpse in its coffin. And when her grandparents and her uncles had died, she had excused herself from the contemplation of corpses with the heartfelt thought that she would rather remember people as they had been in life than as they lay in death. Yet now it was she who had been chosen to come here to study a particular body, to inspect it carefully and determine for the official world that this was indeed Verna Hume, the sister with whom she had shared a room through the years of her adolescence, and whom she had watched for hours in front of the dressing-table mirror as she grew into a teenager and studied what seemed the incredibly sophisticated ways of her dark-haired and beautiful older sister.

Everyone around her was very understanding; she could feel them watching her for signs of distress. They had brought her here in a police car when she told them she had no transport of her own. Now a uniformed policewoman—she had said in the car that they were all just police constables now, but it would take Sue time to get used to that idea—stood discreetly beside her at the desk, ready to offer whatever support was needed. She was younger than Sue, probably ten years younger, but she seemed, in this place, immensely more experienced in the details of death.

They waited a moment until the word came that things were ready for them. Then they were conducted into a room which seemed to Sue all stainless steel. Verna Hume's body was awaiting identification before being slid neatly away into its deep steel drawer among the other silent occupants. The mortuary assistant drew the sheet gently aside at a nod from the constable, and Sue saw Verna's unmistakable face within two feet of her own.

The eyes were closed. Death had removed all strain from the features, and Sue saw the face again as it had looked when she had awakened early on summer mornings and gazed at the sixteen-year-old countenance which had been so impossibly beautiful in the other narrow single bed beside hers. How dark the hair was! And how smooth the skin. Verna might have been sleeping now, had there been the soft rise and fall of breath beneath the sheet that was so still.

She looked serene and untroubled, like those pictures of saints Sue had seen in the Sunday school of her childhood. Sue was shaken by a sudden impulse to cry out that her sister had not been this saintly figure, that she had been cruel, even vicious. That the husband who was now in prison because of her death was innocent. That the world would be a better place without this dangerous and calculating beauty.

Instead, she said, 'That's her. That's my sister, Verna Hume.'

She was not conscious of getting back to the police car on the gravel outside; perhaps someone took her arm and led her there, but she did not remember it. As they drove her back to her house, she sat stiff and silent as a nun, staring unseeingly at the bright day and the lush greens of late spring. Slowly she returned to a consciousness of the real world around her. But she remained deliberately, stiffly erect, and set her full lips in a resolute silence. The task of identification was over. Another step in the removal of Verna from her life had been achieved.

It would never do if these representatives of the law who travelled with her divined that in her mind she was singing with the joy of that release.

118

Eleven

To Martin Hume the situation still did not seem real, even after he had spent a night in the cells.

Finding the wife he had planned to kill lying dead upon her bed had been shock enough. Then, when they had arrested him, he had had to fight an overwhelming impulse to laugh. The irony of the situation was rich, and the fact that only he appreciated that irony had made it almost impossible to contain his feeling that this was all some ridiculous dream, from which he would awaken in due course.

But the black farce was going on, even in the bright light of the day he had been allowed to glimpse as he was taken to an interview room. That square box with its dark-green walls, its single high fluorescent light, and its scratched table with the tape recorder, should have convinced him at last that this was not only reality but a dangerous reality, as far as he was concerned. Yet he still found it difficult

119

to take his peril seriously.

The man who came swiftly into the room might have been calculated to dispel any remaining illusions Martin had. He strutted in like a bantam cock, bristling aggression from every fibre of his short and muscular frame. Once through the doorway, he stopped abruptly; from just inside the room, he studied Martin without any attempt at dissimulation. This tableau of concentration could only have taken seconds, but it seemed to stretch for much longer. Then the man nodded and sat down in the chair on the other side of the table. Martin, who had half-risen to his feet in automatic politeness as the stranger entered the room, sank back onto his hard plastic chair and felt ridiculous.

'Detective Inspector Peach,' the newcomer said without preamble. He looked to Martin irresistibly like a small version of Oliver Hardy, with his toothbrush moustache, fringe of jet black hair around a bald pate, and expression of disgruntled malevolence. But there was no Stan Laurel lookalike to bring humour into the claustrophobic room. Instead, Peach said, 'And this is Detective Sergeant Blake,' and Martin became aware that a woman had come into the tiny room behind Peach. A woman with dark-red hair and blue-green eyes, which studied him as curiously as Peach's dark ones had done as she took her seat beside her senior colleague.

'Done your wife in, they tell me,' said Peach by way of conversational opening.

'They tell you wrong, then,' said Martin.

'Found in the house with the body. Relationship between the two of you not too good. Quite bad, in fact, I believe. No longer lovebirds.' Percy stretched the scanty information which the police machine had so far gathered with practised ease, then shook his head sorrowfully.

'Doesn't mean I killed her.' To his surprise, Martin found he enjoyed replying to the inspector in his own terse style.

'No. Quite right. Doesn't look good for you though, does it? Many people have been convicted of murder on circumstantial evidence, you know. Popular fallacy that you can't be. Want a lawyer, do you? You're entitled, you know. If you feel you need one.'

'Not at present, thank you.' Martin summoned what dignity he could muster and forced it into the words. It wasn't easy, when they had taken away your tie and belt and emptied your pockets. It was surprising how much of your confidence departed with your possessions.

'So when did she die?' asked Peach, turning a box of matches which had appeared from nowhere over and over between his fingers.

Martin almost ventured a speculation about that, then realised that the question was a trap. He must be careful with this man. It wouldn't do to let him know how much he had hated Verna, how much he had wanted her out of his way. He wondered what the man already knew about him. He said, 'Are you telling me you don't know when she was killed? And yet you're holding me on suspicion of murder?'

For a fleeting moment. Peach looked discomfited. Then he grinned for the first time, revealing that his upper canine teeth were missing from an otherwise perfect, very white set. His grin was not only unpretty: generations of Brunton criminals had found it positively disconcerting. He said, 'Nice one, that. I can see why you think you don't need a lawyer, Mr Hume.' He turned suddenly to the officer at his side. 'That's a good point Mr Hume makes. Why are we holding him, Sergeant Blake?'

Lucy, who had thought that Peach was no longer capable of surprising her, was caught off guard. 'Well, Superintendent Tucker considered that there were reasonable grounds for an arrest. I'm sure—'

'Ah, yes. Superintendent Tucker, Mr Hume. Head of CID here. Very senior man, you see. Very experienced man. Clearly must have very good grounds for suspicion if he bangs you up so promptly, as I'm sure you'd agree. Wouldn't do that unless he was pretty sure he had a case against you. You'd have grounds for complaint, you see, on the score of wrongful arrest, if he couldn't justify the action he ordered. So I expect there must be more to this than meets my innocent little eye. I think you—'

'I didn't do it.' Martin felt that if he didn't arrest the flow of words from this squat little man it would sweep over him, drowning his judgement and his capacity for independent thought.

His interruption at least stopped Peach. But it brought another of his pauses for study of the face opposite him, which were so disconcerting to the subject of his scrutiny. And another of his smiles, which was worse.

'So convince me,' said Percy Peach.

'I don't know when Verna died. And you won't tell me.' Peach beamed blandly at him; his mouth seemed wider and his teeth whiter than ever. He was certainly not going to admit that he didn't know yet. Martin pressed on. 'But I was away for the whole of the weekend.'

'Ah! Where?'

'In Oxford. At a conference on Investment Planning. Attended by almost a hundred accountants.'

Peach winced visibly at the thought, as if a convocation of crocodiles had swum before his vision. 'You mean a hundred bloodsuckers can bear witness to the fact that you were somewhere else at the time of your wife's death? We may have to ask one or two of them to do just that, in due course. Where was this gathering of financial wizards, Mr Hume?'

'At the Radley Arms Hotel in Oxford. Over two hundred miles south. I measured it on the milometer of my car when I drove back on Sunday night.' Martin found it difficult to keep a note of triumph out of his voice.

Peach too found the thought satisfying. It looked more and more as if Tommy Tucker had made a right arse of this one. But his instincts would not allow him to foster any complacency in his present victim. 'Just the right distance to allow a convincing alibi, I'd say. But wait a minute: if you left at midnight on Saturday, when all your fellow accountants should have been tucked up in their virtuous beds and expecting you to be in yours, you could have been back in Brunton by three in the morning. Ten minutes at the outside to smother an unsuspecting wife. Then three hours back, on an empty M6 and M40. Time for a stop and a snack on the way if you wanted, and still be back in your bed before the randier lads were back in their own rooms.'

Martin grinned a sickly grin back at Peach's broad one. 'It's hardly likely, is it?'

'On the contrary, lad, that and more has been done. Chap drove from further south than Oxford to Wastwater in the Lake District and back one night a few years ago. Dumped his wife's body in the lake in a plastic bag and hightailed it back south. Well over six hundred miles, that was. Very nearly got away with it, too. It was years before he was arrested. Whereas you're safely inside straight away, thanks to our vigilant Superintendent Tucker.'

'But I didn't do it,' Martin insisted weakly.

'So you say.'

'And it was I who reported Verna's death.'

'Yes. Convincing touch that. Just as it would have been if you had really returned all unsuspecting on Sunday night and found your wife lying dead.'

'No, Inspector! Just as it was.' Martin was suddenly enraged by this aggressive little man who delighted in his murky allegations. 'What I've told you is exactly what happened. Now you prove it wasn't.'

'I'm just doing my job, Mr Hume. There's nothing in the regulations to say I shouldn't enjoy it, you know.' Peach flipped his matchbox a few inches into the air, caught it expertly between his thumb and first finger, and made it disappear as abruptly as it had arrived.

Martin wondered afterwards if it was some sort of sign. For the girl, who had not spoken, whom he had almost forgotten during the minutes of his torment by Peach, now leant earnestly forward and said apologetically, 'Forgive me, Mr Hume, but you hardly seem to be devastated with grief by your wife's death. Would you tell us about your relationship with her, please?'

Martin had known this must come at some stage, but he found himself unready for it, nevertheless. His composure had been shattered by this bald turkey-cock of an inspector who had arrived so abruptly upon the scene. 'Is this really necessary? Surely my—'

'I'm afraid it is, yes. Unless you're going to confess, of course. Because if you really didn't kill Mrs Hume, we shall have to find out who did. And the way we work is to build up as full a picture as possible of the deceased and her relationships with those around her, you see.' Lucy Blake was as patient and low-key as a social worker explaining to an old person what was going to happen, or as a doctor explaining the process of a fatal illness, thought Martin with sudden apprehension. He began to wonder if he needed that lawyer, after all.

He deliberated for a moment whether he should refuse to speak. Or whether he should pretend that all had been better

127

with Verna than it really had been. But that wouldn't work. They were going to go and talk to other people about this, weren't they? Shouldn't he encourage them to do that, since he wasn't guilty?

The pause stretched so long that Lucy Blake said gently, 'Mr Hume? You understand why we need to ask about these things?'

'Yes.' Martin found that his throat was suddenly and ridiculously dry, when he wanted to be at his most assertive. 'Verna and I didn't—well, we weren't close.' He looked up at the two expectant faces, the one concerned, the other ghoulishly gratified, and said suddenly, 'We didn't sleep together. Had separate rooms.'

'I see.' DS Blake was low-key and sympathetic; Martin did not dare look at Peach. 'Do you have a serious sexual relationship with anyone else, Mr Hume?'

Martin thought of his wonderful, fair-haired Sue. Of the marriage they had planned when he had got rid of Verna. Of the marriage they would still have, when this nightmare was over. And he thrust from his mind the canker that had eaten its way into his brain during the long hours of solitary darkness in his

128

cell: the thought that Sue might have done this, might have killed her own sister to release him from her. He drew in a long, slow breath. 'No,' he said. 'No, I haven't got a serious relationship with anyone else.'

He felt like Peter denying his Christ in the market place. But he was only trying to protect Sue, wasn't he? To keep her and Toby out of this awful business, until the real killer was discovered.

Rather to his surprise, they didn't press him further about the matter. Instead, Peach said abruptly, 'Resented that, did you? That you weren't sleeping with your wife, I mean.'

Martin felt more composed, now that they weren't grilling him about his feelings for Sue. 'I suppose I did,' he said carefully. 'But if you mean did I resent it enough to kill her for it, no. Sorry to disappoint you, but I got over any jealousy about the way Verna went on years ago.'

'Went on, did she? With other men, I suppose.' You could never tell which sex was involved, these days. Terrible world we live in, in Percy Peach's opinion. Lots of work for policemen, though.

'She did, yes. But I couldn't tell you

who they were. I'd lost interest in what she did, years ago.'

Percy didn't believe that. But you could never tell. He said, 'We'll need to investigate them. They might be involved.'

Martin saw a chance to score a small point of his own in this contest. 'You accept that I didn't kill her, then?'

'Not at all, Mr Hume. Not yet, anyway. But we're always anxious to see justice done. No stone unturned to discover the whole truth, and all that.'

'So are you going to let me out of here?'

'Might do, later. When we've checked out one or two things. That will be up to Superintendent Tucker, of course. He was the one who thought there was enough evidence to put you in here, you see.' Peach smiled his satisfaction. 'Must go, now, Mr Hume. See what the scene-of-crime team has turned up at your house.' He rose. 'Interview terminated at nine fifty-nine,' he said into the microphone, and switched off the recorder.

He led his detective sergeant back to the safety of his own room and shut the door carefully behind them. Lucy Blake said, 'You don't believe all that nonsense about him driving back through the night from Oxford.'

'Course not,' said Peach delightedly. 'That bloke didn't kill her. Tommy Bloody Tucker has shot himself right up the arse this time. And I hope Hume sues him for wrongful arrest!'

He exploded into laughter at the thought.

Twelve

'Got a confession out of him, did you?' asked Superintendent Tucker.

'No, sir. Afraid not. Your Mr Hume was unwilling to cooperate, I'm afraid.' Percy Peach was as inscrutable as the Chinamen he had read about in his school days.

Tucker felt his first wave of uncertainty. Peach should have been grovelling by now in the face of his chief's efficiency, yet he seemed distressingly unmoved by any sign of envy. Tommy Tucker peered suspiciously at his detective inspector. 'Gave him your customary third degree, did you, Percy?'

131

Peach smiled, and Tucker's disquiet increased with the sight. 'You will have your little joke, sir. Helps to maintain the CID section's sense of proportion, your sense of humour does. I questioned Martin Hume with my usual thoroughness, yes, sir. Offered him a lawyer of course, but he said he didn't require one. Seemed quite confident of his innocence, in fact, even when DS Blake and I pressed him hard. Putting up a front, I suppose. But I must say it was quite a good one. I was glad you were so confident of his guilt, or I might have begun to have my own doubts.'

'Yes. I see. Well, it's only a matter of time. If Martin Hume won't confess to killing his wife, we'll just have to find more evidence and confront him with it.'

'My sentiments exactly, sir. I believe I gave him to understand just that. I expect the scene-of-crime team have got some juicy stuff ready for us, have they?'

Tucker shifted uneasily; the leather seat of his directorial chair seemed suddenly uncomfortably hot against his executive buttocks. 'Scene-of-crime team are at the house at the moment, as a matter of fact. Moved in this morning. Well, there didn't seem any great hurry yesterday for them: I thought the bugger would have confessed by last night.'

Hoped he would have, you mean, thought Peach. So that you could have confronted me this morning with a completed case and shown how clever you are without me. Instead of which, Tommy Bloody Tucker, you've got a man who says he's innocent, and no SOC team findings to support his arrest. Ho ho ho.

Percy raised his dark eyebrows no more than a couple of millimetres towards the wrinkles of his white forehead to register his surprise at this irregularity in police procedure. Tucker squirmed again. The superintendent had got to his exalted position through keeping his nose clean and playing things by the book. These were the cardinal virtues to Tucker, and he had often had cause to rebuke the ebullient Peach for ignoring them.

Now here was his DI underlining his own failure to observe sacred police protocol in his haste to secure an arrest. There was a pause which stretched for several seconds, as the enormity of his omission swelled in Tucker's vision into a dark balloon above Percy Peach's impassive head. Then, as Tucker's throat struggled at last into sound,

Peach said with impeccable timing, 'You know best, as always, sir. But I think I'll just go over to the house and see how the SOC team is getting on. With your permission, of course, sir.'

'Yes. Do that. Right away, please.' Tucker tried to rap out the orders briskly, as if it was Peach and not he who had been at fault in not dispatching the SOC team more promptly.

Peach stood up unhurriedly. 'Pity I wasn't here yesterday, sir.'

Tucker, who yesterday had been delighted by his absence, squirmed anew as he found himself agreeing with the sentiment.

Lucy Blake was a good driver. That had been another prejudice which Peach had been forced to abandon early in their association.

She drove without haste through the tree-lined avenues which led to the house where Verna Hume had died, while Percy tried not to observe the movements of her shapely nylon-sheathed knees. Plain clothes had always seemed a contradiction in terms for him in the case of female personnel.

This was the west end of Brunton, the

134

area where the owners and managers of the mills had built their solid Victorian and Edwardian mansions, in the great days of King Cotton. The burghers had built a municipal park of which they and the town could be proud. It had a row of bronze cannons on the highest of its terraces, from which the grimy panorama might be surveyed in all of its industrial might; it had green slopes where infants might escape from the dark streets to play; it had a broad lake where toddlers could feed ducks and swans, and a stream which tumbled down from the lake to a place of fountains and stone lions with water issuing from their jaws. The Victorian planners had set within their park a broad gravel walk, where people of all classes could saunter in their Sunday best and the world might view its neighbour. The citizens of Brunton could pretend, on the one day when the scores of chimneys in the town below them did not belch their smoke, that they wandered in some English Florence. Or at least in Hyde Park.

By Percy Peach's time, the grand days of the park were long gone. The red squirrels had given way to the ubiquitous greys in the willows by the lake. You were more likely to find litter than parasols among the chestnuts which lined the Broad Walk, more likely to find used contraceptives than Sunday finery among the straggling rhododendrons. The park was no longer a place to stroll at twilight, unless you went there in search of forbidden substances.

But the houses in the quiet roads around the park, where horses and carriages had once trundled over the wide gravel drives, were still thought highly desirable. Although some of the largest ones had been converted to flats, most of these solid residences had been modernised and preserved. There were increasingly complex security systems built into them, of course, but it was now fashionable to preserve those very turn-of-the century features which had been anathema to the interior designers of the fifties and sixties. Victoriana flourished anew instead of hiding its head.

Wycherly Croft, the house where Martin and Verna Hume had carried on their strange existence over the last few years was at the end of a lengthy cul-de-sac. Here the purple of the *Rhododendron ponticum* which flourished on Brunton's clay soils had generally been replaced by expensive modern varieties of the same shrub, which now formed an avenue of pink, white and crimson as the police car rolled slowly to its goal.

Sergeant Jim Burke looked up briefly from his work and greeted DI Peach. He had plainly been expecting him. Burke was a man of forty who looked ten years older. He had headed many a SOC team over the last eight years. He knew what to look for, and it was an advantage to have a man who could be trusted to organise the first, highly important stages of any investigation without supervision.

'Should have been here yesterday, by rights, Percy,' he grumbled. Burke was a good grumbler, and in the modern police force you had to play to your strengths.

'So why weren't you?' asked Peach.

'Day off. Like you. Work just piles up while you're away,' Burke said gloomily.

So that explained why Tucker had delayed the SOC investigation. Without the reliability of Burke he might have had to do some work himself—even if it had only extended to selecting a different team to undertake the work. 'Photographer finished?' asked Peach.

'Yes. He was in before they moved the body, of course. Which is when we

137

should have been here.' Burke watched his two constables moving on all fours over the floor of the bedroom where the body had lain, picking up hairs, fibres, anything which might suggest a presence other than the victim's. 'The bedlinen's all gone off to forensic.'

'Did you spot anything significant on it?'

Burke shook his head gloomily. He knew what Peach meant. Any traces of semen might have indicated a crime of passion. An intruder, perhaps. Something salacious to get your police dentures into, anyway. And something to indicate that Tommy Bloody Tucker had been barking up entirely the wrong tree in arresting Martin Hume. Both of them would have liked that. Burke was as bolshy as Peach beneath his lugubrious exterior. But not so brave, nor so good with words, so that he rarely confronted Tucker directly.

Lucy Blake wandered into the dressing room next door to the bedroom. It was always interesting to know what another woman kept in her cosmetics cupboard, and Verna Hume had used an impressive array of implements in the fight against the advancing years. Thirty-five, she had been,

138

apparently. To Lucy, who was almost a decade younger, that was early middle age. All these tubes and bottles, these depilatories and mascaras and powders which made cosmetics the most lucrative of contemporary crafts, were useless now to that flesh which lay preserved in the frigidity of the mortuary, waiting until the law determined that it could be burned or buried.

Lucy smiled at the female constable who had been tabulating the contents of this tiny room, 'Anything unusual?'

The girl hesitated. She was a probationer constable; a CID sergeant seemed to her impossibly far up the hierarchy, so that she was afraid of saying the wrong thing. The pleasant freckled face confronting her, divined more than she knew of her uncertainty, gave her another encouraging smile, and the girl said, 'Nothing that seems very significant in the bathroom or the dressing room. But we did find something in the top drawer of the dressing table which I think might be important.'

She handed over a small, blue-backed book with a tiny metal ballpoint pen in its spine. A diary, obviously. Lucy flicked quickly through the pages. There were entries on most of the days, the majority of them just initials and times. But the single name 'Hugh' recurred on several pages, sometimes without a time against it, sometimes with one. The only complete name she found was against 2.30 on a Tuesday afternoon. 'Richard Johnson' was written in a neat, easily legible hand. Looking more closely at the subsequent weeks, she found 'R.J.' recurring four times in all.

It was something, perhaps. Two names to add to those they had already listed from the family.

Thirteen

The pathologist still wore his rubber boots when he spoke to Percy Peach. He had removed his cotton cap and the microphone into which he had spoken softly of his findings in the hour during which he had cut the corpse and investigated the organs of the late Verna Hume. He had washed his hands, Percy was pleased to note. But in the room beside them, the water still ran over the stainless steel, washing away the detritus of scientific investigation, removing the blood and gore which had issued from what was now no more than human meat.

'Straightforward enough, to my mind,' said Doctor Binns. He was a tall, lean man, with the beginnings of a tall man's stoop, although he was only forty-one. Like many people of his calling, he was resolutely cheerful about death and its consequences. Perhaps he compensated for the strains of what most laymen considered a grisly occupation with this graveyard humour. The dead were gone; no one could touch them now. One had to consider the feelings of relatives, but there was no need to put up false fronts for anyone else.

'She was smothered?'

'Asphyxiated. Quickly and efficiently. Almost certainly by means of the pillow found beside her. Forensic will confirm that in due course, but I have no doubt of it. There were traces of saliva and lipstick in the centre of it.'

'So a woman could have done it?'

'Certainly. Very little strength needed, once you have the victim lying flat on her back and the pillow in position over her face. Quite a preferred method among females, in fact, over the last few years. But that would include a few so-called mercy killings, of course.'

'When?'

'Ah, the perennial CID enquiry!' Binns seemed almost disappointed to have to release what would no doubt be useful information. 'At least twenty-four hours before her husband reported the death on Sunday night. Probably rather longer than that.'

'So she was killed some time on the Saturday.'

'Almost certainly on late Saturday afternoon or evening, I'd say. I don't think a medical witness for the defence would dispute that, though he might if I tried to be more precise.'

'Right.' So Martin Hume was in the clear; he could surely demonstrate that he was in Oxford with his fellow course members at the time of his wife's death. In a perfect Peach world, Hume would sue Tommy Bloody Tucker for wrongful arrest. But Percy had learnt long ago that the world rarely revolved to his command. 'What else?'

Mark Binns sighed. 'Not a lot. She'd had a light meal not long before she died. Perhaps two to three hours earlier.'

'Any recent sexual activity?'

'Not immediately before death. No traces of semen in the vaginal area. But she was sexually active. Plenty of rumpety in the last few months, I should say.'

'Not with her husband, there wasn't. Not according to what he told us this morning, anyway.'

Mark Binns shrugged his high shoulders. *Cherchez l'homme,* Inspector. It doesn't have quite the same ring as *Cherchez la femme,* does it?'

Peach was thoughtful as he left his cheerful scientific colleague. A killing that might have been accomplished by another woman. A victim who had been putting it about a bit with lover or lovers in the months before her death. There was going to be something for a keen DI and his team to get their teeth into here, once he had released Martin Hume and told Tucker all about it.

Derek Osborne had seemed relieved to hear of his daughter's death. Alice had been secretly shocked to see how little

143

he grieved for her, how contented he seemed to be after the policewoman who came with the news of her death had left them.

She could read her Derek like a book, she told her friends, and she was proud of it. They had no secrets from each other; or rather she had always thought that was the case. Recently, she had been less sure of it. And it was when that beautiful witch of a daughter was around, or even in his thoughts, that the barriers went up and she felt he was concealing things from her.

So Alice Osborne had rejoiced when that sinister presence had been so abruptly removed from their lives. She had felt guilty, because Verna was Derek's daughter, and she had stood behind her husband's chair with her arms around his shoulders when the young policewoman had gone, leaving the two of them alone with the knowledge of this death.

But she had known within two minutes that Derek was elated rather than stricken by the news which had been brought into the neat little bungalow. She had stood with her chin on the top of his head, looking through the big window of the lounge at what he saw, at the white horses on the breezy, distant sea. She had felt relief, not pain, flowing through the quietness of his chest and arms as the two of them had stayed wordless for a few minutes. And when she had whispered softly, 'You're better without her, love, really you are!' Derek had not made even a token protest of his grief.

He had planted out his geraniums and lobelia on the afternoon of that Monday. Although neither of them acknowledged it in words, they both knew that this was a kind of celebration. Both of them felt the freedom of release as they moved in the garden beneath the sun-whitened clouds; it was as if a burden, invisible but heavy, had been lifted from their comfortably ageing shoulders.

'Bit early to risk putting these out, most people would say,' said Derek as he looked up at the racing clouds. 'But we don't get late frosts at the seaside. We'll be safe enough now, I reckon.'

It seemed like an assertion of the freedom which had been brought to both of them by the removal of the spell cast over their lives by his dark-haired daughter.

Yet now, scarcely a day later, Derek again seemed to be troubled. She wondered if it was the prospect of the funeral that worried him, so she forced herself to raise the subject while they were eating their sandwiches at lunchtime. But it wasn't that. He was preoccupied, at a distance from her because something was now concerning him, something which kept him from her. Something, she was sure, connected with this wretched stepdaughter whom she had tried so hard and so unsuccessfully to like. It was a relief to be able to acknowledge how little she had cared for the woman, how glad she was, in fact, that she was not going to be coming into their house ever again.

But that was going to be of scant consolation, if Verna Hume exerted a baleful influence over Derek even now that she was gone. His sinister daughter was still threatening him, even in death. But perhaps that too could be changed.

'Of course I'll sit beside you on the platform—it's generous of you to want me there,' said Percy Peach to Superintendent Tucker. 'But you must take all the credit for the early arrest. I wasn't even on duty at the time.' Percy smiled the generous, self-deprecating smile which was perhaps the most disturbing one in his repertoire.

Tucker grimaced and got slowly to his feet, preparing himself reluctantly to leave the safety of his comfortable office. He wished he had never announced this press conference. But he knew that you couldn't call a thing like this off once you'd announced a time for it. These journalistic wolves scented a cockup faster than anyone he knew. Except for DI Peach, he thought unhappily.

His heart sank when he entered the big room near the entrance which he had set up for the briefing. Not only were the crime reporters of the national and local press there in force, but the Radio Lancashire girl, Sally Etherington, was setting up her microphone on the table in front of his central position. There were blissful smiles on the experienced journalistic faces in the rows of chairs behind her; they studied her rounded blue-denimed buttocks with the lustful relish of accumulated experience.

The fourth estate found Percy Peach unexpectedly affable. He greeted three of them by name. But when questioned about progress, he shook his head and refused to comment, saying officiously,

'Superintendent Tucker will tell you all about that. He's in charge, you know.' But he pursed his lips in a manner which indicated that there could be juicy information to come, for those with the patience to seek it out.

Tucker thanked them all for their attendance. His audience leant collectively forward, interpreting this immediately as a defensive attitude. The superintendent licked his lips and smiled nervously. 'A suspicious death at a house in South Park Road was brought to our attention on Sunday night,' he said. He looked at his watch. 'Some forty hours ago, now.'

Seventy-three eyes regarded him balefully. (The single eye of Alf Holdsworth, the reporter for the local *Evening Dispatch*, glittered brightly enough for any two others.) Tucker cleared his throat. 'I have to tell you now that foul play is suspected. In fact, I can reveal now that we are treating this as a murder case.'

There was not the little stir of excitement he had hoped for. They had known all this for twenty-four hours. They wouldn't have been called here without a murder. Peach gave them his widest and most affable grin from beside his chief. Tucker looked at the microphone in front of him, at young Sally's alert, expectant face behind it, and reached for a handkerchief to mop his brow.

From the second row, Alf Holdsworth, too old to be bothered with that most unreporterlike of virtues, patience, called, 'We hear you've already made an arrest.'

Tucker looked helplessly at Peach. Usually, the superintendent was effective with the media, but this time he had brought them here with too few shots in his locker. A rare mistake, but one for a humble DI to savour. Peach said, 'Superintendent Tucker ordered an arrest, yes. The credit for that is all his. I hope some of you chaps who moan about how we drag our feet will note that. A man was arrested within three hours of a suspicious death. And not on the basis of anything as simple and straightforward as a confession. Make a note of that, please.'

They did. Tucker watched thirty-seven ballpoint pens move swiftly over paper and thirty-seven heads rise to confront him expectantly. Sally Etherington sprang from her front row seat towards the microphone on the table in front of him and said breathily, 'Could you give us the man's name, please, Superintendent Tucker?'

Tucker, scenting that he might after all escape without too much damage, said, 'I'm afraid we are not able to do that at the moment, Miss Etherington. For reasons I'm sure you will all understand.' He looked at the rows of unresponsive countenances. 'Legal reasons,' he said desperately.

'Is it the dead woman's husband?' said a florid-faced man in the back row.

'You must understand, ladies and gentleman, that I cannot at this juncture reveal anything which might prejudice the course of—'

'Then why have we been brought here?' said the red-faced man, looking at his watch. There was a murmur of support from the benches in front of him. Tommy Tucker's over-active imagination heard the tumbrils beginning to roll towards him. It must have upset his judgement, for he turned in desperation to the man beside him. 'Detective Inspector Peach will bring you up to date on the latest state of the investigation,' he said. 'He's more in touch with the hourly development of the case than I can be, as I'm sure you all appreciate.'

Seventy-three eyes turned speculatively upon the toothbrush moustache and the domed white head of DI Peach. Percy gave them his widest, most encouraging smile, so that the gaps where his upper canines should have been made him look like a laughing cavalier with blacked out teeth.

'Superintendent Tucker is generous with the credit, as always. I wasn't around in the early stages of the inquiry, so I can take no credit for the rapid moves which were made then. But we are pursuing the case now as vigorously as the superintendent has indicated. Perhaps the best thing I can do at this stage is to invite your questions.'

Over half the people there knew Peach from previous such occasions over several years. It was the first time they had ever heard him encouraging media questions. There was a moment of stunned silence, during which Percy took the opportunity to assume again the wide grin he had not been able to maintain while he spoke. Then a young man with acne and no shorthand said from the first row, 'This man you're holding for the killing. Has he been charged?'

'No.' Percy's teeth flashed white. His

eyebrows rose towards the white dome above them, positively inviting a supplementary question.

The florid-faced veteran was the first to respond. 'Is he about to be charged?'

'No.' Percy watched Tucker's arm move instinctively in front of him, then drop helplessly out of his vision.

'How long do you expect to hold a man without a formal charge?'

Before Percy could make his unhurried answer, the acned youth, anxious to demonstrate his fledgling knowledge of criminal law, called, 'Have you made application to the magistrate's court to keep the man in custody for a further period?'

Percy shook his head regretfully. 'No. We have not.'

There were murmurs of excitement through an audience that had begun to think that there was not a decent headline to be had from this. Police malpractice was always a runner, if there were going to be no details of sex and violence made available to them. There were mutters about the Birmingham Four and cutting corners. The tabloid press prepared to mount its high moral horse.

The complexionally disadvantaged young man became quite animated. 'You mean you're holding a man and denying him his legal rights?' He rose to his feet, would have clasped his lapels if he had not been wearing a polo-necked sweater, and said, 'Detective Inspector Peach, are you seriously telling this media conference that you are holding a man without observing the due processes of English law?'

Percy ignored the murmurs of assent which ran round the rows behind this latter-day Camille Desmoulins, allowing the excitement to build upon his silence until he judged the moment of maximum impact was at hand. Then he held up the stubby fingers of a neat white hand in a gesture that was oddly magisterial. 'No,' he said, 'I am not telling you that at all.'

'Then what the hell are you telling us, Inspector?' roared the young man. He would record that line in his copy, he thought. There was no reason why he should not give himself a leading role in his account of this exchange, beneath the headline of his clarion call to British justice. He felt the blood pulsing in his temple.

'I'm telling you that the due courses of

the law have been meticulously observed,' Peach said calmly.

The young man should have seen the warning signs of a Peach coup, but he was too excited to back off now. 'Oh, come on, Inspector! How can you say that, when a man who may be innocent, who by the most sacred tenet of our legal system is certainly innocent until he is proved guilty, is being held without even any consideration of—'

'Because he isn't.'

The silence which dropped upon the hall was wholly satisfying to Peach. He smiled down at the acned youth as that deflated champion slowly resumed his seat. That particular reign of terror had been neatly overthrown before it began, Percy thought.

It was Sally Etherington of Radio Lancashire who said, 'But I thought you said a man was being held in connection with the death of Verna Hume.'

'No.' Percy's smile was inexorable. 'We said that a man had been arrested.' He turned his head sideways to look at Tucker, without moving his body at all, like a parrot looking curiously at some new source of amusement. 'That is correct, isn't it, sir?'

Tucker nodded weakly. The bright young woman from local radio resumed with the words which were always music in Percy Peach's ears. 'But I don't understand. If that man is still in custody and hasn't been charged, then surely—'

'But he isn't, you see.'

'Isn't in custody?'

'No. He was released two hours ago.'

'Released?' Seventy-three eyes widened. Sally Etherington said, 'Why was this?'

Peach shrugged. 'The due processes of law.' Peach looked down with pity upon the deflated young man below him. 'What I think our young friend here called "the most sacred tenet" of our legal system: a man is innocent until proved guilty. We did not have enough evidence to hold the man, so we released him. Quite simple and straightforward, really. Any more questions?'

There were, of course. Questions about wrongful arrest, and precipitate police action. About the identity of the man who had been held, and his reactions to it. The press switched tracks with accustomed skill to a new attack on police inefficiency. Peach let Tommy Bloody Tucker field these enquiries as best he could.

No sense in saying too much to these lads and lasses, once you had made it clear to them where the blame for a cock-up lay.

Fourteen

'Why "Osborne Employment Agency" when we're told Verna Hume was the owner?'

Detective Inspector Peach looked at the large, impressive letters which ran down the whole length of the double-fronted premises while they waited for an opportunity to cross the busy street.

'Osborne was her maiden name, apparently. It's not unusual for women to preserve their own identity in their business ventures,' Lucy Blake pointed out.

Percy sniffed but did not comment. He had learnt to exercise an uncharacteristic caution in discussing feminist issues with his detective sergeant. 'Must be prosperous,' he said. 'They've just opened another new branch, according to the telephone directory. But then, with three million unemployed, people who say they can get you a job are in a good position, I suppose.'

The most remarkable thing about the woman who came to meet them was her luxuriant crop of chestnut hair. It was not as rich a red as Lucy Blake's—Peach, with his absence of cranial hair, was something of a connoisseur of these things—but it was dark, lustrous and altogether remarkable. Peach did not examine the roots as his sergeant automatically did. It was part of being a detective to observe things accurately, Lucy told herself when she felt uncharitable.

'Barbara Harris,' the woman said, and offered each of them in turn her hand. People meeting the police were often unsure of the niceties of introduction, but this one showed no hesitation.

Ms Harris took them through a bright room where three girls worked quietly at computers and into her private office at the rear of the building. 'Good of you to keep to the time we arranged, when you must be busy with the case,' she said. 'I've arranged for tea in five minutes.'

She expected this exchange to take a little time, then. And presumably that it would be completed within the half hour she had allotted them when Lucy rang her. That was all right. Percy didn't mind punctuality and afternoon tea. As long as this tall, efficient woman cooperated equally readily in volunteering information to them, there should be no problem.

She ignored the upright chair behind the big desk and sat down with them in one of the three comfortable armchairs the carpeted room contained; they were set so that none of them directly faced the light from the window, and Percy wondered if they had been carefully arranged that way for their meeting, so that no one should feel at a disadvantage.

He said, 'I'm afraid I have to tell you that we are now certain that your partner, Verna Hume, was murdered—she was your partner, by the way?'

'Yes.' There was the slightest hesitation before this confirmation, but no sign of grief at the death or excitement at the mention of murder. Often the very voicing of the word brought a *frisson* of horror into people's reactions. A cool one, this.

The tea came then, and she took the tray from the girl, shut the door firmly behind her, and busied herself with pouring and distributing the amber fluid, in what in more gracious centuries they used to call 'the ceremony of the tea', Percy recalled. But women with the leisure for such things would have patronised him in those days of class divisions; and he could never have become a policeman then, let alone a detective inspector with considerable powers at his disposal.

'We don't know who killed her, yet. As a matter of fact, we don't know as much as we would like to about Verna Hume. That's what we have to do in a murder case, you see: build up as full a picture of the victim and her habits as is possible, from those who knew her. It's the one crime where the victim can't speak for herself. A prime suspect usually emerges from those who knew the deceased if only we can get enough information about him or her.'

And that prime suspect might even be you, he thought. She was too intelligent a woman not to make that deduction for herself, but her hand was very steady as she offered him a biscuit from the oval china plate. She said, 'Well, our relationship was mainly a business one. But a close one: we'd known each other for fifteen years. Verna and I used to work together as secretaries, and we set up Osborne Employment within a couple of years of meeting each other. Well, it was Harris and Osborne then.'

She looked into Peach's dark eyes, expecting a reaction to that. But he let it go. First things first. 'You obviously got on well.'

'We built a successful business together. We thought very much along the same lines, and it worked for us.'

She hadn't quite answered his question, and both of them knew it. Peach asked, 'Did you associate much outside the business?'

'No.' The word came a little too quickly and she hastened to soften the denial. 'When you work together all day, perhaps you need to get away from each other when you leave work behind. Don't forget, we worked very long hours together, in the early days.'

Barbara found she was nervous about this, now that the time had come. She had prepared these phrases in advance; she wondered if that was obvious as she delivered them. Were her answers coming out like prepared statements? This dapper, muscular man and the quiet girl at his side were studying her quite openly, and she found it disturbing. In a social exchange, people would not have looked at her so directly, but this pair were not even pretending that this was anything of the kind.

Lucy Blake asked, 'Did your partners meet much?'

Barbara had not expected this. 'Our husbands? No. Scarcely at all.' She looked briefly at the print of Venice on the wall behind her questioner, then said, 'You might as well know: Verna and Martin didn't get on at all. I couldn't see why they stayed together. Whereas Michael and I ...'

'Your marriage was a happy one?'

Barbara noted the past tense. They knew Michael was dead, then. She wondered with a sudden shaft of fear how much more they knew about her life and her feelings. 'Yes. Very happy. Until Michael was killed in a car accident. Five years ago, that was.'

'Yes. That must have been a difficult time for you.' The girl was not unsympathetic but it was a statement which invited comment, and she left it hanging in the air like a challenge.

Perhaps they knew everything she was trying to conceal, were merely hoping she would make the mistake of lying to them about it, Barbara thought, with a rush of panic.

'It was difficult, yes. In all kinds of ways.'

'Financially difficult?' asked Peach, whose dark eyes had never left her face while his sergeant had introduced this subject.

Barbara was suddenly annoyed with these people who came on to her own ground and asked her about things no one else would have dared to raise with her. 'Look. I can't see how this can possibly have anything to do with Verna's death. It's my business, and no one—'

'Possibly. Possibly not.' Peach enjoyed interrupting her, relished the opportunity to do a little bullying. He was at his least likeable in these circumstances, thought Lucy, as she watched him from the corner of her eye, but possibly also at his most effective. 'We shall find out in due course whether it's our business or not, Mrs Harris. Verna Hume has been callously murdered, by person or persons unknown—for the moment. If it's not to remain that way, we need to find out as much as we can about her relationships with everyone around her. You knew her better than most, as you've already admitted.'

Barbara took a sip of her tea, watching her hands, surprised that they still moved so competently. She felt at the moment as if they belonged to someone else and were directed by some brain other than her own. She said, 'I heard you'd arrested Martin Hume.'

'Yes. And now we've released him. He didn't kill his wife, Mrs, Harris. Were you hoping he had?'

'No. Well, I sort of assumed ...'

'It would have made things simpler for everyone, wouldn't it? Us most of all. We wouldn't need to be sitting here prying into your feelings about your dead partner, for a start.'

'She wasn't my partner.' Barbara stared into her half-empty cup, holding the saucer tightly in both hands, glad to have something that would anchor them as she threw away her plans for concealment. 'I know I said she was, but she wasn't. Not now. She was until five years ago. That was when the firm was Harris and Osborne.'

'It changed after your husband died?'

'Yes. Verna lent me money to tide me over a difficult time. Said I could pay it back when it suited. I paid it all back, but she'd taken over the firm, legally, and she wouldn't let me back in.'

'Awkward.'

She flashed Peach a look of hatred for the word, then controlled herself. 'More than awkward as far as I was concerned. I was left working as Chief Executive—a well-paid employee of the firm I had set up with Verna and worked all hours God sends and a few more to develop.'

'And that was still the situation at the time of Mrs Hume's death?'

'Yes. She wouldn't budge.' Barbara thought of the blazing row she had had with Verna on the day before she had died, of the way the girls in the outer office had looked at her afterwards, of her certainty that they had heard the raised voices and the high passions in this very room. The girls knew, and if they were questioned by this awful, persistent man and his attentive sergeant, they would tell. So there was no point in trying to conceal that dispute.

Barbara forced herself to speak of it. 'As a matter of fact, we had a serious disagreement about it on the day before Verna died.'

'Really. And how do you know that Verna Hume died on that Saturday, Mrs Harris?' Peach's tone was quiet, polite, deadly accurate.

'I—I don't. I should have said just before the weekend when she died. I was upset. I was preoccupied with the row I had with Verna. You must see … ' She stopped, aware that she was saying too much, that there was nothing she could do now to retrieve the blunder she had made, that the two near-black eyes and the two ultramarine ones were studying her stumblings with an analytical interest.

They allowed the pause to stretch in the quiet room; the noise of a car horn on the other side of the building came to them unnaturally loudly through the double glazing. Lucy Blake thought that these silences in interrogations, when confused people willed them to speak, were almost the cruellest thing they did. But detection fed on confusion, and Peach had taught her to foster it whenever it appeared.

Peach eventually said, 'All right. Let's

get back to this "serious disagreement". What exactly was it about, Mrs Harris?'

'About the company. About the partnership issue. Verna told me when she lent me the money that I could buy back into the firm whenever I was ready. Last Friday, she refused to honour that agreement.' Barbara's tone was even, exhausted. She wanted to get the facts about this out and have done with it. She tried to speak evenly; she was aware even in her distress that it would be as well to conceal what she could of her burning sense of grievance.

'That must have made you very angry.'

She flashed him a bitter smile, a recognition that he had pinpointed what she had sought to hide. 'Yes. Of course it did. I was very angry. And very frustrated. Because we'd never written anything down about it. I knew I had nothing to fall back on, if she chose to deny me what she had promised at the time of Michael's death.'

'So you parted on bad terms?'

'Very bad.'

They paused again, waiting to see whether she would offer any more. Then Lucy Blake said quietly, 'We shall need an account of your movements over the weekend. Can you start by telling us where you were on Saturday afternoon and evening, please?'

'I was on my own at home. I live alone. I do see a man fairly regularly, but not on Saturdays.' She looked up at them with a bitter little smile. 'He's married, you see, with a family.' And now he can't even provide me with an alibi for this, she thought. She could picture the apprehension on his face at the very thought of any involvement in a murder inquiry.

Barbara watched Lucy Blake record the information in a neat, swift hand in a small notebook. She used a small gold ballpoint pen, a surprisingly decorative and female touch amid all this police efficiency. Barbara, drawn by the silence to speak when she had never meant to, asked, 'Is that when Verna died?'

'We think so. You appeared to think so yourself, a little while ago.' Peach smiled a predatory smile at her, returning briskly to the attack after the softer female tones of his partner. 'If you think of anyone who could confirm your whereabouts at that time, it would be in your interests as well as ours to let us know about it.' He flashed her a brief, mirthless smile. 'Assuming, of course, that you didn't go round to Mrs Hume's house and kill her.'

'No. I didn't do that. Even though on Friday I would have liked her to disappear from my life for ever.'

'Then you must help us to find who did kill her. By definition, a murder victim must have at least one serious enemy. Most people have more. We should like help from you with some names.'

Barbara had given up smoking ten years and more ago. Now, for the first time in many years, she found herself longing for a cigarette, for the long, slow inhaling which would draw the smoke and the drug into her lungs, settling her nerves and her brain which raced too fast within her head. She looked down at her fingers, imagining the slow curl of smoke at the end of a freshly lit Benson and Hedges, even twitching the first two fingers of her right hand as if they held that solace. 'Verna Hume had plenty of enemies, Inspector Peach.'

He was surprised she had remembered his name: most people didn't, under stress.

Part of her job, he supposed; but it showed her mind was still working hard. 'We need to know about them, Mrs Harris. In confidence, of course. And as you'd expect, we shall be asking the same question of other people we see.'

Barbara shrugged her elegant shoulders. 'You make enemies in this business, inevitably. People are unrealistic about their own abilities: they think you should have got them jobs which were way beyond their range. But no one resented things enough to kill Verna, I'm sure.' Except me, she thought, except me, whom Verna cheated out of the business which had been our whole life.

Peach, who was considering exactly the same thought, said, 'What about her life outside the firm? Her husband has already told us there were other men.'

'There were.' Even now, even with herself as a suspect and owing the woman no favours, she found it difficult to talk about Verna and her men. Some vague feminine code seemed to make it more difficult for her than if she had been speculating about a man and his mistresses. 'Verna had lots of men. Seemed almost to need a succession of them, as if she was proving something to herself.'

Peach said, deliberately provocatively, 'We need names, not psychology, Mrs Harris. The more time that elapses after a murder, the less likely we are to find the killer. And people who have killed once and got away with it often feel bold enough to murder again.'

That usually got them going, hastened things along a bit. Especially when the first murder victim had been a woman. Percy watched with satisfaction the sharp intake of breath beneath Barbara Harris's expensively brassiered breasts.

'Most of them I didn't know. Didn't want to know. Verna kept business and pleasure strictly apart, and that suited both of us. But there seems to have been one particular man in the last month or two. Almost for the first time, really, I began to think there might be something serious and long-term in it.'

Lucy Blake gripped the gold ballpoint point. 'We need a name, please.'

'I'm sorry, I don't know the surname. But I think his first name was Hugh.'

It was the second time that mysterious monosyllable of a name had been recorded in DS Blake's book.

Fifteen

'Golf is a bloody stupid game!' shouted Percy Peach. He shouted it vehemently, but to no one in particular. None of his companions troubled to deny such a self-evident fact. Percy glared at his ball, contemplated the distant green, and perpetrated a shot which sliced extravagantly to the right and confirmed his opinion. 'Golf is a BLOODY STUPID game!'

Yet he delivered the thought with less than his normal vehemence, and trudged into the rough to seek his ball quite philosophically. The North Lancashire Golf Club, with its views over the Ribble Valley and its distant prospects of Ingleborough and Pen-y-Ghent, was not a bad place to be on a balmy summer evening after a trying day. Indeed, if pressed hard enough, Peach, who was not given to overstatement, would have confessed that he thought there were few better places to be in the whole world. And if his golf

171

was bad, he could always remind himself that the North Lancs had shown the good taste to reject Tommy Bloody Tucker's application for membership.

Nevertheless, Percy felt it was a pity he had to spoil the peace and the panorama with such execrable golf. The feet which had once danced down cricket pitches so effectively, which had on one never-to-be-forgotten occasion put him in position to hook the fearsome Curtley Ambrose for four, now only got him into trouble at golf. In this silly game, his feet had to remain rooted to the earth while the whole of the rest of his body moved. His left heel kept lifting from the ground on his backswing, despite his best efforts, so that he lost control of his swing path in returning it to base, just as the pro had told him he would. Stupid game. BLOODY STUPID game. Sod it.

Then, as he swung a five-iron without hope or preparation, everything magically and mysteriously came together. The golf ball which had been so maddeningly wayward sprang away from the clubhead so smoothly that he hardly felt it. It was effortless, akin to the sensation he had previously enjoyed only on those rare occasions when he had lifted a cricket ball out of the ground off the very middle of his bat.

The small white ball soared high against an azure sky, then hung there for so long that it seemed the action had moved into slow motion. When it finally descended, it plummeted softly to earth on the emerald carpet beyond the greenside bunker. Percy studied its position by the distant flagstick for a stupefied moment. 'Bloody 'ell!' he muttered softly to himself.

'Bloody 'ell, Percy!' shouted his partner appreciatively from the other side of the fairway. Peach waved a modest, self-deprecatory acknowledgement, trying to convey in the gesture that this was his normal game, despite all previous evidence to the contrary. Two minutes later, he holed the putt for a most unlikely four, and the world was suddenly a perfect place. Then, with three wins and a half on the last four holes, the rejuvenated Peach and his partner halved a match which had seemed irretrievably lost.

In that last hour of summer daylight, Percy walked on air in a perfect male world. The cares of work and the complications of personal relationships alike dropped away as he concentrated on his game and enjoyed the view to Longridge Fell, over fields and hamlets which might have been set out as a background for Gray's elegy. Here, there was no need to worry about the disturbing Lucy Blake; about the personal complications which were impinging upon a working relationship; about making a fool of himself with an attractive woman ten years younger than he was; about the tenderness which could so easily compromise his steely image.

The figures who moved beside him were indisputably male, middle-aged and undesirable. They had that indefinable scruffiness which overtakes men towards the end of a round of golf, that boyish capacity to devote themselves to things which are essentially unimportant as if the whole world depended upon them. As his companions walked ahead of him with their trolleys, they were reassuringly without grace in both form and movement. Percy was free of that disturbing curve of Lucy's perfectly rounded and engagingly mobile rear, which impaired his concentration by day and agitated his dreams by night.

The North Lancs still had a men's bar, so that the male ambience which Percy

174

had found such an uncomplicated comfort could be preserved after the golf was over. The four sat at their own table, indulged in hilarious exchanges about the game they had just completed, and reviewed their performances with a robust humour which women might have thought cruel. After the first two pints, the conversation began to seem a model of wit and invention.

As the twilight dropped into darkness beyond the windows, the men's bar emptied and there was much noisy leave-taking. Peach's four-ball had been the last one in, and presently there remained only one other group in the bar with them. It was a larger one than theirs: eight men clustered around a table at the other end of the small room with its red leather chairs, swapping jokes and reminiscences.

As the anecdotes dried up, they moved on to local topics. Percy Peach kept his end up in the conversation at his own table, but his alert policeman's ear picked out scraps of what was happening at the other end of the room.

'You knew the woman, didn't you, Hugh?' asked a young man in a Pringle sweater, speaking more loudly than he realised.

'I did, yes,' said the blond man he addressed. He had been dominating the group; now he spoke more quietly. His apprehensive glance at Peach's table revealed more than he knew.

'Bet you had 'er knickers off, then!' said the voluble one. He was the youngest one in a group who were all under forty, wanting to be laddish with the rest and yet unsure of himself. He sniggered at his companions in a way which was meant to be wholly complimentary to the man he addressed. Sexual conquests were the surest mark of status in this company.

'Leave it, Matt,' the fair-haired man said urgently. He snatched another nervous glance at the only other occupied table in the bar. 'The woman's dead, isn't she?'

This vague attempt to appeal to the good taste of a drunken man was unsuccessful: Matt gaped at him uncomprehendingly. Nor did it save Hugh from the intervention he feared. Percy Peach was at the speaker's side as he looked up.

'We're talking about Verna Hume, aren't we?' he said quietly.

The fair-haired man looked up, simulating a calmness he no longer felt and anxious to preserve the stance he had always adopted within the group. 'We aren't talking about anyone,' he said, insolently. 'I wasn't aware that anyone had asked you to join in our private conversation. Of course, if—'

'Your name Hugh?'

'Yes, it is. Not that that's any business of—'

'Detective Inspector Peach. We need to talk.'

The man smiled. He had a complete set of expensively dentured teeth and an elaborate haircut. Percy had neither, and both were red rags to his bullish advance. He thought the copious yellow hair beneath him might even be permed, though he disdained any expertise in such things.

Now the man glanced at the steward, who was watching them from behind the bar, and tried to assert himself. 'We don't talk in here, especially to PC Plods. This is a golf club, Mr Peach, where we come to relax. We don't like people who bring business here. Especially business like yours. I don't—'

'Quite right, too. Your place or mine, sunshine?'

Hugh put his hands on the edge of the small round table in front of him, feeling his way carefully among the empty glasses. He was intensely conscious of his image among the men around him, who were suddenly silent after all their noisy hilarity.

'Well, I'm certainly not coming to Brunton Police Station. I shall be at my place of work, Pearson Electronics, tomorrow morning as usual, but you should be warned that I've no intention of—'

'Right. I'll be there at eight thirty. Look forward to hearing what you have to tell us. Murder inquiry it is. You'd best be frank, sunshine, if you know what's good for you.'

Percy was back at his table, smiling his satisfaction, almost before his three companions realised he had been away.

PC Darren Wall was trying hard to look alert and in control. You never knew who was watching you. That was the trouble with being in uniform. You had to keep up the image of the force with the public at all times, as they told the rows of rash young faces at training school. Smart. Vigilant. Confident, without being arrogant. In control, without being aggressive. What a load of bollocks.

As the warm summer darkness cloaked

his actions, Darren moved into a gateway between two cypresses and tugged at his boxer shorts; they had been riding up as usual beneath his black uniform trousers. They told you all those other things at training school, but never mentioned the effect of police trousers upon boxer shorts.

He looked up at the quiet houses, where bedroom lights were beginning to go on behind the curtains as people prepared for bed. Not much chance of anything happening around here to enable a young constable to make his name. (At nineteen, PC Wall was still young enough to think in these terms, like a reporter looking for a scoop.) There was always the possibility of a burglary in these big houses near the park, he supposed, but there wasn't much chance of glory, even in that. Burglary was too common a crime to carry any glamour these days, and you had to radio in for assistance; that was the official procedure. And a right prat you could look then, if you brought out a carful of police muscle to pick up some pimply unemployed school-leaver who was just trying his luck in an empty house.

And yet. And yet you could never be sure. Hadn't there been a murder in a big respectable house at the end of this very road a few days ago? At the weekend, of course, when he was off duty. Just his luck. Mind you, CID would have muscled in on it pretty quickly anyway, even if he'd been around. But at least he might have got in on the house to house.

Darren took out a strip of chewing gum from the pack which had to last him the week. He unwrapped it slowly and methodically, stretching the moment into a ritual which only a man with too much time on his hands could have devised. Refusing to contemplate whether his mother might after all have been right when she had tried to dissuade him from becoming a policeman, he thought again of the new blonde Venus at the station, PC Julie. He was hoping to introduce her to the tricks of the trade, if only he could persuade an uncooperative station sergeant to adjust the duty rosters.

A lissome, athletic, lust-inducing figure, that PC Julie was. It was clearly Darren's duty to protect her from the lubricious advances of the old sweats and afford her his own lechery-free advice and experience. She would be off-duty now; he tried not to think of her changing out of her uniform. And failed.

A little desperately, he began to patrol the deserted road, walking with exaggeratedly slow, regular paces in an attempt to exorcise all libidinous thoughts. God, but she was desirable, that Julie. And he would be entirely considerate of her, absolutely the gentleman. Just to touch the nape of her neck beneath that straight yellow hair would be quite enough for him. Of course, if she herself should be excited, should find herself eager for a little more than that ...

He quickened his pace, trying furiously to think of football and the prospects of the Rovers when the new season should begin. The golden days when they had had Alan Shearer to lead the attack and score the goals were gone for good now. But they were a good team still, with youngsters to come through. Perhaps PC Darren Wall would be on crowd control duty there this year, instead of shouting his head off in the seats behind the goal. He imagined himself announcing to his friends on the night before the match that he would be at the ground in his official capacity, that he wouldn't be with them, though he would of course be seeing the match for free in the line of duty.

He might even be paid overtime to go to the ground which had been the repository of his dreams since his boyhood; might even be policing the players' entrance, nodding casually to his heroes, touching them briefly on the shoulder as he shepherded them through the excited crowds.

But even these soccer images, entertained so often since he had first put on his police uniform four months ago, failed to excite him on this occasion. They could not distract his thoughts from the entrancing Julie, with her wide blue eyes, her neat nose and her soft, ingenuous mouth that was so obviously in need of protection. He marched still more quickly, thrusting his hands hard into his pockets, clutching at his torch, masticating his gum with a fierce resolve.

Stupid idea this patrol was, anyway. Get the policemen out of the cars and back onto the beat, the chief constable had said to the press. Let the public see its police force; let the criminals as well as the innocent be aware that the enforcers of the law were around the town and were vigilant. An experiment, the CC had said, which would be implemented across the borough if it proved successful.

What he hadn't announced was that it was a very small experiment. Six constables, in fact. All of them young suckers like him. Or so it seemed to Darren. Once the maximum publicity had been wrung from it, the experiment would be quietly dropped. PC Darren Wall was beginning to learn the ways of authority.

Well, it would be good to be back in a patrol car. At least there you had a mate to grumble with, and the time passed more quickly. That mate might even be Julie, if he played his cards right. He almost swallowed his gum at the thought.

The fit of coughing this caused made a dog bark as he passed a darkened house. The door of the house opened, allowing a shaft of orange light to cut a swathe through the darkness. An invisible man pushed a springer spaniel out into the night and ordered, 'Seek him out, boy!' The tones were obviously meant for the ears of some imagined intruder in the garden shadows rather than the dog itself.

Darren moved hastily on down the road. The dog, after a single bark, confined its efforts to urinating on the trees within the boundaries of its territory. A snuffler, not a bared-fangs canine, thought Darren with some relief. Three houses down the road and safe, he found he had moved too swiftly in evading this potential threat to police authority: he had to melt into the shadows to ease the tightness of his boxer shorts.

He looked at his watch. Time he was checking on Wycherly Croft again. It was part of his brief to check on the now empty murder house every couple of hours. God knew why. The scene-of-crime team had long since finished their examination of the premises; anything interesting must have been dispatched to forensic some time ago. But the ways of the CID were not to be fathomed by simple uniformed minds like his.

Wasn't there some old saying about the murderer returning to the scene of the crime? But there surely wasn't anything in that notion; no one would be so foolish, in real life, would they? PC Wall, walking tall and squaring his shoulders in the darkness to give himself confidence, felt the summer night suddenly chilly around him.

He had tried the doors of the murder

house earlier, when it was still daylight. Perhaps he wouldn't bother going right up to the doors and windows this time, whatever the regulations said he should do. It was a waste of time, really: he'd be better employed looking for someone breaking and entering elsewhere. Or even showing a police presence by the boisterous pub at the bottom end of the park, at the other end of his beat.

From the gate, the silhouette of the house looked menacing against the blue-black sky, like a building in those horror films he had laughed at so bravely with his friends as they asserted their adolescence. The moonless late-spring night felt colder still, as if there might be a touch of frost before he went off duty in the clear dawn light.

Then, as he looked at the house, Darren could scarcely believe his young eyes. There was a light inside the place. A dim light, appearing and disappearing, but a light, he was sure. He gulped; it was the kind of incident he had been praying for half an hour earlier. Now it had come, he felt the hairs prickle on the back of his neck, as they had not done since he was a child.

He spoke softly into his radio, his eyes glued to the light flickering behind the windows of the dark slab of a house. 'PC Wall to Control. PC Wall to Control. Come in, please.' No answer. The blasted thing was on the blink. It had been faulty earlier when there had still been full daylight. Then, for a while, it had worked impeccably—when there was nothing to report. Now that he needed it, it was dead. Dead as a Dodo. Darren was not sure he liked that phrase.

He was standing under a big chestnut tree at the gate, by the sign with the picture of a witch beneath the name, Wycherly Croft. Perhaps he should move out into the open, try the radio again. But he knew in his heart that it was the instrument that was faulty. Shitty bloody thing! Should have been chucked away years ago. And he didn't want to take his eyes off the house. This was real policing at last, even if it was scary. Darren was vaguely aware that he would never forgive himself if he missed out on it. And he'd get a right bollocking if he let an intruder get away through moving round the corner to try again on a bloody radio that he knew was shot.

There was a car in the drive, just to the left of the house; he saw it as he moved a pace or two nearer. Not very professional, that: it could have been hidden round the side of the building. And it was scarcely a getaway car. An old Fiesta Popular, 950 cc. It didn't look the kind of car to contain massive men with baseball bats and balaclavas. Without his radio, he could not even check out whether it was a stolen vehicle. It was white, and the letter he could see on the number plate told him that it was eight years old.

Darren crept past the car, down the last yards of the drive, stooping to use the cover of the rhododendrons, despite the darkness. The light was more definite now that he was close, but intermittent. For an excited moment, he thought someone had set fire to the place, that flames were beginning to get a hold on the downstairs rooms. Then he realised what the source of this illumination must be. A torch. And whoever held it was moving from room to room. That was why the illumination sometimes disappeared altogether, then reappeared in a different place.

Darren gripped his own rubber torch firmly. It was reassuringly solid as he drew

187

it from beneath his tunic. He'd have this bugger: get him when he came out of the front door to go to his car. He'd have surprise on his side, wouldn't he? He didn't allow himself to entertain the thought that there might be more than one intruder.

He didn't have long to wait. He slipped behind the square shape of the hatchback as he heard the front door of the big house open, trying to ignore the pounding of his heart. He had somehow assumed that this sort of reaction would be removed when you became a policeman and got your uniform. He had a long moment to feel the blood thumping in his head before he heard the click of the Yale lock as the door was pulled carefully shut. Then a dark figure appeared at the corner of the house and crossed the few yards to the driver's door. Darren was too busy hiding himself to see much, but he knew at least that there was only one bloke to tackle—and he hadn't looked huge. Wiry and strong perhaps, ruthless no doubt in his panic, but not huge.

Darren made himself wait for the sound of the key in the lock. Men were always vulnerable when they had one hand occupied with the door lock and were off balance.

He had been right about the size of his adversary. As he sprang, he was conscious of a reassuringly diminutive figure. He shouted only, 'You're nicked, mate!' leaving the words of the formal caution until he should have the man's arm up his back and his charge at his mercy.

He had both hands on that arm before his quarry could even try to turn. He was conscious of how thin and unresisting it was in his grip, even as the shriek of alarm from his victim rang in his ears.

It was a thin, high scream of fear. Too thin. Too high.

PC Wall looked down unbelievingly into the frail face that turned in terror to look up into his. A female face. An elderly, pop-eyed, female face, set in a small, frightened head, with a feathered hat on top of it.

'Oh, bugger!' said Darren.

His radio still wouldn't work. He had to get his arrest to drive them to the station in the ageing Fiesta. She took a long time to do it, following his directions with elaborate concentration, trying to stop her hands from shaking with the shock of her capture.

The station sergeant who watched prisoner and escort entering his nick had seen most things, but his face told Darren that this was a first for him. He listened to PC Wall's breathless account of the arrest at Wycherly Croft, then put the old lady in a cell. Apologetically.

Turning back to the arresting officer, he said simply, 'Bloody 'ell, Max!' Max was PC Wall's nickname, after the late lamented comedian. It looked as though he was going to keep it.

Sixteen

'I wish you'd eat a proper breakfast!'

It took a mother to hit that anxious, resentful tone, thought Lucy Blake. She said, 'I'm all right, Mum. Really, I don't need it. Just the opposite actually—I need to watch my weight. I've put on six pounds since I moved into the flat, you know.'

'That's that body-building course they

put you on when you went in for this police job, that is.'

'It was a fitness check, Mum, that's all. Can't have our detectives unfit, can we?' She sneaked a look at her watch. Almost seven already. She'd be in front of the Brunton rush hour, though; and she could use the lanes for the first part of the fifteen-mile journey.

'Made your shoulders too big, that body-building did!' said Mrs Blake resentfully. 'Not ladylike, that isn't.' She moved round behind her daughter, who sat at the breakfast table, studying those shoulders and the straight neck beneath the soft auburn hair, reflecting with that universal maternal regret on the vulnerable schoolgirl who had sat at this table so short, so very short, a time ago and resenting this sturdy, independent young woman who had come so brusquely into her place.

Knowing that she should not say it, that it would produce only irritation in this girl she loved, she was still driven to raise the issue yet again. 'I don't know why you needed to move into that flat. You could have travelled from here in the car.'

'Need to be on the spot, Mum. Irregular

hours, now I'm in CID. Have to be available at short notice.'

They both knew that wasn't the real reason. She would have moved out anyway by now, even without the transfer to CID. She needed to be independent, to come and go without a parental watchdog. It was the modern way, but it made Agnes Blake suddenly feel very old, when she was scarcely fifty. But you couldn't go admitting your loneliness to the young. She said, acknowledging defeat, 'I bet you eat a lot of junk food. That's why you're putting on weight, you know.'

Lucy felt uncomfortably that there was something in that, though she would never admit it. 'I don't eat as well as I do here, Mum, that's true. But I'd put on even more weight, if I had your baking to tempt me!'

They left it at that, each with a little smile at the other which an onlooker would have noted as facsimiles. Lucy drove the bulbous little Vauxhall Corsa away into the morning sun with a cheerful, valedictory wave, and her mother went back into the house with a sigh to listen to the news on Radio Lancashire. They didn't seem to be any nearer to catching whoever had murdered this Verna Hume woman in Brunton.

Mrs Blake hoped her Lucy wasn't involved in dealing with things like that.

The sign over the door read 'Pearson Electronics'. It was edged with glass tubing, so that it could light up in green neon at night. The sign sat most uneasily over the pillars of a Georgian door and beneath the elegant rectangular windows of a building that was two hundred years old.

Hugh Pearson saw the look of distaste that Peach cast at the sign as he came into the building. 'It pays to advertise,' the director of the business said brightly, 'even when your headquarters are in a building like this.'

Peach did not comment. His black pupils were as bright and vigilant as a bird's as he followed his quarry through a room with two secretaries and into his private office. So the mysterious Hugh's surname was Pearson. It had taken them until last night to find a murder suspect's full name; there was much ground to be made up here.

'Do sit down,' said Pearson, his smile as bright and automatic as a politician's. 'I'll arrange for some coffee.' He made for his desk and the intercom.

'Don't bother,' said Percy. 'Too early in the morning. Too much to do.'

'Ah. Well, if you won't be staying long ...' said Hugh Pearson.

'That will depend on you. We shall be here as long as is necessary to find out what we want. This is Detective Sergeant Blake.'

It was to be one of Percy's aggressive interviews then, thought Lucy, as she sat down at his side. She was rather pleased about that: she had not appreciated the oleaginous smile Pearson had poured over her when she was introduced.

Hugh Pearson sat down rather awkwardly behind his desk, put his hands together, steepled his fingers, and said, 'How exactly can I help you, Inspector Peach?'

Percy stared at the man behind the big desk in silence for a moment. He looked as if he had turned over a stone and found something unpleasant but interesting beneath it. 'You can start by telling us why you did not come forward earlier,' he said.

Hugh Pearson had not expected this to be easy, but he had thought he would carry it off without too much difficulty. The filth might be a nuisance, but they were not very intelligent, for sure. His plan had been to run rings round them, then be thanked for his cooperation. He controlled his anger, forced a smile, and said winningly, 'Look, Inspector, perhaps we got off on the wrong foot last night at the golf club. I didn't like being disturbed with my friends—we have what may seem an old-fashioned view that business shouldn't be brought into the golf club.' He glanced at Lucy Blake's blue-green eyes, and offered her another of his wide smiles. 'We're old-fashioned enough to think that the men's bar in particular should be sacrosanct, you see.'

Percy Peach studied him without a word, his face as expressionless as it had been since Pearson began. Hugh found this absence of reaction far more disturbing than he would have thought possible. He faltered on, trying not to lose the thread of his argument. 'What I'm saying is that if I was in any way offensive last night I—'

'Fine. Now would you answer the question, please. This is a murder inquiry. Why didn't you come forward to help?'

Pearson was suddenly aware of DS

Blake. The woman's neat hands were poised over a notebook at Peach's side; the gold ballpoint pen hovered above the naked page to record his reply to this verbal assault. He gathered himself and said with an attempt at truculence, 'Now look here, Inspector—'

'No! *You* look here, Mr Pearson. A woman has been brutally murdered. Several days ago, now. Two days ago, we put out a request for anyone who had been in touch with her in the days before her death to come forward to Brunton CID. You choose to ignore that call. Why?'

'Well—well, it seemed to me that anything I had to tell you couldn't possibly be of much interest. That a perfectly innocent association such as I had enjoyed with Mrs Hume couldn't have anything to do with her death ...'

Pearson's words tailed helplessly away. Just when you expected this man to interrupt you again, he let you go on, tying yourself up, sounding increasingly feeble even to your own ears. Hugh was used to being in control of things, to ordering other people about. It was too long since he had been an employee and had been put on the spot like this, for him to cope with it.

For his part, Peach was reflecting that he thoroughly disliked Pearson; that it was eminently satisfying to him that he did not have to conceal that dislike.

'Do you wish to see the person who murdered Mrs Hume apprehended?'

'Well, yes, of course I do, but—'

'Then you have a very strange way of going about it. Surely you see that it could only help our investigation forward to have your statement? To hear what you can tell us of the victim? To eliminate you from our inquiries? If that is what we are able to do, of course.'

'Now, look here. If you're saying I'm—'

'I'm not saying anything, Mr Pearson. Not yet. The trouble is, neither are you. But in police thinking, your conduct is suspicious. The behaviour, wouldn't you say, DS Blake, of someone who has something to hide?'

He turned his round face abruptly upon Lucy, and she had to conceal her surprise. 'Yes, sir. Highly suspicious.' She had not removed her disturbing eyes from Hugh Pearson's face. 'The name "Hugh" has appeared in various places.' She was proud of her vagueness here; almost Peachian she thought. It made it sound as if the name

197

had been springing out at them from everywhere, instead of being picked up from the dead woman's diary and from Barbara Harris. 'And yet, despite appeals in the press and on the radio, you have not come forward. Bound to seem suspicious, that.' She picked up Peach's word and used it like a recurring chorus.

Even the bloody woman was getting at him now, Hugh thought bitterly; probably a dyke, to be doing a job like this. He said sullenly, 'There was no appeal to me by name. Just a general demand for anyone who had known Verna to come forward.'

Peach looked his disgust, studying Pearson for several seconds with practised, silent distaste. It had its effect. It was the man behind the desk who broke the silence. He said weakly, 'Well, I'm here now, anyway.'

'Yes. We've ferreted you out.' Peach looked round at the high, ornate ceiling of the Georgian room, at the prints of Chester and York in their neat gold frames on the walls, at the decanters of port and whisky on the Pembroke table beside the window, at the mahogany desk and the ornate inkstand which was never used. And finally at the anxious face above that inkstand, at the man who normally controlled events in this elegant room. 'Time to make up for lost time, Mr Pearson. What was your relationship with Verna Hume?'

Hugh had planned to dissimulate, to pretend that he had not known Verna very well, that their meetings had been random and sporadic, their friendship rather casual. He comprehended now that he would not get away with that; that this Rottweiler of a man would take him and shake him until he gave up his secrets. Or most of them. He must revise his assessment of the filth if he was to keep the most vital facts of all to himself. These two were not as stupid as he had expected them to be.

'Verna and I were lovers. I expect that's what you wanted to hear.'

'The truth is what I wanted to hear. Rather earlier than this, for preference. How long had this association been going on?'

'Well, I'd known Verna for about six months. I suppose we'd been going to bed together for most of that time. But you mustn't assume that our relationship was all that close. Verna's marriage wasn't a happy one. I didn't think I was treading on any toes when I slept with her. And—and as I say, we weren't really all that close. Verna liked a good time. I wasn't the first lover she'd had, and I'm sure I wouldn't have been the last.'

Hugh stumbled on, repeating himself, wanting to be stopped, finding that now, when he expected to be interrupted, this awful man let him gabble on, going he knew not where, revealing, he was sure, far more than he intended. When he finally forced himself to stop, he felt Peach's black pupils boring like gimlets into his mind; they seemed the only things alive in the Inspector's stony face. Hugh thought he would be able to see this round white face long after their meeting was over, looking down on him during the night like a Francis Bacon portrait. Outside, a heavy lorry passed along the street. The sounds of its ponderous progress were louder through the double glazing than he would have thought possible; its passage seemed impossibly slow as the noise of it faded and died.

Peach said, 'How often did you see her?'

Pearson's shrug of the shoulders, exaggerated because of his tension, made Lucy

Blake suddenly hate him. He was trying to shrug away this dead woman whom he had bedded and caressed, who had surely been tender with him, who had brought him intimacy and delight. Detective Sergeant Blake, who should have been professional and objective, hated him for that.

'I met Verna once a week. Sometimes twice. Probably more often than twice in the last few weeks.'

'Where?'

'At my flat, mostly. We had a weekend away, once. About five weeks ago, that would be.'

'When did you last see Verna Hume, Mr Pearson?'

Hugh licked his lips, gathering himself like a highjumper for the biggest leap of all. He had rehearsed the answer to this question, because he had known it was inevitable; now he found the words he had chosen would not come when he needed them. 'On the Tuesday. The one before the Saturday when she died.'

Peach's features, previously so immobile, sprang now into vivid animation. 'You seem very certain about the exact time of the lady's death. It is information we haven't yet released.' He smiled upon

Pearson like a cartoon cat upon a cornered mouse.

And like a cartoon smile, this one seemed to Hugh to stretch and stretch, until it threatened to fill the whole of this familiar room. He said, 'You said four days ago, yourself, just now. I'm sure you did.'

'I said *several* days ago, Mr Pearson. Quite deliberately.'

'Oh. Well, I—I suppose I just assumed ...'

'Hmmm. You're sure you didn't see Mrs Hume after Tuesday?'

'No. We spoke a couple of times on the phone, but I didn't see her after Tuesday.' He repeated the day again, like a man anxious to convince himself of an unlikely fact. Searching desperately for some detail which might make it convincing, he said, 'Verna rang me at the office, at least once. On the Friday, I think. My secretary could confirm that for you.'

'Yes. Secretaries are often able to corroborate things. Bit like wives, really.' Peach contrived to imply that even confirmation of facts was highly suspect, in his view. 'So we've established that you were bedding the lady. Regularly. How close

202

would you say the relationship was, then?' Again, Percy produced the only phrase he had accepted from the social workers who were such anathema to him.

Again the shrug from Pearson. This time Hugh managed to transfer some of the physical relaxation it brought into his own voice, and Lucy Blake hated him a little more for that as he said, 'Difficult to say, really. She was available, and I'm single. As I say, I wasn't the only man she slept with, by any means.'

Lucy, looking up from her notes, said acidly, 'Easy lay, was she, Mr Pearson?'

Hugh, taken by surprise because he had almost forgotten her in his contest with Peach, was more than ever convinced that this was a dyke. He said peevishly, 'I didn't say that, did I? She liked sex, and her marriage was a disappointment to her. I didn't kid myself I was the only one to enjoy her favours.'

'So she meant very little to you?'

'I didn't say that either, did I?' Hugh felt suddenly more confident, even truculent, with this younger, female adversary, who clearly knew nothing about the delights of life between the sheets with a man like him. 'We knew the score, both of us. I wasn't ready to settle down, and Verna was taking pleasure where she found it.' The look on the open features beneath the dark yellow hair said that Hugh Pearson didn't think Verna would have found any greater pleasure than with him.

'We found your name in Mrs Hume's diary,' said Peach. 'Why would she bother to write it down, do you think, when there were so few other names there?'

For a moment, Pearson fought with his vanity, as Percy had intended he should. But he was enough aware of his danger to resist. 'I couldn't say, I'm sure.'

He wondered what Verna had written there; whether there had been any indication of the pressures she was putting upon him to shack up with her. That was one of the troubles with these CID people: they gave nothing away. They could trap you into lies, if you weren't careful. Probably the less he said the better. 'Perhaps she just wanted to make a note of when we were due to meet. She was very methodical, you know.'

'No, I don't know. We're still building up a picture of our murder victim, you see. Were you expecting to meet her at the weekend?'

The abruptness of the question almost caught him off guard, even as he told himself that he should have been prepared for it. 'No. Well, not definitely. I was expecting her to ring me, to make some arrangement.'

'And yet you didn't ring her, when you heard nothing from her?'

'No.'

'Didn't you find her silence even a little worrying? You say you were expecting to be in contact with her.'

'Puzzling, rather than worrying. I might have rung her, I suppose. But I had plenty of other things to do at the weekend.' Belatedly, he tried to recover a little of his swagger, to imply that he was confident enough of his appeal not to have to chase after women.

Peach studied him for a moment as if he disbelieved every word of this. Then he said, 'You say there were other men in her life, as well as you. Do you think one of them might have been responsible for this death?'

It was a chance to throw them a red herring, to divert the hunt from his own trail, which these two seemed to find so attractive. But, despite all Peach's implications, Hugh Pearson was not stupid. This pair he had planned to treat so lightly had won a reluctant respect from him, and he hesitated to lie to them more than he needed. Taking care this time to leave the day of the killing open, he said, 'I doubt whether Verna made any move to contact another man on Saturday or Sunday. She'd become rather attached to me, if you must know. And to be honest, we were rather closer than I implied earlier. She—she'd told me she was going to divorce Martin and marry me.'

'Really.' Peach's eyebrows shot alarmingly towards the ceiling. 'And that pleased you, did it?'

Hugh fought fiercely to ignore the contempt in Peach's voice, forcing himself to think about what his reaction to this should be, about how he could best get himself off the police hook. Verna wasn't around any more to dispute anything, thank God, and he didn't think anyone else would know much about this.

He said carefully, 'I wasn't averse to the idea. Quite attracted to it, in fact. Perhaps I've played the field for long enough. Perhaps it's time I settled down. And she was a good-looking woman, you know.' Even in his own danger, his vanity came out in that last phrase, as if he needed to defend his choice, to preserve his reputation as a womaniser.

'And of course she had her own business,' said Peach, his tone this time carefully neutral.

Before he saw the trap, Pearson had nodded his serious agreement. Then he said hastily, 'But that wasn't a consideration.'

'Of course not.' Again the man behind the desk was accorded that long, disconcerting moment of estimation from Peach's dark eyes. 'Who do you think killed Verna Hume, Mr Pearson?'

'I—I've really no idea. You can't expect—'

'Someone did, you see. Suffocated her, quite deliberately and cold-bloodedly, with a pillow. If you've any ideas on the matter, you'd better let us have them now.'

'No. No. I haven't.' Hugh felt again that he was being offered a chance to divert them, to set them on a scent other than his own. But he could think of nothing other than getting them out of this room where he was normally in command. He wanted only to be alone, away from these four inquisitorial eyes and their unflinching scrutiny.

Peach rose to his feet with apparent reluctance. 'Don't leave the area without informing us of your movements, Mr Pearson. And when you think of other information which might be of interest to us, get in touch immediately, please.'

'When', not 'if', thought Hugh. But he was too relieved by the prospect of their departure to raise any objection.

Pearson's tormentors had driven half a mile away from Pearson Electronics before either of them spoke. Then Lucy Blake said, 'I didn't like him.'

'I realised that. I make it a practice not to like many of them: you might have noticed. But you mustn't let it affect your judgement.'

'No. But I still don't like the turd. From what we've learned of Verna Hume so far, he seems a fitting mate for her. I shall make him my leading suspect. Is he yours?'

Percy knew that he should have told her immediately that she should proceed from facts, that she should beware of prejudging certain issues, and that there were suspects they had not even seen yet. Instead, he was silent, for as long as he had been in some of the intervals which had so unnerved Hugh Pearson. But this time he was genuinely weighing a proposition.

Eventually he said, 'I thought a man should be more upset by the death of his lover than our Mr Pearson appeared to be. Especially when he claims that he was intending to marry her.'

Seventeen

Martin Hume discovered his wife's body on the night of Sunday, 19th May. The news broke in the press and on radio on Monday May 20th.

Richard Johnson watched the brief local television announcement of the news on the evening of that Monday. On Tuesday, he worked through his day at the hospital as usual. If he wondered whether and when the call from the police would come, he gave no sign of his apprehension to the series of anxious faces he sought to reassure during his ward round and his out-patients' clinic. And there was no contact from the police, though the hours seemed to stretch endlessly as he waited to find out if his connection with Verna Hume would be brought to light.

There was no need to ring home: his wife would contact him immediately if there was any enquiry there from the police. He knew that: he could almost hear her bewildered and troubled voice in his ear. Yet he still had to resist the urge to pick up the phone whenever he had a moment between patients, to confirm to himself that Carmen had heard nothing.

When he eventually arrived home at five thirty, he knew from a glance at his wife's placid face that nothing untoward had broken the tenor of her day. Carmen had a serene, unlined, black face which had been one of her chief attractions when he had first met her and they had been students. It had filled out a little, and that serenity which had been so attractive in a teenage countenance now seemed dull, even bovine, when he was in his least charitable moods.

'I thought we'd have tea in the conservatory,' she said. 'It's only quiche and salad. I let the boys have theirs, because we didn't know how late you'd be.'

She'd ask him presently how his day had been, he thought, and he'd give his standard reply. They would watch television later. And then, at the end of the evening, they would make love, if he required it. There would never be a rejection for him, never a complaint if he did not feel amorous. He knew he was being unfair, that the dullness he complained of was as much of his making as of hers. Yet, as he watched her carefully cutting the portions of quiche and sliding them on to the plates in the modern, aseptic kitchen, Richard Johnson wondered whether he now hated his wife.

And that name, Carmen! You couldn't get much further from Bizet's passionate and tempestuous heroine than this woman he had tied himself to. So long as the children were happy at school and she had enough money for her modest housekeeping needs, she was contented enough. Certainly she would never complain.

You could not have a much greater contrast to the sensual and impulsive Verna Hume.

Like many a selfish man, Richard

Johnson required those qualities in his wife which would have made her an excellent mistress for someone else. And like many an intelligent, educated, professional man, he was totally incapable of applying the objectivity which was a habit of his working life to his own private emotions. He was a good surgeon: he knew that. And he was a considerate and humane practitioner, bringing comfort as well as expert treatment to those he saw each day. Yet in more intimate and personal relationships, his life was in a turmoil.

Wednesday was one of his operating days. He found himself looking forward to it. In the closed, sterile world of the hospital theatre, there was no room for anything but absolute concentration upon the task in hand. He had always enjoyed that absorption, and on this day it was a positive support for him. He found his involvement in his work, his determination to do it well, were factors which eased the tensions of another long day of waiting and watching.

In the latter part of the afternoon, when he had finished operating, he saw three patients and discussed the results of their

X-rays with them. He saved the easiest one, the one where he could offer welcome news, to the end of the day; keeping the best until the last was a habit he had cultivated as a schoolboy and had never rejected.

On that Wednesday, it meant that the last person he saw was a woman of sixty-eight, who had been suffering from stomach pains. Audrey Capstick came into his consulting room white-faced with pain and anxiety. She was disciplined by her background to be polite to medical specialists, even in the extreme fear which now clutched at her throat and made her voice husky as she tried to keep it even. 'No. No, the pain hasn't gone away,' she said resolutely. Her husband had made her promise that she wouldn't minimise things in her embarrassment, wouldn't behave as if she were merely an unwelcome hindrance to a man with more important illnesses than hers to consider. But she heard herself saying, 'I—I expect I make too much of it, Dr—I mean Mister Johnson.'

She reddened suddenly with embarrassment, the blood filling her strained face as if it had been poured in from outside. She knew you had to call a surgeon 'Mister', not 'Doctor', had known it for years. Yet to her, it still seemed odd to find a black man in such an exalted position. There had been no black men in the town when she had played as a girl in the stone-flagged playground which was now long gone, when the world seemed an unchanging place and hospitals were mysterious places where the old went to die.

The very black face with its regular, handsome features and its gold-rimmed glasses smiled reassuringly at Audrey Capstick, and suddenly she knew that everything was going to be all right. 'You shouldn't apologise for feeling pain, Mrs Capstick. Gallstones are a very painful complaint.'

Her heart leapt at the words. Her eyes must have been misted a little by tears; for a moment, the rest of the consultant's face disappeared and she could see only the wide smile and the beautiful, regular teeth, which seemed so very white. 'It's not—not anything more serious, then?'

She couldn't say the word even now, and Richard Johnson said it for her, gently, slowly, releasing her softly from the malign grip it had kept on her for weeks. 'Not cancer, Mrs Capstick, no. Certainly not.

Painful enough, but curable, completely curable. More easily now than a few years ago, in fact.'

She was massively relieved, then absurdly grateful to him, as if he personally had banished the canker which had threatened to eat away the trunk beneath her best two-piece and the new underslip she had bought for this visit. Though he was not sure how much she was taking in, Johnson took her through the details of keyhole surgery, explaining how much easier it was now to pinpoint the source of the pain, how much smaller the incision, how much more quickly she would recover and be herself again.

They arranged that she would come into woman's surgical on Thursday and be operated on on Friday. For a moment, her face clouded again, as if the urgency suggested that he was still concealing something from her, that she was after all in some desperate condition, as she had been sure she was when she was wracked by pain in the small hours of the night.

But Richard Johnson laughed away her fears. 'It's because you're in pain you're a priority, not because what you have is life-threatening,' he said. 'I think you've waited quite long enough already to have this put right, don't you, Mrs Capstick?'

And Audrey, thinking again of all those useless paracetemols and the muted weepings as she waited for the dawn to reach her bedroom windows, had to agree with this friendly, reassuring man, who carried his knowledge so lightly, when compared with the doctors of her youth.

'You'll be on your feet again a few days after your op. Rushing about again in six weeks,' he reassured her.

It was too good to be true. They might even manage a holiday in September. Down to Sidmouth or Torquay, perhaps. Paul would like that. She couldn't wait now to get back to the waiting room outside and tell him. They'd said he could come in with her, but he hadn't wanted to, and she'd understood that.

Richard Johnson shook her hand before she went, just as if they were equals. He said he'd see her when she came in on Thursday, before the operation. If she should have any questions, she could put them to him then. As if she would have! As she turned to go, the familiar pain stabbed sharply at the left of her stomach, making her wince. But even the pain seemed a friend, reassuring her that it was not the awful thing she had feared for so long. She clutched the spot for a moment with gentle, welcoming fingers, and went happily out to the husband who would tell her that he had been right all along.

Richard Johnson smiled after her, glad that he had been able to help her, delighted by her eagerness to relay her good news to the dour, loving man outside. He was again glad that he worked not in one of the great city hospitals but in this grimy town with its stalwart, friendly folk.

He was tired at the end of a crowded day, but pleasantly so. Perhaps tonight he would drive Carmen out into the Ribble Valley, so that together they could enjoy the peace and beauty that was so close at hand. He didn't hate her at all. That had been one of his stupid overreactions. Of course, he didn't love her as he once had, but passions cooled in all marriages over the years. And all the faults were on his side. It was time he put his life together and made the most of it. With Verna gone for ever, he could begin to do that.

He gazed out for a full minute at the crowded ribbons of terraced houses beyond the disused canal, to the heat-hazed hills on the skyline. There was no reason why he should not make his life outside this place as happy and confident as the one he enjoyed in the hospital.

When he went into the adjoining office, he found that his secretary had switched off her computer and gone home, as he had suggested she should while he was with Mrs Capstick. He glanced at the memo she had left in his in-tray.

It informed him that a Detective Inspector Peach would like to see him. Urgently.

Eighteen

Death affects people in all kinds of ways they do not anticipate. Murder is more severe than mere death: it seeps around those involved like a toxic gas, poisoning relationships which were once secure and unthinking.

Martin Hume was immensely relieved when he was released from captivity. It had been an unreal period, when he knew he was technically innocent, yet felt there was a justice in his detainment and questioning. Had he not planned Verna's murder, been thinking of how he could best encompass it at the very moment when he found her body? He had tried hard to disguise the fact that her death was immensely convenient for him from the succession of policemen who saw him, but he was not sure how successful he had been. Certainly that bouncing ball of aggression who called himself DI Peach and who had finally released him, had seemed to realise that Verna's death had caused her husband elation rather than grief.

And now, when he rang the woman he had been freed to marry, their conversation was curiously muted. Perhaps Sue Thompson's heart lifted when she heard him, but her voice stuck in her throat. Their first exchanges might have been the polite small talk of distant acquaintances.

'Are you at home?' she asked.

'No. I'm at Alison's. My sister's,' he added unnecessarily.

'Are the police still at your house?'

'They may be. They explained that they have to go over everything with a fine toothcomb, because it's what they call the scene of the crime. I expect they'll have finished their work by now, but I didn't fancy being in that house on my own, somehow. Not just yet.'

'No.' She wondered what to say to him next, as she had not needed to do for months. Verna's death was like a wall between them; she felt that she had known it would divide them from the moment she first heard of it. What was it he had said to her all that time ago, on that fatal afternoon, when he had taken her to the station in his car and they had first kissed? 'There are ways of making things happen. Just trust me.' In the weeks which had followed, as their love had developed, she had hugged those words to her, in the small hours of the night when she was lonely, in the evenings after he had left her.

And now her sister was dead. Very conveniently, for both of them. The first time anything connected with Verna had been convenient for a very long time. Too convenient? The question nagged at her, however roughly she tried to thrust it away. And all Martin's confidence that things would work out for the two of them seemed suddenly sinister.

'How's Toby?' asked Martin. He had

220

heard a slight click on the line at the beginning of their conversation, and he wondered if the phone was bugged. Perhaps he was just feeling persecuted. They wouldn't have bugged Alison's phone, surely? But they had wanted to know where he was going when he left the police station, had taken details of the address, and had warned him that he was not to move out of the area without letting them know his whereabouts. Did they bug the phonecalls of people in his situation? Was it legal for them to do so? He didn't think it was. But he realised that he was really hopelessly ignorant of police procedures and police powers, and his ignorance made him feel vulnerable. He must watch what he said to Sue, just in case.

She was telling him about the things Toby had been doing at school: it seemed an impossibly distant, innocent world. Martin reminded himself again to be careful of his words, just in case there were listeners other than his lovely Sue. 'They seemed to realise I couldn't have done it, in the end. The police, I mean.' He heard himself giving way to the little nervous giggle he thought he had left behind with his adolescence.

'I had to identify her, you know.' Sue spoke as if she had not heard him.

'Oh. That must have been unpleasant for you.' The word was thoroughly inadequate, but he couldn't be spontaneous.

'She looked very peaceful. Almost as though ... well, you know.'

'Yes.' Almost as though she'd died naturally, Sue meant. Instead of being brutally murdered. 'There'll be an inquest, of course.'

'Yes, I suppose so.'

'I expect you'll have to be there because of identifying the body. I will, of course, because I found her.'

'Yes.' She tried not to picture what had gone on in that house. 'Have they given up all thought that you might have done it?'

'Yes. Well, I think so.' He thought again of that little click on the phone. Perhaps he was being watched, as well as overheard. Perhaps there was some plainclothes man discreetly positioned outside the house even now. Or perhaps he was becoming paranoid. The police were vastly experienced in this business of murder—how had he ever thought he might deceive them? He said, lowering his voice in the empty house,

'Perhaps it might be better if we didn't meet for a little while. Until we know how things are going.' He wasn't sure what he meant by that last lame phrase.

'All right. I wouldn't want Toby to be drawn into any of this, anyway.' She was glad to have her son to offer as an excuse; then she felt ashamed to use him like that. Did murder always make people behave shabbily?

She had agreed too readily, with too little argument.

'Perhaps I'm just feeling persecuted. But we can keep in touch by phone easily enough.'

'Yes. We'll see each other at the inquest, anyway.'

They rang off then, without any of the loving endearments which they had used before this thing happened. Each of them was left feeling deflated by a phone conversation they had eagerly anticipated.

It was her own fault, not Martin's, Sue Thompson told herself. It was ridiculous that she could even have entertained the idea that Martin might have killed Verna. She had dismissed it long before the police agreed with her and let him go, she thought.

But the murder had deadened her responses when she had wanted to be warm and loving. And Martin had been guarded with her when she had expected him to be relieved, to lift the foreboding this death had brought to her. She sat for a long time looking at the silent phone. She still believed that Martin Hume was in love with her, but the idea which had crept bleakly into her head would not go away.

Did he now seriously think that she might have killed her own sister?

Percy Peach's interviewing technique was not designed for elderly ladies. It had broken many a brash young mugger or car thief, but it was not suitable for people who were already almost speechless with apprehension and embarrassment.

He said to his detective sergeant before they went in to see her, 'Just come into the questioning whenever you feel it might be useful, Lucy.'

DS Blake nodded, carefully suppressing the smile which threatened. He used her first name when he wanted help from her, she had realised. And he used it more and more these days. He had almost dropped the 'Sexton' which was her inevitable nickname around the station. It was probably very unfeminist in her even to notice such things, but she was pleased when he called her Lucy and put her on a par with the male detective sergeants.

In the small, warm cube which was the interview room, the two of them sat down unhurriedly. Percy Peach contemplated the anxious face with its frame of grey hair on the other side of the square table for several seconds before he said, 'Well, Mrs Alice Osborne, this is a turn-up for the books, and no mistake. Breaking and entering. And at a house where a murder took place only last Saturday. A real turn-up. And a night in the cells to follow. Breakfast all right for you, was it?'

Alice gave a nervous little grin. She said almost apologetically, 'Your people did their best to make me comfortable. I had my own key. That's not breaking and entering, is it? And I drove my own car to the police station, with your officer giving me directions.'

She wasn't from round here, then. She had a light, attractive Geordie accent. Percy grinned back at her. 'Not the usual way to be arrested, I have to admit. But you were in a strange house at dead of

225

night. Gave an innocent young copper quite a turn, I expect. PC Wall was probably quite relieved when you didn't clobber him.'

Alice Osborne considered this. She could see how things looked bad for her. But eleven o'clock wasn't quite the dead of night. And it hadn't been entirely a strange house. She said, 'He's a canny lad, your young copper. I'm sorry if I gave him a shock. But I hadn't broken in: I had a key. It was my stepdaughter's house, Inspector.'

Peach nodded. He'd found out that much before he came into the interview room. 'Verna Hume. Who was brutally murdered last Saturday night.'

'Yes.'

'Where were you last Saturday night, Mrs Osborne?'

'At home. At our bungalow, in Lytham St Annes.'

'With your husband? Who can no doubt vouch for your presence there?'

'No.' Alice Osborne's moist grey eyes opened a little wider, then suddenly blinked three times.

'I see. Can anyone else confirm that you were at home, Mrs Osborne?'

'No. I don't think so. Derek was visiting a friend, you see.'

He noted that she had volunteered information about her husband, the dead woman's father. Not usual, that. It seemed incredible that this slight, elderly figure could have been involved in a murder, even as an accessory, but stranger things had happened. You had to remind yourself about that constantly, when dealing with murder. That was one of its attractions for a man like Percy who was easily bored. So he reminded himself now that a much frailer woman than Alice Osborne could have pressed that pillow onto Verna Hume's face until she ceased to breathe.

It was Lucy Blake who said softly, 'What were you doing in the house last night, Mrs Osborne?'

Alice wrung her fingers hard together beneath the square table. She had done this since she was a child when she was agitated, and she knew it. That was why she had made sure from the start of this meeting that her hands were out of sight; she had known that this moment must come. When she spoke, she was surprised by the steadiness of her voice. But she would trust it with as few words as possible. 'I was looking for something, bonny lass, wasn't I?'

'Were you? We don't know, so you'll have to tell us. But tell us everything, Mrs Osborne—it's much the best thing to do, in the end.'

The girl's face seemed to Alice incredibly young. Could this pretty, earnest girl really be a detective? Alice fought down an urge to confide everything to her, and made herself look back at the hostile dome of the moustachioed man who had begun the interrogation. It would be easier to lie to him, even though he looked so disbelieving. 'I thought there might be photographs. Of the three of us together, you see. Verna used to visit us, fairly regularly.'

Peach looked as if he might explode with derision. But it was Lucy Blake who said swiftly, 'Did you need to go secretly to the house where she had been killed to get photographs, Alice? An empty house where murder had been committed, and during the night? It must have taken an awful lot of nerve to do that.'

Alice nodded. It had. She'd been petrified as she crept from her car to the front door and put her key in the lock. And creeping from room to room with her torch had been ...

'So you weren't just looking for photographs, were you, Alice?'

It was the girl who had trapped her, after all. Those soft, compliant features, that voice so full of understanding, had merely underlined the stupidity of the story she had thought up so hastily as she waited in that cell, where the high, whitewashed walls seemed designed to inhibit thought. Alice fought down the urge to nod, to weep, to tell all, to enjoy the delicious relief of confession. But she knew she must deny herself, must give them some other, more convincing story. 'No. I was looking for jewellery, really.'

There was a long silence. She felt them weighing this new idea, testing whether it had anything more to be said for it than her first, abject lie. Lucy allowed a little surprise to creep into her voice as she said, 'You wanted to steal your daughter-in-law's jewellery?'

Even in her turmoil, Alice bridled at that word 'steal'; she could not let it go by. 'No. I was only looking for what was mine. I—I'd lent Verna a ring and a pair of earrings. Diamond ones. I thought I

229

wouldn't get them back if I didn't collect them myself. There was nothing to say they were mine, you see, and I thought they'd just be put in with the rest of Verna's things.'

Lucy took her time: it was something she had learned from Percy Peach. She looked at the cheap bangle on the ageing wrist, at Alice Osborne's clean but well-worn blouse, at the short coat she had taken off in the overheated room. And, as she watched the worn hand steal too late towards the C & A label, she thought of the clothes she had seen in Verna Hume's wardrobe, clothes from shops which this woman would never have entered. An infinite sympathy for this anxious, elderly woman who was so patently out of her depth stole over her for a moment. Then she reminded herself that this most unlikely candidate could still be their murderer: Peach had taught her to remember that as well.

Lucy looked at the lobes of Alice Osborne's ears. 'Clip-ons, were they? The earrings?'

The colour drained from Alice's face, which made the lines on it much more apparent. 'Yes. Not Verna's normal style, really. But she was very taken with them.'

'I see.' They both knew she was lying. Verna Hume's ears had been pierced, and she would never have worn earrings of the type Alice was describing. Lucy smiled at her, making ready to exploit this moment of her weakness. 'What were you really looking for in that house, Alice?'

It was the older woman's turn to pause for a long time before she spoke. But she looked not at her tormentors but at the table between them, as if she hoped that if she stared at it long enough some plausible explanation would emerge from its blank Formica surface. But no inspiration came. She said eventually. 'She had things of mine. Things I wanted back. Things I didn't want other people to see. That's all.'

'What things, Alice? You must see that we need to know, in these circumstances.'

She did. But she couldn't think of anything to tell them. She was suddenly, overwhelmingly, tired. Exhausted. She wanted to be cradled in her mother's arms and carried up to bed, as she had been sixty years ago after playing out on long summer nights in the cobbled Tyneside street. She said stubbornly, 'Just—things, pet. Things I didn't want other people to see.'

She swayed gently on her hard chair, her eyes cast down, her features clear now of all anxiety and suffused with an infinite fatigue. She looked as if she might collapse at any moment, keeling over gently and falling to the uncarpeted floor without even the softest of cries. That would look well, thought Percy Peach: an old biddy collapsing under the pressure of interrogation. He asked quietly, almost apologetically, 'Did you kill Verna Hume, Mrs Osborne?'

The almost bloodless lips gave a little smile. 'No. I'd never have done that to her. And I don't know who did. I don't think poor Verna had many friends, though.'

It was almost the first thing she had said that they could accept and agree with. They sent her back to her cell with a policewoman and a mug of tea. Half an hour later, she was released, and Peach watched unseen from the window of his office as Derek Osborne helped her carefully into the passenger seat of the old white Fiesta and drove her away.

That old lady had outsmarted him, he

thought, as a young tearaway would never have done. They still did not know exactly what she had been looking for in Verna Hume's house.

Nineteen

'The public wants results. And it's our job to provide them, Detective Inspector Peach.'

Chief Superintendent Tucker, Head of Brunton CID, brought in the full name and title for his rebukes, like a primary school teacher checking a recalcitrant child.

Percy thought that if this was the best bollocking Tommy Bloody Tucker could muster, it wasn't going to be a contest worthy of his talents. 'Yes, sir. I see, sir.' He stood to attention and looked over the head of his chief at the wall behind him, like a soldier on a charge.

Tucker was irritated. He had been prepared for an argument, had wanted some hooks of resistance on which he could hang his planned pep talk. 'Sit down, for God's sake, Inspector Peach.

You're here to bring me up to date on the Verna Hume murder. I've got a press—no, a full media conference this afternoon, you know.' Tucker tried to look modest, but his chest swelled a little despite himself at the importance of it all.

'Yes, sir. Wouldn't want you to look silly in front of the cameras, sir.' Peach pulled up a chair carefully, as if it was important to place it exactly an inch outside Tucker's designated space, then positioned himself upon it equally carefully, with his knees together and his back bolt upright. 'What exactly would you like to know, sir?' He threw his most benign smile across the big desk; it flooded his features, expelling every wrinkle from the face beneath the white dome of baldness.

'Well, just fill me in, that's all.' Tucker couldn't admit how little he knew about the progress of an investigation he was supposed to be directing. 'I've got an overview, of course, but I need—'

'Ah, yes, the Tucker overview. One of the most valuable factors in Brunton CID success, that is, if you don't mind my saying it. We beaver away at things on the ground, but it's your overall grasp of the issues, your view from the clouds

234

above, which gives balance and direction to the enterprise. But I expect you must know that, sir. It's part of the strategy which informs the whole of our work, just the top part of the system which is your creation.'

As often with Peach, Tucker found himself knowing quite well that he was being taunted, but not quite sure which phrase he could fasten on as an insult. This damn fellow kept such an earnest exterior over his hostility that you couldn't pin him down. And when your reputation was dependent on the bastard's work and both of you knew it, it made things even more tricky. He tried the friendly and encouraging tack. 'I think you should just run me through the details of the suspects,' he said. Then he added daringly, 'And perhaps give me your latest thinking on them.'

'Certainly, sir.' Peach's smile, which had disappeared with the exaggerated concentration he gave to Tucker's most routine phrases, now returned. 'And perhaps I might have the benefit of your thoughts on the problems of the investigation. Your overview, as we might say: most valuable, that would be. If you have the time, of course.' Percy snatched a glance at his watch. He had just twenty minutes before he was due to visit Richard Johnson, whereas this windbag had no doubt nothing useful in mind before the afternoon's press conference.

Tucker said limply, 'You've released the husband. I suppose you're satisfied he had nothing to do with his wife's murder?'

'Martin Hume? Oh, yes, sir. It would have been difficult for him, as we now know he was at least two hundred miles away at the time of death. Must admit I wondered at first why you'd pulled him in so promptly. Then I realised that it must be to put chummy at his ease. Or her ease, of course. The real killer, I mean.'

Percy was very satisfied with the look of bewilderment and apprehension on Tucker's face. It reminded him of Lady Macbeth's warning to her husband that his face was as a book wherein men might read strange things, but he decided this wasn't the moment for a quotation: his quarry was quite baffled enough.

Tucker said defensively, 'But I believe he didn't get on with his wife.'

Peach shrugged. 'That's matrimony for

you, sir. Blissfully happy marriages such as your own are unfortunately very much the exception, I'm afraid.' Rumour had it that Tommy Bloody Tucker was a domestic wimp of seaside postcard dimensions under the domination of his formidable spouse. Percy leant forward. 'Verna Hume was playing away, I'm afraid, sir. Frequently.'

Tucker strove for an idiom which would get him on this man's wavelength. 'Prick-teaser, was she?'

Peach nodded vigorously, as if it was the first time he had heard the expression and it fitted perfectly. 'Worse than that, sir. A drawer-dropper. Upstairs, downstairs, over most of East Lancashire, from what I can gather.'

'She was an attractive woman,' said Tucker wistfully. He sounded as if he was sorry he had missed his chance with the lascivious Verna.

'Yes, sir. But as you will appreciate, that isn't making our job easy.'

'Who've you got in the frame, so far?'

'Three men and three women, sir.' A neat division: Percy had only just fixed on this number, but he spoke with complete confidence.

Tucker's face fell. He had been hoping to

announce breezily to his media conference that an arrest was imminent. He leant forward, producing the new phrase he had learnt with modest pride. 'No prime suspect, then?'

'No, sir. And the list is by no means comprehensive: we may need to add to it in due course. That's the trouble with drawer-droppers: they get around.' Percy smiled brightly again. It was not the least of his annoyances to Tucker that he seemed to find the very things which depressed his chief quite cheering.

'I understand the uniformed boys made an arrest at the house where the woman was killed. Surely that must have provided you with a lead? Surely the villain concerned must be the murderer, or at least an accessory?' Superintendent Tucker drummed his fingers hard upon his desk; it was a move which seemed to intimidate all his staff save DI Peach.

'That's interesting, sir. The lady in question is a pensioner. A Mrs Alice Osborne. She may have deceived us, sir—she seemed a frail old lady on the point of collapse when we interviewed her, but she was probably conning us. I wish we'd had you in at the time, now. You'd

238

probably have seen through her in a flash. Perhaps we—'

'Don't be stupid, Peach!' A spurt of genuine temper warned Percy that he could go too far. 'What did this woman say she was doing in the house?'

'Alice Osborne, sir? Well, she said she was looking for photographs at first. But we wouldn't wear that, so then she claimed she had been looking for jewellery. A diamond ring and a pair of diamond earrings, she said.'

'And you believed her?'

'No, sir. Not when she said they were her own things that she'd lent to Verna Hume, we didn't.'

'So what was she really after?'

'We don't know, sir. Not yet.'

'And yet you let her go!' Tucker was triumphant in his surprise.

'Yes, sir, we did. She seemed on the point of collapse, you see. And we thought it unlikely she was the murderer.'

Tucker shook his head sadly at such naivety. 'She must be a suspect. Anyone could have suffocated Verna Hume with a pillow, you know. It didn't need much strength.'

'Yes, sir. Shall we pull Mrs Osborne in

again? Before this afternoon, so that you could announce it to the press and TV?' Percy was full of eager energy.

'No! No, don't do that. Just bear in mind what I've said, that's all.'

'Right, sir. We will indeed, sir.' Peach brightened with a sudden brainwave. 'Should we put a tail on her, sir? Follow her into the underworld, if necessary?' He wished Tucker had the imagination to see the beautiful picture he could see of Alice Osborne with her shopping bag on her arm, pursued around the highly respectable shopping square of Lytham St Annes by a diligent police shadow.

'Not for the moment, no. But bear in mind what I've said. Who else have you turned up? Let's have the women first.'

'Yes, sir. Logical as always. Well, there's the dead woman's younger sister, sir. Susan Thompson.'

'And why do you have reason to suspect her, Inspector?' Tucker switched to heavy patience.

'They don't seem to have been particularly close as sisters, sir. And—'

'Oh for God's sake, Peach! Can't you come up with anything better than that? Two days of intensive activity from you

240

and your team produces the idea that a sister didn't 'get on' with the murder victim. Really, I sometimes wonder—'

'And she seems to have been carrying on an affair with Martin Hume, the dead woman's husband, sir.' Peach was as inscrutable as a carved Buddha in a temple as he delivered his bombshell.

Tucker knew he had been set up, but couldn't quite pinpoint where. 'Then why for God's sake didn't you say so earlier, man? What's her story about the killing?'

'Don't know, sir. I shall find out later today, I hope. She's given a statement to a DC, of course. But she needs to be interviewed by a senior officer. If you should be available yourself, sir ...'

'No! No, I'm tied up today with the media conference, as I said. And you know it's my policy not to interfere with my officers. Just—just get on with it, that's all.' Tucker waved a hand vaguely at the air over Peach's head.

'Yes, sir. We've already seen the dead woman's business partner, Barbara Harris.'

Tucker leant forward, switching to eager efficiency. 'Motive?'

'She gets the business back. According to her, Verna Hume conned her out of her share of the partnership some years ago. But the deed they agreed when they set up together hasn't been rewritten: the death of either partner means that the other gets the entire business.'

'Ah!' Tucker sighed with deep satisfaction, as if he had just seen the significance of something his obtuse inspector might have missed. 'Opportunity?'

'Mrs Harris has as yet no satisfactory alibi for the time of the death, sir.' Peach spoke as carefully and impersonally as if he had been in court.

Tucker nodded and spoke confidentially, 'Off the record Percy—and I won't throw your opinion back in your face in the future, you know, it's not my way—did this Mrs Harris strike you as a ruthless sort of woman?'

Peach considered the adjective carefully. 'Yes, sir.'

'Ah!'

'But then most women strike me as ruthless, sir. In the right circumstances. I haven't the same happy experience of wedded bliss as you, of course. I suppose my divorce is bound to affect my views, even now. And I expect businesswomen have to be especially ruthless, don't they?'

Tucker had the uneasy feeling that he was being taken for a ride again, without being able to say exactly how. 'She'll stand watching, if she has so much to gain, this woman. You mark my words.'

'Yes, sir. Thank you for the overview, sir.' Peach made a note on a piece of card he produced from his pocket, held it at arm's length to inspect it, then returned it to his jacket. 'That's the three women, then.'

'Right. On to the men. I haven't got all day, you know.'

'No, sir.' You've got exactly seven minutes more of my valuable time, you old fraud, thought Percy. 'Derek Osborne,' he said abruptly.

Tucker looked puzzled, then said triumphantly, 'Alice Osborne's husband?'

'The very man, sir. And thus the dead woman's father.'

Tucker leant forward and looked over his glasses again, and Peach inclined his head in eager anticipation of the coming pearl of wisdom. 'Don't rule him out on that account, Peach. Eighty per cent of murders are committed by close members of the family you know.'

'Really, sir? I shall certainly bear that in

243

mind.' Percy shook his head in amazement at this best-known of all crime statistics.

Tucker peered at him suspiciously. 'Yes. Well, it's well worth remembering. It wouldn't surprise me at all if this Derek Osborne and his wife were in this together.'

'You smell collusion, sir? And yet Alice Osborne was most anxious her husband shouldn't know she'd been arrested at his daughter's house. I see it all now, of course. Just a bluff to put PC Plods like me off the scent. They were in it together all the time, I expect.'

'I'm not saying it's like that at all!' said Tucker irritably. 'Just keep an open mind, that's all I'm saying.'

'A welcome reminder, sir, all the same. Sometimes one is too close to the investigation and the people involved in it to see these things.' Percy put his hand to his pocket, as if he planned to make a further note of this latest gem, then thought better of it. He frowned with concentration and nodded vigorously several times, as if he hoped thus to hammer Tucker's adage into his dull brain.

'Who else?' asked his superintendent hopelessly.

'We seem to have found the only man Verna Hume mentioned by name in her diary, sir. A Hugh Pearson. Member of my golf club, actually.' Peach grinned apologetically; it was another chance to remind his chief of how the exclusive North Lancashire GC had rejected Tucker's crude hackings but accepted his own developing skills.

'Hugh Pearson? I know that name,' said Tucker suspiciously, as if that meant a deception was being attempted.

'Very probably, sir, with your awareness of local issues and people. Runs his own successful business, our Hugh does. Pearson Electronics. May well be a member of the fraternity, too, but I wouldn't know about that, of course.'

Tucker looked as shifty as he always did when there was a reference to his Masonic connections. That was why he knew the name of course: Hugh Pearson was a member of the Lodge. Quite a winning young fellow he had always seemed to Tommy. He said stiffly, 'Whether or not Mr Pearson is a Freemason is neither here nor there, of course.'

'No, sir. But he seems to have been knocking off Verna Hume all right. Here, there and everywhere. She seems to have had what I believe they now call 'the hots' for our Mr Pearson. Though he's trying to make out now that it didn't mean all that much to him. Not very gallant that. But then Hugh didn't seem much of a gentleman to me.'

Tucker wasn't going to rise to the bait of defending a fellow Mason. He said, 'Knocking a woman off doesn't automatically mean you have to kill her, you know, Peach.'

'No, sir. Worth remembering, that.' For an awful moment, Tucker thought his DI was going to make a note of another of his banalities as if it were a pearl of detection. But all he said was, 'My impression is that he wanted to shake Verna Hume off but she didn't want to go. Perhaps she was serious about a man, for once. Wanted a commitment he wasn't prepared to give. Pearson has not so far given any convincing account of his whereabouts on Saturday night.'

'You must treat him the same as any other suspect, of course. But for what it's worth, my impression of young Pearson is that he wouldn't be involved in murder.'

'I see, sir. Thank you for that different

perspective, sir.' Percy realised that he had already been hoping that the egregious Hugh Pearson would prove their man. He wished it now with a renewed, wholly unprofessional fervour which only Tommy Bloody Tucker could have roused.

The superintendent turned briskly efficient. 'Now. You said there was yet another man in the frame. A far more likely candidate than Hugh Pearson, I expect.'

'Yes, sir. Probably, sir. He's a consultant at Brunton Royal Infirmary, sir.'

Tucker's face fell, as Peach had known it would. A professional man, and a highly successful one at that, involved in serious crime? It always meant trouble: they knew how to pull strings, these professional men. 'You're sure he's a real possibility?'

'Oh yes, sir!' Peach's enthusiasm was in inverse ratio to Tucker's dismay. 'Good bit of detection work, actually. Only one mention of his name in the dead woman's diary. That and his initials once or twice: R.J. But we've tracked him down. Matter of following through the CID procedures you've laid down for us in such detail. Careful groundwork and elimination. Paid off again.'

Tucker looked understandably puzzled. What Peach and his colleagues applied at Brunton CID was no more than standard police procedure—nothing to do with any directive from him. 'And you say the man's a consultant.'

'Yes, sir. A surgeon, actually. Richard Johnson. Has a national reputation, apparently. Be a pity if we have to lock him up, won't it?'

Tucker shuddered. He could see hostile headlines already. 'The sooner you can eliminate him from your inquiries the better. And do it quietly, for God's sake. The man may be a popular local figure.'

'He is, sir, by all accounts. You may know him.' Peach suddenly slid a postcard-sized picture across the desk, like a conjurer producing a dove from his sleeve.

Tucker stared at it in astonishment. 'He's black,' he said dully.

'Yes, sir.' Perhaps it was Tucker's amazing powers of observation which had secured him his present rank, Percy thought. 'Apparently his origins are Caribbean, but he's spent almost all his life in this country. Educated at Radford and London University. I expect he can use a knife and fork. He's certainly adept

248

with the surgical sort of knife, by all accounts.'

Tucker looked thoroughly unhappy. He was trying to reconcile the man's colour with the job he did, and finding it difficult. Imaginative leaps were not his forte. He sought for a statistic to fling at his DI, and clutched at the only one which swam across his vision. 'More than half the violent crime in some of our big cities is committed by blacks, you know, even when they represent a much smaller section of the population than that,' he said, desperately.

'Yes, sir. Of course, a high proportion of young blacks are unemployed and living in slum conditions.' Percy thought he might throw a fact of his own in to annoy his chief, though he couldn't see what relevance this had to Richard Johnson, FRCS.

'I don't want any left-wing political claptrap, Peach. Just stick to the point.' Tucker looked at his DI severely over the top of the gold-rimmed spectacles. 'And handle this Johnson fellow with kid gloves. I don't want the ethnic lobby round my neck, you know.'

Percy paused for a moment, savouring

the picture of Tucker disappearing like Gordon at Khartoum under a welter of coloured faces. 'No, sir. I see, sir.' He stood up, regaining with that single movement his normal bouncing energy and eagerness. 'Well, if you'll excuse me, we're just off to see the bugger now. I'll bear in mind what you said about the predominance of his brethren in urban crime statistics. Might be a useful thing to quote at him, if he isn't immediately cooperative. Rest assured, this Johnson fellow won't get an easy ride from me!'

'No. No, that's not what I said!' Tucker too was on his feet, but Peach was gone. The Head of CID called from his door at the back which was disappearing down the stairs, 'Use some diplomacy, Peach, for once in your life!'

Percy smiled to himself as he reached the car park. He could have used the last twenty minutes to gather his thoughts for the coming interview with Johnson, rather than in baiting Tommy Bloody Tucker. But a person was allowed to indulge himself occasionally.

Hobbies are the things which distinguish man from the beasts around him.

Twenty

She was a protective secretary. She watched them as they entered her office with observant, resentful eyes, and greeted them with, 'Mr Johnson is very busy. He always is.'

'So are we. And murder doesn't wait,' said Percy Peach briskly.

'Neither does disease. And disease can be arrested, if it is attacked in time. The dead are in no hurry.'

Miss Williams smiled the superiority of this sentiment at the CID intruders. She had heard it voiced in the hospital, and it seemed appropriate now. She stood four-square before them, a sturdy crusader in a tweed skirt, a defender of the citadel where her icon resided, an acolyte who would sell herself willingly on his behalf. A worthy opponent, thought Percy, but one he mustn't waste his fire on now. 'Those murderers who aren't caught within a week usually get away with it. And I'm sure you wouldn't want that.'

'And we do have an appointment with Mr Johnson,' said Lucy Blake.

It was an argument Miss Williams, who lived her life around the great man's appointments, could not refute. 'I know. I spoke to you myself, last night. I'm just asking you to be as brief as possible, that's all.'

The man she was trying to protect appeared at that moment in the door of his office, immaculately erect in a dark-blue suit, smiling his approval of her attempts at protection like a man commending a favourite watchdog. 'That's all right, Patricia,' he said. 'We mustn't hold up the due processes of the law, must we?'

He led them into the big room beyond the mahogany door, which seemed impeccably tidy after the filing cabinets and the letters scattered over the surfaces of Miss Williams' workplace. The bustle and hum of the busy hospital outside was shut away as Richard Johnson closed the heavy door behind them. The canal and the terraces of mean nineteenth-century houses built for the subjects of King Cotton were silent and unpeopled beyond the double glazing of the wide window; nothing moved in that industrial landscape.

It was like a Lowry print with added sunlight and without his stick people.

This was a room for quiet consultation, for serious reassurance and, on occasions, for the revelation of tragedy to those who sat helplessly awaiting it.

The central figure here was handsome, urbane, and yet not quite at ease. He seated them in chairs which faced the light, then sat opposite them in a matching armchair, carefully eschewing the swivel chair behind the protective desk. Peach studied him, allowing the tiny pause of preliminary embarrassment to stretch imperceptibly. This job made you good at assessing people's ages, but he always found that difficult with black men, and prosperous black men were the most difficult of all. Their faces seemed to have fewer lines, and those lines were less revealing than those in similar white faces. Did that mean he was prejudiced? The simplest thoughts were politically incorrect nowadays: it was safest not to voice them.

He decided that Richard Johnson must be in his early forties. Although he looked younger, he could scarcely have reached this position of eminence and acquired his excellent reputation much earlier than that.

So he was not that much older than the delectable and amorous Verna Hume. With his well-cut suit, his handsome, intelligent features, his wide and liquid brown eyes, he could well have been attractive to a discontented wife. A randy discontented wife, taking her pleasures wherever she found them, he reminded himself firmly: the world at large might choose to sentimentalise the dead, but detectives must not do so.

Johnson snatched a surreptitious look at the gold watch beneath his stiff white cuff. 'What can I do for you, Inspector?'

'You can tell me about Mrs Verna Hume, who was murdered at the weekend.'

Johnson smiled, a wide, forced smile, which displayed perfectly formed front teeth and no humour at all. 'You must be under a misapprehension if you think I can tell you anything of value about Mrs Hume. I don't know why—'

'Your initials were found in her diary, Mr Johnson. There was more than one entry.' This was Lucy Blake, making the most of the few brief inscriptions they had found in the little book in the dead woman's bedroom.

'Really?' But he wasn't surprised, nor

did his raised eyebrows convince them that he was. 'Well, I'm sure you'll understand that any exchanges between practitioner and patient are completely confidential. Just as—'

'Are you saying that Mrs Hume was a patient of yours, Mr Johnson?'

Lucy Blake's wide eyes looked very green with the full daylight upon them. To Johnson, a man susceptible to young and beautiful female eyes, they seemed like pools luring him to destruction. He checked himself, then adopted the man-of-the-world expression he thought appropriate for the revelation which he realised had always been inevitable. He was finding this acting a part far more difficult than he had anticipated. When he had planned his tactics beside his sleeping wife in the quiet, restless hours around dawn, he had convinced himself that it would be easy to deceive. People who are used to being believed often make that mistake.

He licked his lips, forced them into a reluctant smile and admitted, 'No. She wasn't a patient. My limited meetings with Mrs Hume were of a purely social nature.'

Peach looked stern, noting how it accentuated the other man's discomfort and relishing this moment of breakthrough. 'We shall get through this much more quickly if you are completely honest, Mr Johnson. When did you first meet Mrs Hume?'

Richard had never heard her called by this formal title until this morning. It made his Verna seem like a different person. But she wasn't his Verna: he must stop thinking of her like that. 'It must have been about four months ago, I think. I couldn't be exact.' Only four months! How his life had been changed in that time! But again, he mustn't recall it, even to himself: all that was finished now.

Peach's small black eyes watched him steadily, like a ferret waiting for a rabbit to make a false move. 'I see. And where did this first meeting take place?'

Richard Johnson had no false bedside manner: that sort of medicine had disappeared with his generation. His smile when he spoke to his patients was warm, genuine, caring; it took over his face without his even thinking about it. Now, when he tried to force that same smile, it would not come.

'Look, Inspector, I'm not proud of some things I've done. Not many people can be completely open about the whole of their lives. Do I have your assurance that what I now have to tell you will be kept confidential?'

It was a familiar plea. Usually it meant men wanted their wives to be kept in the dark about philandering. And usually Peach did his best to meet it, though he often wrested a little more cooperation in return. But this was a murder investigation, with its own set of unwritten rules.

He said, 'We shall do what we can, if what we find is not relevant to our inquiries. But there can be no guarantees.'

Peach savoured that formal language as he dropped it stiffly from his tongue; turning the screw on professional men was not always as easy as this. But a restless prick made a man vulnerable; Percy thought he might put that in his book of wise sayings. It was the kind of aphorism they should have in *Readers' Digest* but didn't.

'Yes. Well, this isn't relevant to your investigation. You'll find that out soon enough.' Again Johnson found his normally ready smile elusive as the two pairs of eyes watched him intently. He realised suddenly that he had not been studied so steadily and unemotionally since he had been quizzed for part two of his FRCS twelve years ago. He still remembered that as an unnerving experience; but it had been a professional examination on his own ground, whereas in this bizarre game the opposition set the rules.

Peach smiled at last, a little wearily, making Johnson feel that he had heard all this before, that he saw through every petty subterfuge his victims might be unwise enough to attempt. 'Where did you meet Mrs Hume for the first time?'

'It was at the Northern Ritz. That's a nightclub in Bolton Road.'

'Yes. I know where it is, Mr Johnson.' It was a tawdry set-up in a converted cinema, offering mild striptease, a 'floor show' with third-rate comedians and singers, and cheap champagne at enormous prices. A place where the mildly criminal, the tawdry rich and the easily deceived could be found in almost equal numbers. Peach guessed that Johnson would be in the last category. Strange how the highly intelligent could sometimes have no common sense at all. In his experience, they deceived themselves much more easily than less gifted people. 'Did you arrange to meet Mrs Hume there?'

'Oh no!' For a moment, Johnson was aghast at the idea of a deliberate assignation. Then he smiled, genuinely for the first time, and at his own expense. These distinctions could hardly be important in the middle of a murder inquiry. 'We met by chance. I went there to unwind after a busy day. Verna was with a party of about half a dozen people. We danced. And that was all we did, that first time.'

Peach let the last phrase hang for a moment in the air, watching it rise like an invisible smoke ring towards the ceiling. Then he said, 'But you arranged to meet again.'

'Yes.'

'And the relationship developed,' Percy searched for a diplomatic phrase, 'became more intense.'

'Yes.'

'You slept together.'

'Yes. Not as often as we'd have liked, but yes.'

Not as often as *you'd* have liked, anyway, thought Percy. For an unguarded moment,

Johnson had been almost like a young lover, proud of his conquest, anxious to assert the depth of the emotion. Interesting. 'Where did you meet, Mr Johnson?'

For a moment, he thought the consultant was going to wax indignant, protest about the invasion of his privacy. Then, with a little sigh, Johnson said, 'Wherever we could. At her house, when we knew her husband was safely out of the way. In motels. In the back of my car, when there was no other way. We managed an occasional night away from here, in the Lake District. Just twice we did that, actually.'

For a moment, Richard Johnson's dark face was riven with the passion and the pity of it. So much it had meant, so much he had promised himself would come from it. And now it was over; Verna was dead and waiting to be put in the earth. Or worse: for the first time, he contemplated the idea that the perfect body he had explored so fervently might be burnt, and its ashes scattered to the heedless winds.

'And this relationship was still alive at the time when Mrs Hume was murdered?'

Johnson's dark, handsome features winced a little at the word. Then he nodded, almost eagerly, his brown eyes upon Peach's face. 'That is correct.'

Lucy Blake, her gold ballpoint poised over her notebook, said, 'And when did you last see Mrs Hume, Mr Johnson?'

Johnson paused, appearing to give due weight and attention to his reply. It was a mistake, for they all knew that he must have considered his answer to this stock question many times before. 'It would have been on the Monday night of last week. Five or six days before she died, I suppose.' He was carefully ignorant of the exact time of the death, they noticed; it was perhaps a little too elaborate. 'We saw each other for an hour or so in the early evening.'

Peach studied the ceiling again for a moment. 'Was there any dispute between you? Then or on any previous occasion?'

'No. Far from it! We were getting on very well!' The little nervous laugh which bounced against the last word was a strange sound. It was also a highly inappropriate one for a man who, by his own account, should now be desolated by this death.

Peach allowed himself a moment of surprise; Lucy Blake raised a startled face from her notebook right on cue.

Percy said slowly, 'Presumably you're going to tell us you didn't kill Mrs Hume. Have you any idea who might have done so?'

'No. I wish I did. I—I didn't know most of the people she mixed with, you know. We didn't meet all that often. Probably it averaged out at about once a week, I suppose.'

Once he was released from talking about his own feelings for Verna, he dropped back into the caution he had intended to use to the CID throughout this meeting. The man who had seemed eager only a moment ago to assert the depth of his passion now seemed anxious to distance himself from the dead woman, thought Percy. But drawer-droppers often had that confusing effect on men, especially when they looked as delectable as the late Verna Hume.

'Where were you last Saturday night, Mr Johnson?'

He took his time, appearing to puzzle a little over a straightforward answer. 'I was at home with my wife, Inspector Peach.'

'And the children?'

'No. They were out.'

'But your wife will confirm that you were at home all evening, no doubt.' Percy managed to slide a little cynicism into the neutral statement. Wives who provided their spouses with alibis were an occupational hazard in CID work. But usually it was for breaking and entering, or the odd bit of GBH, not homicide.

'Yes, I'm sure she will. But Carmen knows nothing about my relationship with Verna Hume, and I'd like it to stay that way.'

'That may not be possible, Mr Johnson.'

'No. But I'm asking you not to reveal it unless it is absolutely unavoidable. It would harm my marriage. And my marriage and my family are important to me, you see.' Richard thought to himself that this was the one bit that had come out exactly as he had prepared it in those restless hours of the night.

Lucy Blake thought, He's saying now that Verna was just a bit on the side. A bit of fumbling and tumbling. The wives always win, in the end. Aloud, she said, 'The hospital says you came in here that night.'

He was shaken by that. Not by the fact, which could surely only be in his favour, but by the thoroughness of their checking. Someone must have spoken to the night sister, already. 'Yes, I popped in for a few minutes. There was a patient I wanted to check on. A young man who'd had a bone marrow transplant on the Friday. He was running a temperature, you see. But it turned out he was stable. He's doing fine now. Sitting up today.' He found himself wanting to enlarge on this, to draw attention to his care and his competence in the complex world in which he worked.

Peach asked, 'What time was this, sir?'

'I'm not sure of the exact time. About nine o'clock, I should think.'

'The night sister says it was five to ten,' said Lucy Blake.

Johnson smiled, caressing this attractive, earnest young woman with the warmth of his approval. 'Then I'm sure she's right; no doubt she made a note of the visit in the patient's record at the time. I did say I wasn't sure, you know.'

'Indeed you did, sir,' said Peach. He stood up. 'If anything occurs to you which you think might help us, please get in touch right away. No doubt you are as anxious as we are to know who killed a woman for whom you had such a great affection.'

Johnson glanced at him sharply, but there was no trace of irony in the inspector's impassive features. They left him then, and he stood at the big window for a few moments, until he saw the police Mondeo glide into view. He watched it turn onto the main road which ran by the canal and back into town. It was as if he needed confirmation that they had really left the place before he could resume his normal day.

In the car, Peach said, 'We have two men who claim they were the current boyfriend, Hugh Pearson and Richard Johnson. God knows how many others there've been in the past few months, all of whom who might have done it. Dangerous women, drawer-droppers. Cause a lot of trouble.'

'They still have a right to life, sir. And a right to have their killers brought to justice.'

'I know, Lucy. We'll find out who did it.' Where a few months ago he would have bridled at her reminder, he now put his broad hand for a moment on top of the more slender one which rested on top of the gear lever. 'We'll need to check out with the wife that Johnson was at home on Saturday night as he says, of course. As delicately as possible. You'd better do that: it's a job for a woman, if you agree there is still such a thing.'

She didn't argue, as he had expected her to do.

Back in the quiet of his consulting room, Richard Johnson was wondering whether he had been detected in the most important lie of all.

Twenty-one

The coroner was brisk and businesslike in his conduct of the proceedings, but not unkind.

The death of a woman of thirty-four was always distressing. When the deceased was a victim not of a road accident or a deadly disease but of murder, you had to be prepared for even more distress than usual among the relatives and friends. They sat before him grim-faced and darkly dressed.

But the coroner's experience and his

266

legal background, the talk he had had with his coroner's officer on the previous day, made him fully aware that on this day there was drama as well as tragedy in his courtroom. Somewhere among the quiet ranks of attentive faces, there might be sitting the person who had killed Verna Hume.

Sue Thompson gave her evidence of identification in a clear, low voice. She looked to Martin Hume a little older than her thirty-one years. He had never seen her so formally dressed before: the grey worsted two-piece suit, a little out of fashion because she had had it so long and worn it so seldom, seemed almost like a uniform. She stood sturdily erect; with her dark blonde hair and blue eyes, her light make-up concealing any hint of girlish freckles, she seemed to him more attractive than ever.

But they did not look at each other in court, observing their pact to be careful until any hint of police suspicion of Martin had died. They were behaving, he thought, as if he had really killed her, instead of merely planning that he might. It was an enormous relief to him that someone else had stilled Verna's taunting mouth for ever, but he was weighed down by the enormous, inescapable fact of her death. The feeling of guilt was as strong as if he had done the deed himself.

For the first time since Verna's death, Martin felt that his head was clear and his brain beginning to work in its normal rational way. He began to speculate about who had done this thing.

The proceedings were almost over now. The pathologist was giving the evidence from his post mortem examination about the cause of death. The coroner listened in silence to the steady recital of medical terms. Then he asked the single, vital question. No, the pathologist replied in a clear, steady voice, it was not possible that this asphyxiation could have been accidental. Not in his considered, professional opinion. The traces of saliva on the pillow beside the corpse's head suggested that this was almost certainly the instrument of the abrupt ending of this life. And that pillow had been deliberately applied to the face of a woman who lay on her back at the time.

The proceedings were over surprisingly quickly. Martin had not expected that there would be a jury in this court, but there was. They brought in a verdict of murder, by person or persons unknown. As yet.

When the coroner expressed his sympathy for the bereaved husband, Martin took a second or two to realise that the remarks were addressed to him. He bowed his head in embarrassed acknowledgement. Then he looked up to see whether the policemen present were watching his reaction. He found that Detective Inspector Peach was studying not him but the people further along the row.

Peach ran his eyes rapidly over the faces in the front seats of the quiet courtroom. The face of the younger sister, Susan Thompson, who had been so composed in her evidence of identification; of the father and stepmother, Derek and Alice Osborne, sitting close together with grey, strained faces; of Barbara Harris, the business partner, leaning forward in rapt attention; of Hugh Pearson, who even in this assembly could not rid himself of that slight, supercilious smile which was perhaps by now his normal expression.

Peach noted also that Richard Johnson's dark, handsome face was not here. You wouldn't have expected him to attend, really. Johnson was a man with a busy hospital schedule, and sick people depending upon his efforts. Moreover, cynics would remember that he was anxious that Mrs Johnson should know nothing of his connection with the dead woman. And CID men were professional cynics.

It was almost like standing outside the church after a funeral service. The relatives stood in a little knot together, with other interested parties a little way further off, as if anxious not to intrude upon the family mourning.

The Osbornes talked with Martin Hume and Sue Thompson, relieved that the proceedings in court had not been as harrowing as they had feared. After the preliminary remarks, an embarrassed silence fell upon the group, punctuated only by meaningless comments about the weather. They should have been commiserating with Martin in his loss, as the coroner had indicated they might, but each of the four knew that he was glad to be rid of the wife who had died.

With sidelong, surreptitious glances, all four of them recorded the movements of Barbara Harris and Hugh Pearson, who obviously knew each other a little. The pair exchanged a few sentences twenty yards further down the pavement, then made for their respective cars. It was impossible to be certain if anything other than polite small talk had passed between them.

Eventually, Alice Osborne seized eagerly upon Sue's son as a safe topic of conversation, and Sue talked happily of Toby's progress at school, her eyes lighting up and her face clearing of the cloud of caution which had shadowed it.

'You must bring him over to see us again,' said Alice. 'He'll be old enough now really to enjoy the seaside.'

Sue promised that she would. She liked her father and his new wife and felt guilty that she did not visit them more often. It had not been easy during her divorce and the years that followed to make the journey to Lytham St Annes; it wasn't much more than thirty miles, but nothing was easy without your own transport these days. She wanted to assure them that it was genuine when she promised to visit them now.

'I'm sure Martin will bring me over, once all this is finished with,' she said impulsively, waving her hand vaguely at the court they had just left.

'I'll be delighted to!' he said quickly, smiling his pleasure. It was time to begin acknowledging the connection between the two of them, he thought, especially within the family. 'I'm sure Derek would like to see more of his grandson.'

'And so would Alice,' said Derek Osborne, asserting the right of his second wife to the family circle, as he had grown used to doing with the sisters over the years. Both he and Alice noticed that Sue and Martin were still avoiding eye contact with each other. It was as if each of them knew something they were determined to withhold, even as they moved closer to the older couple.

Sue Thompson smiled at the anxious, lined faces of her father and her stepmother, thinking how the death of her sister had released all four of this group to a new and happier life. She did not see the stocky man who had stolen almost unnoticed to her side.

'I'd like a few words with you, Mrs Thompson,' said Percy Peach. 'At the station or wherever you like. But as soon as possible, please.' He gave her his neutral smile.

Back at Brunton nick, DI Charlie Bancroft was beavering away in the CID Section.

He was a man to toe the line and keep his nose clean, was DI Bancroft: he never pretended otherwise. It was the standard way to make progress in the police force, and it had already taken him as far as inspector. Covering up Chief Superintendent Tucker's blunders made even a determinedly unimaginative man like Bancroft grind his teeth at times. But reliability is a huge virtue in the police bureaucracy, and no one was betting against it carrying Charlie even further up the hierarchy in due course.

And his methods had their virtues. Bancroft was solid and thorough, more at home with documents and paperwork than people. As part of a team rather than as a leader, he could be a strength. He was happy to beaver away at his computer, entering and cross-referencing all the material that gathered so quickly around a murder case. Although neither would have admitted it, and each professed a hearty contempt for the methods of the other, he and Peach were complementary to each other as the senior members of a team. Percy, with his determination to be out and about and his penchant for taking chances and following his insights, needed an organiser back at the station to cover his back and keep control of the accumulating detail of a serious crime case.

Now, in the quiet of the murder room, while he sorted the documents on his desk and made his entries on the computer files, DI Bancroft permitted himself a quiet smile. What he had spotted in the sheets which had come in from the bank might or might not be significant in the end. He would need to follow it up with old Muirhead, the manager.

But it was most interesting. Even that arrogant sod Peach would be forced to admit that.

Barbara Harris had never liked Hugh Pearson. She had not seen him more than three times while Verna had been alive, but he had always struck her as a man on the make. A man not to be trusted in business or in the rest of life. Sex had made Verna blind to his danger. It was ironic that her infatuation should have upset her judgement, when she had so often used her charms to lead men into rashness and bad decisions.

Now, in a context where she would least have expected it, Barbara's impression of Hugh Pearson was suddenly and dramatically confirmed as correct. The conversation in low voices which the group of Verna's relatives had witnessed but not overheard had not been a desultory exchange of pleasantries.

Hugh Pearson had communicated one vital piece of information to Mrs Harris in those two short minutes outside the Coroner's Court. Then he had gone away, with his silly smile a little wider, and Barbara had decided that he was not just smug and untrustworthy but a thoroughgoing bastard.

She drove slowly to the quiet of her house, not back to work as she had planned. She was shaken: she admitted as much to herself. It was not a normal feeling for someone whose life revolved around cool efficiency and foresight, but she had experienced it often during the events of the last week. From the moment when she had endured that blazing row with Verna over the partnership, life had not been normal. This development, when the worst had seemed to be over, was

275

something she had never foreseen.

And she could not see what she was to do about the vile Mr Pearson. Sitting with a forgotten cup of coffee going cold on the table in front of her, Barbara Harris, now sole owner of Osborne Employment, ran both hands through her chestnut hair in something very near panic.

Twenty-Two

'The last few days must have been very upsetting for you,' said Lucy Blake.

'Yes. They haven't been pleasant. I'm glad the inquest is over,' said Sue Thompson.

This was just the conventional opening, she thought, the ritual exchange of the first pawns in the game. Considering it was a game she had never played in her life, she felt surprisingly calm. She took her time and looked round the small room, with its harsh green windowless walls, its single square table with the cassette recorder, its spartan upright chairs, its stark and shadowless fluorescent light.

And she looked last of all at the two people who were to be her adversaries here. The woman who had spoken the polite and orthodox opening words was younger than her, attractive in the unconscious way which energetic people so often carry with them. She had a slightly square, attentive face and a lock of dark-red hair which strayed over the left-hand side of her unlined forehead.

The man beside her was like a medieval gaoler, she decided, with his short, powerful frame; his fierce, almost black eyes; his bald dome with its fringe of jet-black hair; his small mouth partly hidden by the toothbrush moustache; his air of muscular watchfulness.

They looked a more formidable pair in this enclosed space than they had done in the coroner's spacious courtroom. Sue determined that she would keep calm, would not be intimidated. 'Do we have to have that thing turning?' she said, pointing at the tape recorder.

It was the man who replied, as she had somehow known it would be. 'Not if you don't want it, love. You're just helping us with our inquiries. We shall want you to sign a statement in due course, though.

This could form the basis of it for our stenographer.'

Sue knew women who would have told him that they certainly weren't his 'love'. But it had fallen naturally enough from his lips, no more than a northern form of friendly address, and she did not resent it. It was a long time since she had heard anyone use the word stenographer. She nodded, accepting the explanation without relinquishing any ground, maintaining the formalities. 'I have no objection.'

Lucy Blake said, 'So you now know officially that your sister's death was not accidental.'

'Yes. But I didn't need an inquest for that. I've known from the start that Verna was murdered. You arrested her husband as soon as he reported finding her body.'

'Martin Hume was detained for a while, yes. We are now satisfied that he had nothing to do with this killing.'

'No. He was in Oxford at the time.' Sue allowed herself a smile.

Peach silently cursed Tommy Bloody Tucker and his talent for getting the wrong end of any criminal stick. He said quietly, 'Many a jealous husband has employed someone else to do his

278

dirty work, Mrs Thompson. But we don't think that happened in this case. We're beginning to get a picture of the victim now ... But you can help us to put in more detail. We need to know about your own relationship with your sister. Were you close?'

'No. We never had been very close. And we grew further apart over the last few years.'

'I see. How much do you know of her life in the year before her death?'

Sue wondered how much they already knew about Martin and her. Were they trying to trap her? She said, as calmly as she could, 'I know that her marriage had failed. That she spent very little time at home. That there were numerous other men. I don't know any details.'

'That's a pity. It's detail we need, if we're to find out who killed her. I'm sure you appreciate that.'

Sue shrugged, aware that they were studying her, handling their scrutiny better than she had thought she would. In the ninety minutes between the inquest and this meeting, she had changed into the blouse and skirt which she had brought, and the summer breeze had disturbed

279

the formality of her dark-blonde hair. She looked younger, more vulnerable than she had when giving her evidence of identification so calmly in the high room where the coroner held his court.

She smiled at them, holding Peach's formidable eyes for a moment with her own bright-blue ones. 'Other people can give you more detail than I can, Inspector. For instance, they have probably already told you that Martin Hume and I have grown very close over the last few months.'

'How close?'

She smiled again, apparently completely calm. 'We are planning to marry. We should have done so even if Verna had still been around. But it's simpler now.' She was telling herself to be careful, to say nothing that would incriminate her, but she was finding the confession of her love for Martin an unexpected relief. Living with a young child has its conversational drawbacks as well as its joys; Toby was the only person close to her, and you could not talk to a five-year-old about a developing sexual love.

Peach studied her demeanour; his assessment was so open that it was almost insolent. Then he said, 'Making difficulties was she, your sister?'

'She made difficulties about anything that would have made other people happy!' The words came vehemently, a self-justification which sprang out before she could stop herself. Sue was not calm now; she could hear her own breathing, see beneath her eyes how her breasts rose and fell as she gasped. Damn Verna, she thought, she's a menace to me even when she should be safely dead. Well, they would have prised this out of me anyway, she consoled herself, soon enough. She hadn't done any real harm by volunteering it.

Lucy Blake said softly, encouragingly, 'Yes. Other people have told us much the same thing. She stood in the way of your happiness, then?'

'Her enjoyment was to stop other people's happiness. That's the way it seemed, anyway, most of the time. She certainly enjoyed torturing Martin. She threw her own affairs in his face, but that didn't stop her taunting him about me, I'm sure. I know her of old, you see.'

Peach looked at her, watching the small hand rise to her face and try to brush away a tress of hair that had never strayed forward, and felt a little surge of excitement as he saw the cracks in her composure. He allowed a slow-burning smile to cross his lips beneath the black moustache, until he looked to her more than ever like a sixteenth-century torturer. 'So you hated your sister. And she had the one thing you wanted—her husband. Did you kill her, Mrs Thompson?'

Sue heard a rasp of breath; it was a full second before she realised that it was her own. She had known this would be an issue, but she had not expected such directness as this man Peach was using. She was rattled now, but she was obscurely aware that he might have wanted that. 'No. Of course I didn't kill Verna, any more than Martin did. She wasn't going to make life easy for us, but we'd have beaten her, in the end. It would have taken a little longer, that's all.'

Lucy Blake remembered reading some-where that murderers were often people in a hurry. Impatience overrode logic and led to rash actions. And this woman had confessed to hate of the victim and love for her husband: both emotions that could lead to violence. Trying to calm the resentment which she felt building in the woman on the other side of the table,

282

Lucy said, 'All right, Sue. You're saying you didn't like her but you didn't kill her. You may not be surprised to know that we've had similar statements from other people. We shall need to know where you were last Saturday night, though. You can see that.'

'Yes. I was at the cinema in Brunton. The Rialto.'

They hadn't expected that. They obviously thought that all single mothers should be at home with their children, Sue thought. She did not know that it was the classic weak alibi of those who had been where they should not have been at the time of a crime. Peach gave her the slightest and most sardonic of his repertoire of smiles: she felt that it should be a warning to her, but she was not sure of what. He asked, 'Alone?'

'No. I had a woman friend with me.' Against her inclination, she began to give explanations. 'I'm in a baby-sitting circle, you see. We all have young children. I've built up quite a lot of credits, because when Toby was smaller I used to take him with me in his carrycot. I still take him with me to other houses, sometimes, if I'm getting a lift home in a car: he goes off to sleep anywhere, so long as I'm with him.'

She smiled a little of her pride in the relationship with her son, wanting them to comment, to arrest the flow of her words, because she knew she was speaking too much. Neither of them did and she was compelled to go on. 'Well, I haven't had many places I wanted to go to myself, in the last few years. I've only begun to use my credits up since I met Martin.' Again she found she was asserting this new presence in her life, when she had not meant to call attention to it.

'And what is the name of the woman who was with you at the cinema on Saturday night?' asked Lucy, quietly.

'Margaret Ashton. She'll confirm it, if it should be necessary.'

'It will be,' said Peach, grimly. He looked at her dispassionately for a few seconds, then said, 'If you didn't kill your sister, who did, do you think?'

Sue managed a smile, though her heart was racing. They were going to let her go soon, she felt sure. But she mustn't overplay it, mustn't make any mistakes in the excitement of her relief. 'Isn't that for you to find out, Inspector Peach?'

His smile was broader than hers, but completely without mirth. 'Detection is our job, yes. It's also the duty of the public to give us every assistance. We shall check your story of course, Mrs Thompson. Just as thoroughly as we are checking those of anyone else who had dealings with the deceased in the weeks before her death.'

'I've already said that Martin couldn't have killed Verna. You obviously think that yourselves. I can hardly—'

'You have a father and a stepmother. What are your relationships with them?'

Sue swallowed, trying not to rush into words she might regret. 'I get on well with both of them. There was a bit of resentment of Alice when she took my mother's place, but she's a nice woman who has always made me welcome. And she's just right for Dad. Mother had been dead for years when he met her; it was a bit of a shock, I suppose. And I was younger, then: more puritanical—and more selfish.' She smiled wanly at that young woman who now seemed so far away from her as to be a different person.

'How much do you see of them?'

'Not as much as I'd like. I've no car, or I'd go over to Lytham St Annes more often. Toby loves it there—they both make a great fuss of him.' In her new life, she knew she would visit them more often, would build up the relationship between her child and his grandparents. And they must come and see Martin and her in their new home. She knew Derek and Alice got on well with Martin; they would enjoy seeing more of him. Everything was going to be easier and happier now that Verna was out of the way.

It was the torturer, of course, who dragged her back to the present and the business of Verna's death, which must be dealt with before this bright future could evolve. Peach leant forward, until his eyes seemed to look into her very soul. 'Do you know of any reason why either your father or your stepmother would have sought to kill your sister, Mrs Thompson?'

The suddenness of it took her breath away for a moment. 'No,' she said automatically. Then, feeling that more emphasis was needed. 'That's a preposterous idea!'

'Is it? Someone suffocated your sister some time last Saturday night. We can't be precise about the time. Perhaps it was while you were in that cinema.'

It sounded to her like a direct accusation.

Though she tried to return his unblinking stare, her eyes eventually fell to the table and the silently turning tape. The recorder seemed to demand some response from her. She said, 'I'm sure my father didn't do this. And nor did Alice.' The words seemed to reach her ears from a long way off, as if someone else had spoken them.

Peach studied her face for a full half-minute before he spoke again: she had a vision of sitting here, exhausted, hours from now, confessing her lies and throwing herself abjectly upon the mercy of these representatives of the state. But they couldn't conduct things like that, could they? Not in Britain, not now?

Then Peach said, 'Did Verna Hume have any jewellery which belonged to Alice Osborne?'

It was such a strange, unexpected question that she almost laughed. 'No. Well, not that I know of. No, I'm sure she didn't.' It was ludicrous. Her sophisticated sister, with her cultivated tastes and the collection of expensively set stones she had acquired as gifts from men over the last few years, would have looked with contempt on any of poor Alice's paste trinkets. Sue wanted to ask them why they had such ridiculous ideas, but she knew that they would tell her nothing except what they wanted her to know. In any case, she did not trust herself to speak. She felt her face burning with the tension; it was really very unfair that her colouring should be so revealing of her emotions.

'And your father, Mrs Thompson. Had he any reason to wish his daughter dead?' Peach's voice creaked in her ears like the turning of the rack.

She wondered why they kept harping upon the closeness of the blood ties in this death. They said most killings took place within the family. Were this pair convinced that Verna's murder was one of those? Did they really think that her father had killed his own daughter? Well, it was a plausible theory, with such a daughter as Verna. Hadn't her father seemed on the point of confessing something to Sue when they had last been together three weeks ago? She wished now that she had conferred more closely with Martin and her father and Alice after the inquest, so that they might present a united front to these probing enemies who seemed so anxious to divide them.

Sue made herself speak very slowly. 'You

must know by now that Verna was not a likeable woman. You've already said I hated her, and I haven't denied it. I'm sure she gave our father reason to hate her, too. That doesn't mean that he killed her.'

'No. We realise that. But you will see that we have to consider every possibility, which is exactly what we are doing.' The cool, soft voice came from the woman at Peach's side; Sue had almost forgotten that she was there in the intensity of her contest with the inspector. DS Blake went on quietly, 'And that means we have to include Alice Osborne also as a possible killer, until we can eliminate her from the inquiry. Our forensic people assure us, you see, that a woman, even an elderly woman, could certainly have suffocated your sister with that pillow, if she was taken unawares as she lay on her back on the bed.'

Again the emphasis that the victim was her sister, and this time the details of the death she had heard so recently in the Coroner's Court were emphasised anew, as if they felt that if the picture was vivid enough her control would crack. The image of Verna's desperate dying eyes, wide with surprise and horror, swam before her and would not be banished. She said, like one speaking through an anaesthetic, 'I'm sure Alice didn't kill Verna.'

Peach said harshly, 'Whether she did or she didn't, she has done things since the death which can only excite suspicion. So has your father. We're asking you to give us any information you possess about either of them, that's all.'

'I can't.'

'You mean you refuse?'

'I mean I don't know of any reason why they should have killed Verna.'

He regarded her for another long moment; he was as cool and objective as she was hot and ruffled. She hated him, wanted suddenly to scream her loathing at him, but no words came. She listened to her own breathing, trying hard to impose some rhythm upon it. Peach said, 'When did you last see Verna Hume?'

The fierce formality of the question, the use of the full name after all these references to family ties, almost made her laugh. But she was aware that it would not be easy to stop, if she let laughter start. 'Not for three weeks at least. I thought it best to keep out of her way. She knew about Martin and me, you see. She wasn't the type to let it go.'

'I see. We shall incorporate these things in a statement for you to sign, in due course. If you have second thoughts about what you have said, it would be best to put it right before you sign anything.' He nodded briefly at the woman beside him; from that moment, Sue Thompson, who had occupied his most concentrated attention for the last twenty minutes and more, might have ceased to exist for Peach.

Lucy Blake said, 'We can make you a quick cup of tea before you go, if you've time.'

But Sue only wanted to be out of this place, to be back in her bright little home, to sweep Toby up into her arms and clasp the innocence he represented against her body.

Lucy Blake saw her out, then went back and sat with Peach in his office. These were the best times: that thought came unexpectedly into her head. The times when they conferred, wonderfully united by the hunt, when she was taken into his mind and they swapped ideas as equals.

Percy gave her that small, welcoming smile that was so reassuring. The early days of his resentment at being given a female sergeant seemed now years rather than months behind them. This time he was silent for quite a long time, while she voiced her own thoughts about the interview with Sue Thompson.

Then he said, 'I wonder where she really was on Saturday night.'

Twenty-Three

'You'd no need to get up at this time, you know. I'm quite capable of looking after myself!'

Lucy Blake heard the petulance in her voice as she poured milk over a modest portion of slimline cereal. She was never at her brightest first thing in the morning; you'd have thought a mother might have known that after twenty-six years. It would have been nice to eat her hurried breakfast alone, to collect herself for that other, working world she should never have left.

There was no need for her to have come: she realised even through her bad temper that that was what she really resented. You thought you'd cut the old

292

ties, made yourself a thoroughly modern career woman, and then here you were having breakfast with your mum fussing round you, for the second time in three days. Agnes Blake had said on the phone that there was no need for her to come, that it was only a cold. But Lucy had worried about a cold becoming flu, had visualised her mother lying helpless with a high temperature and no one to take care of her.

Instead of which, the cold was on the mend and her mother had been able to say that there was no need for all this fuss. Lucy glanced up at the clock. Twenty to seven already. But it would be five minutes fast: all the clocks in this house had been set thus as she knew from the moment she had learnt to decode them as a four-year-old.

Her mother sniffed, blew her nose dramatically on a tissue, and said, 'I used to get up at this time every morning, when your dad was alive. We were used to early starts, in my day.'

Lucy smiled up at the housecoated figure with the thickening waist and the greying hair. 'Your day isn't that long ago, is it, Mum? And it's not over yet. They tell me you can still run rings round the younger staff at that supermarket.' No one *had* told her that, but it was a fair enough guess. Had she been born a generation later, when the working-class woman's place was no longer taken automatically to be in the home, Agnes Blake's sharp mind would have taken her at least as far as her daughter had gone.

And was going to go. Lucy wondered for a moment quite where that might be. Sometimes, when Percy Peach was charging about producing results and she was his willing assistant, there seemed no limit to her progress. She had a good base already: there weren't too many women who made detective sergeant at her age, as her mother was proud to remind her neighbours when the occasion arose.

But in the privacy of her early-morning kitchen, Mrs Blake was in disapproving mode. 'Too tight, that sweater is,' she said pontifically. 'There's no call to show off your curves to the types you have to deal with all day in that job.'

Lucy smiled. The moment took her back all those years ago to her first bra and her mother's critical assessment of her pubescent profile. 'I'm not feeling collars

294

all day, you know, Mum. It's different in CID. Most of the time, I'm dealing with perfectly innocent members of the public. I'm supposed to dress as I would if I were doing a different job altogether.'

'It was much better when you were in uniform, if you ask me. I liked you in that. You used to look really smart in the uniform.' But she hadn't approved at the time, Lucy thought. She had complained about her daughter's loss of identity beneath the dark cloth and silver buttons, had said repeatedly that it was no job for a woman.

Lucy stood up and went to look at herself in the mirror in the hall. Her figure would become positively Edwardian, if she gave it a chance, she thought. She was resigned to having to battle to keep slim for the rest of her life. She pulled the hem of the turquoise sweater her mother had criticised down a little further below her waist, noting with satisfaction how effectively the colour complemented her eyes. Men usually saw her as voluptuous; the lads at the station sometimes indulged in low growlings which were only partly parody. But that was the lustful nature of the male beast: she could handle that.

And if Detective Inspector Percy Peach had been caught out recently in the occasional admiring glance, she could handle that, too—she was almost sure she could.

In the mirror, she saw her mother standing behind her. 'Is that all you're going to eat?' said Agnes Blake in mock surprise. This was a ritual they had played out many times before.

'Certainly is, Mum. Can't afford to make my contours even more inflammatory in this sweater, can I?'

'I despair of you sometimes, our Lucy I do really. You should let me make you a proper cooked breakfast, if you want to do a proper day's work. Everyone knows a good meal at the start of the day is important.'

Agnes Blake didn't really believe it. It was a plea to be useful still to the one person who really mattered in her life, a small attempt to turn back the years to the time when a laughing pigtailed girl looked to her mother for guidance in everything. The daughter could not know how short a time separated now from then for the woman who sighed and brought Lucy her coat.

Lucy put on the coat as her mother held it for her, feeling a sharp pang of guilt she could not pinpoint. She said breezily, 'See you next week some time, Mum. I'll give you a ring to let you know just when.'

'Look after yourself, love. I wonder what you live off in that flat of yours, sometimes, I do really.' Agnes Blake was annoyed with herself. Even now, when the daughter she loved was about to drive off into that working world of which she knew nothing, she could not keep the note of admonition out of her voice. But love strikes a variety of notes, many of them unwanted: she hoped her daughter realised that by now.

Lancashire folk didn't make displays of emotion. Lucy understood that. But now, in the cool of the early summer morning, with the hour still before seven, there was no one else visible in the little row of country cottages. She flung her arms impulsively round her mother's ageing shoulders, discerned the surprise quivering for a moment beneath her fingers, and felt the strength of the older woman's answering clasp.

Then she leapt quickly into the little blue Corsa, started it first time, and drove away, her arm waving through the open window, her eyes watching the foursquare, yet vulnerable, figure in her rear-view mirror. It remained waving by the side of the house, as she knew it would, until the last vestige of her presence was removed, when the car went round the bend of the lane and out of her mother's sight.

As she drove over the deserted bulk of Longridge Fell and turned the car towards Brunton, Lucy tried to concentrate on the murder case to which she was returning. She puzzled over the statements of Martin Hume and Sue Thompson; of Hugh Pearson and Barbara Harris and Richard Johnson; of Derek and Alice Osborne. One of them at least was not telling the truth. Yet despite all her conscientious efforts to direct her thoughts to such issues, her mind kept coming back from these people who should have fascinated her to her fellow officer, Percy Peach.

It was disconcertingly unprofessional.

'Need a word, Percy.'

Charlie Bancroft looked smug. He must, then, have some information, thought Peach. The plodder had his uses, complementing the man who got out and about. And Bancroft was the best sort of plodder, dedicated and thorough. The sort who saved a lot of time for more mercurial characters like Percy. 'Is it about the Verna Hume case?'

Bancroft nodded, quietly confident. That bouncy little bugger wouldn't be able to patronise him about this. It was information gained by patience and by traditional methods, not by leaping about town and country after any lead that flashed upon the scene. And he'd caught Peach at the right moment, without that Lucy Blake around to flash her legs and twitch her comely arse about the place. DI Bancroft was a man who kept his urges under an iron control, and protested his fidelity to his plain wife a little too often to be convincing.

'I've got five minutes, Charlie, that's all. Come in here.' Peach led his fellow officer away from five pairs of disappointed constabular ears in the murder room and into the privacy of the small office afforded him by his status. 'You've found out something new. About one of our suspects.'

'Derek Osborne.'

Peach permitted his expressive black eyebrows to rise a little. The dead woman's father did not seem to have the driving energy that was usually, but not always, a characteristic of a murderer. But Percy knew better than to make assumptions about a crime that was the most individual as well as the darkest of all. 'So what's the old bugger been up to?'

Bancroft had intended to string this out a little. As usual, Percy was too direct for him. 'It may be nothing.'

'Don't piss me about with that line, Charlie. We get it too often from the public.' As you'd remember, he thought, if you went out and met them more often instead of sitting on your inspectorial backside all day. 'What about him?'

'I've been to see Verna Hume's bank manager. As you asked me to. Twisted his arm a little. Called in a few favours. He went through her last year's statements with me.'

Murder overrode even the sacred English secrecies about money. If you pressed hard enough. 'And?'

'There are regular payments from her father into Verna's account. Every month. Three thousand pounds a year in all.'

Not a great sum, for some people. But a huge one for a man with the income

Derek Osborne probably had. 'Are there any indications of the reason for these payments? A debt being repayed, perhaps?' That seemed very unlikely.

'None. I pressed old Muirhead pretty hard about it. He huffed and puffed about confidentiality and the bank managers' code, but I don't think he knew any reason himself.'

Peach frowned. 'I wonder what Derek Osborne's income is. Not a large one, I should think.'

Bancroft allowed himself a small, super-ior smile, For once, Peach had followed the script he had planned. 'His account is at the same branch. I made a few discreet inquiries about that. Leant on Muirhead pretty hard. Osborne has a regular income from pension and insurances of just over eleven thousand pounds per annum.'

Peach whistled his surprise, a sound which made sweet music in the ears of Charlie Bancroft. Eleven thousand pounds was enough to live on in retirement, if you went carefully. But not if you were paying over twenty-seven per cent of it to a domineering daughter. (Percy's dad had insisted on ten minutes of mental arithmetic every night, when it was long since out of fashion in schools.) Violence often leapt out of desperation, and desperation could burn under grey hairs and wrinkles as fiercely as anywhere else. And it was often the old who could see no way out of a desperate situation.

Percy thought suddenly of Alice Osborne and the way he had failed to cut through her deceptions a few yards away from this room. Had she been trying to protect her husband? 'No indication from Osborne's account of why he was making these payments?'

'No. But there was one other interesting thing.' In his excitement, Bancroft forgot his plan to delay this final fact a little longer. 'The last payment, a week before Verna Hume's death, was bigger than the previous monthly transfers. Three hundred, instead of two fifty.'

Lucy Blake had been informed that she was good with old women. Of both sexes. But the police hierarchy told you that sort of thing, when they were dishing out jobs no one else wanted to do, she reflected.

Her practised eye caught the face looking down from the window as she went up the stone steps to the wide front door.

By the time she was climbing the stairs to the first-floor flat in the high-roomed Victorian house, she thought grimly that she might need to be careful as well as competent, with this one.

The man was a probably thirty years older than her mother, she thought. He had very little hair, rheumy eyes, and a head which nodded continually. The first problem would be to determine how much reliance to put on what a man like this had to tell her.

'You said on the phone that you had some information for us, Mr Tattersall.'

He looked her up and down as if she were trying to trick him. 'Not for the likes of you I 'aven't, young woman. No more than for that constable who came knocking at the door on Monday. Still wet behind the ears, he was. I told 'em to send a senior officer round.'

'And that's just what I am, sir. One officer in seven in the force is a woman nowadays, you see.'

The damp eyes opened wide. The nodding head suddenly changed direction and shook disapprovingly. But the loose lips tightened: he was not beaten yet. 'I said someone senior, not a slip of a girl.'

He grinned at her nastily, triumphant in this conclusive rejoinder.

Lucy sighed, then forced a small, automatic smile. 'It may surprise you to know that I am a detective sergeant, Mr Tattersall. That's as high a rank as you're going to get, I assure you.'

She sat down beside the frail body on the sofa which seemed too large for it. A skeletal hand moved like a spider across the two feet of tapestry towards her thigh, warning her that her move might have been a mistake.

But at least her proximity made him abandon any reservations about her sex and rank. 'I saw people, didn't I? going into that house on Saturday night.' The nodding head gave a greater lunge to indicate Wycherly Croft, the yellow teeth flashed wide to indicate the value of his knowledge.

Lucy noted that he had picked up the important hours from the uniformed constable he had talked to originally. If he was sharp enough to have deduced the time of the murder, he was certainly not gaga. So he might have information that was of real value. She felt that little surge of excitement which Percy Peach said was

304

one of the rewards of the real detective.

She took out her notebook and the gold ballpoint pen, sensing that Tattersall might respond to the importance accorded to him by an official recording of his tale. The skinny hand with the brown marks on the back of it stole three inches nearer to her skirt.

'Tell me about what you saw, please,' said DS Blake, in her most official voice.

'We keep ourselves to ourselves round here,' said the old man unexpectedly. Then, realising perhaps that his visitor would not be sitting beside him if that were really the case, he went on hastily, 'But I'm making an exception now, because there's crime involved. Because it's MURDER.' He delivered the word in breathless capitals, his eyes widening and fixing upon her, his voice becoming that of the small boy now more than seven decades behind him.

Lucy leant her head confidentially six inches closer to his, keeping her eye warily on the bony hand on the tapestry. 'There was murder in that house on Saturday night, yes, Mr Tattersall. And you may be in a position to help us to see that justice is done.' She spoke earnestly, as if the aged observer were receiving some special confidence.

It had the desired effect. Horace Tattersall took a long, slow breath of satisfaction, then transformed his ague into a vigorous nod. 'I saw things, didn't I? You should have spoken to me sooner.' He smiled with a supreme smugness.

And he might have a point there, thought Lucy Blake, but she wasn't going to admit it. The fingers on the slender hand straightened like legs beneath it and carried it to within three inches of her leg.

'There was a young woman. A pretty one, with blonde hair.'

'How tall was she, Mr Tattersall?'

'About your height. Maybe a little shorter.' He let his eyes travel slowly from her neck to her ankles, dwelling with pleasure upon what they passed on the journey. 'Good figure, too, like you. *Healthy* girl.' He breathed a wealth of eager lubricity into the adjective.

'And what age, would you say?' Lucy, writing phrases dutifully into her notebook, tried to sound dull and official, so as to douse the fire in these ancient loins.

'Difficult to be certain, from up here. But she was a bit older than you, dear,

I'm sure of that.' And the hand leapt rapid as a lizard towards her groin, fastening with surprising strength upon the highest point of her thigh.

Lucy removed it firmly. She was not scared by the old man: she had learned to cope with lager louts and worse on Brunton's Saturday nights, could throw young toughs around with surprising dexterity. The hand was not moist, as she had expected, but dry and warm, like the skin of a snake a boy had made her touch years ago at school. She said, 'Show me where you watched this from, would you, please?' and the two of them stood and moved over to the window, without any reference to the activities of that mobile, optimistic hand.

'I was here, dear. I can see the whole avenue from here, if I move around a bit. And no one notices me.'

Broadly speaking, it was true. The first-floor sash window had wide panes and commanded an excellent view from its elevated position, while the surprisingly clean white net curtain probably concealed the aged observer from all but the wariest of his subjects. There was an excellent view of Wycherly Croft at the end of the cul-de-sac.

Lucy took details of what the woman he had seen was wearing. The old man was a little vague, but it seemed to be jeans, with a light green anorak above. This could well have been Sue Thompson. Tattersall didn't think he'd ever seen her before but, by her own account, Sue had been an infrequent visitor to her sister's house.

Lucy had reserved the most vital question until the last. She put it as quietly as she could. 'And have you any idea what time this woman came here, Mr Tattersall?'

He cackled delightedly beside her. 'Yes, I have. Not such a dozy old bugger as you thought, am I? It was while that blasted lottery thing was on the telly. I got up to have a walk round—well, to go for a pee, if you must know.' He sniggered at his daring. 'Thought I'd just 'ave a look out, and there she was, just going through the Humes' gate.'

Around eight o'clock, then. Lucy was getting the hang of this. She fed him the line he wanted. 'But you won't know how long she was in there, of course?'

The thin shoulders beside her at the

window shook with triumph. 'Wouldn't I, though? She was in there for exactly a quarter of an hour. I saw her come out again. Watched her walk right down to the end of the road.'

I'll bet you did, you old lecher, thought Lucy. Especially if the jeans were tight; you'd watch her until she was out of sight. Then, for the first time, she was beset by a vision of the hopelessness of old age, of the loneliness of the life that was lived in this room. She said quietly, 'You've been very helpful, Mr Tattersall. Thank you for your cooperation.'

The two of them turned away from the window. She kept carefully behind him. Sympathy need not extend to rashness: it was better not to afford groping opportunities. Tattersall sat down heavily on the sofa, as if exhausted by his evidence. He patted the area beside him seductively with the gaunt hand, but Lucy ignored the invitation. 'Thank you for your help, sir. I'd better be on my way now, so that we can use this information.'

He looked up at her. His sly old face wrinkled mischievously, until he looked so like Mr Punch that she took an involuntary step backwards. He glanced appreciatively

309

at her calves, then returned the moist eyes to her face. 'Don't you want to hear about the other one, then?'

Lucy looked down at him sharply. His head and limbs shook involuntarily, but his lips turned slowly upwards in a devilish grin. He was serious.

She sat down carefully on the upright chair opposite the sofa. 'Of course I want to hear,' she said. 'Tell me all about it, Mr Tattersall. Did you stay at the window for the whole of the evening?'

'No. What do you think I am, a peeping Tom?' He giggled uncontrollably for a moment at such a ridiculous idea. Then he leant forward earnestly, beckoning her close, affording her a gust of stale breath. 'I watched my telly, didn't I? Not that there's much on on a Saturday night. But I always watch *Match of the Day*, don't I? Last Saturday it was on early, for once. Started at ten. Should do that every Saturday, if you ask me.'

Fearing a diatribe against the BBC programmers, Lucy said, 'And did you see something while the football was on, Mr Tattersall?'

He gave her a look of mixed contempt and pity for this feminine ignorance.

''Course not. Wouldn't be missing the football, would I? It was before it started. I got up to shut the curtains, while the news was on. Put the light out first, didn't I? See more that way, you know.'

She did. And remain concealed yourself, of course. And they said it was women who watched over their neighbours like this. 'What did you see, Mr Tattersall?'

'I saw a car. Went right into the drive at the Humes' house. Brought on the security lighting, or I wouldn't have seen much—it was practically dark, you know.' His beaming face indicated that security floodlights were one technological introduction of which he thoroughly approved. 'Clear as day, it was, when that came on. It was a Volkswagen Golf. Smart black job, with a soft top.'

He was obviously proud both of his recall and of his knowledge of modern cars. Lucy had seen a car like this somewhere in the last few days, but she couldn't remember where. 'You didn't get the number?'

His face fell. He'd been delighted to place the name and the model, and yet this insistent young woman wanted more. 'Of course I didn't. Didn't know then that it would be important, did I? Didn't know that I'd be asked all about it by a pretty redhead who says she's a detective sergeant, did I?' He leered horribly at her nylon-sheened knees.

'No, of course you didn't,' said Lucy hastily. 'You've really done very well. Did you see the driver of this car at all?'

He nodded, pacified by her words. 'Another woman, wasn't it? Up to no good, if you ask me, at that time of night. Tallish woman, with dark hair. Could see that when the light came on. Older than the other one, I think, but I couldn't really see much of her face. Couldn't see what she was wearing, either, except that she had a dark coat on. She rang the bell by the door.'

'And someone let her in?'

'Couldn't see that, could I? I expect so. She waited on the step for a bit, then went into the house.'

'And was she in there long?'

'No. She came out again very quickly. Within two minutes, I'd say. The news was still on the telly. And she drove off at a hell of a rate.'

Lucy suppressed her excitement, trying hard to keep it out of her voice as she shut her notebook. 'Thank you, Mr Tattersall.

You've been most helpful. It's good to find an elderly person so observant.'

'I've kept my other faculties as well, young lady!' he said eagerly, pawing the air with his skeletal hands as he levered himself off the sofa. But she was too quick for him, making her farewells from beyond the doorway of the overheated room.

His description of this second woman, who had come to Verna Hume's house with the beginnings of darkness and left it so hastily, had not been detailed. But it had been enough to suggest to her where she had seen that Golf soft-top in the last few days.

It had been at Osborne Employment Agency. Outside the office of the dead woman's business partner, Barbara Harris.

Twenty-Four

DI Peach didn't know it, but he agreed with Richard Johnson on one thing at least. Carmen was not an appropriate name for the surgeon's wife.

She had an unlined, full, black face and a

313

figure which Percy's old mother would have said was built for comfort, not for speed. Too ample for you to imagine her dancing a habanera or clicking her castanets, or flashing her eyes at susceptible soldiers. But Carmen seemed a nice enough woman: she greeted Peach with fresh coffee. He was glad after all that he had changed his mind and come here himself instead of sending Lucy Blake.

Serenity was the word which sprang to mind, he decided, as he watched Mrs Johnson's confident, unhurried movements about her kitchen. Well, Percy Peach might disturb serenity. He was good at that.

'I need to talk to you, Mrs Johnson. About your husband. It shouldn't take long.' Not unless you're going to be as evasive as everyone else involved in this case seems determined to be, he thought.

Carmen Johnson nodded, not at all disturbed. 'Your sergeant said that on the phone when she arranged the appointment. You just need to confirm some facts you've been given, she said.'

Percy approved that. Lucy was picking up the tricks of the trade. Offer just enough information to disturb, without revealing the detail which would allow the subject

314

time to prepare answers.

'I need to ask you a few questions, Mrs Johnson. Get you to confirm something your husband has told us, if you are able to do that. It's just a routine part of our work.'

She looked at him steadily, not frowning, not smiling; it was almost as though she had set up a contest with him, in which her part was not to show emotion. 'I understand that. You are investigating the murder of this woman Verna Hume. My husband knew her, and you wish to check out his story. I would expect that.'

It was studiously deadpan; even on the dead woman's name there had been no sign of a reaction. But she had not asked him how her husband came to be involved in the inquiry, nor why he had been asked to give an account of his whereabouts at the time of her death. This woman knew that Richard Johnson had had some sort of relationship with the dead woman: she had acknowledged that. He wondered how much they had talked about this, how much the consultant had told her about his infatuation with that other, very different woman.

Peach knew suddenly that behind her

mask of indifference she was amused by him, was watching his efforts to tread carefully with a bitter detachment.

'Your husband says that he was here with you for most of Saturday night.'

'I see.' The face was as placid as ever, but he detected a gleam in the eyes which was new. Excitement? Amusement? He could not tell, and the rest of the smooth black face gave him no clue.

Peach retreated into his notes and thought furiously. This kind of exchange was a waste of time, as a rule. The wife confirmed the husband's account of things and, whatever reservations you had, there wasn't a lot you could do about it. Carmen Johnson might at least be a more convincing supporter than most wives. 'We know he was at the hospital, checking on a patient, by five to ten.'

'The young man with a bone marrow transplant, yes.'

Percy thought that he should know better by now than to be taken in by a placid exterior. This woman was as sharp, as concentrated upon what she was doing, as a cat watching a bird. 'But Mr Johnson was with you throughout the rest of Saturday evening, as he says?'

She paused a little, like an actress who instinctively makes the most of a scene's key line. 'No, Inspector Peach, he was not. He left here at half past eight.'

For the first time in their meeting, the broad face relaxed into an unaffected smile. The game was over.

The day was full of surprising women. After Carmen Johnson, Barbara Harris. She rang the station. Asked for CID. Even demanded an appointment with Chief Inspector Peach.

'We were coming to see you in any case, Mrs Harris,' said Percy, concealing his surprise, looking at the mouthpiece of the phone as if it had offended him in some way. He felt a little cheated, as if her phone call had taken the initiative away from him. He was with Lucy Blake, who had come back understandably excited with her news of old Horace Tattersall's sightings of visitors to the Hume house on Saturday night.

He put the phone down and looked at his detective sergeant appreciatively. With her colouring animated by the excitement of the hunt, Lucy made a most agreeable sight. The lock of her dark-red hair which stole over the edge of her forehead in moments of distraction was free now; it was an appealing variation. 'So what do you make of that? The lady is coming to see *us*.'

'She can't know she was seen on Saturday night. I don't see how she can even know that I've been to see old Tattersall. Maybe it's about something else altogether.'

It was logical, and it was right—or almost right. Barbara Harris was with them within a few minutes. And she was severely embarrassed. Not by the thing with which they had planned to confront her, but apparently by something else entirely.

She sat down at Peach's invitation, brushing her hand impatiently over her chestnut hair, though it was perfectly in place. Attractive hair, thought Peach, but nothing like as attractive as Lucy Blake's more definite shade of red. He decided to reserve grilling her about last Saturday night until they had cleared up why she had volunteered to come here so urgently. 'You asked to see us, Mrs Harris.'

'Yes. I'm afraid I've been very foolish.'

It didn't sound like the beginning of a

confession of homicide, but people under stress chose strange forms of words. Peach said gravely, 'It is always foolish to lie to the police, Mrs Harris.'

That was the line to take, he thought with satisfaction. Let her deny that she had lied, if she thought it wasn't true. Whether she accepted it or not, the accusation would put her on the back foot. And on a tricky pitch, with a rearing ball. Percy had been a good batsman in the Lancashire League, but he had never fancied that. He said sententiously, 'I trust you now plan to be completely open with us?'

Barbara Harris's sallow face flushed, an unusual reaction for one of her colouring; her discomfort gave Percy considerable satisfaction.

'That is why I asked to see you. I—I wasn't altogether honest to you when I told you about my last meeting with Verna. At least—well, I think I deceived you about my movements on Saturday night.'

'Tried to deceive us,' corrected Percy. He gave her his blandest, most alarming smile. He really could be quite insufferable, thought Lucy at his side. But it was very exciting. 'You told us you were on your own at home on the evening of the murder.

319

That was a lie. A foolish one.'

Barbara Harris had found this enormously difficult from the start. As a successful businesswoman running her own company, she was used to controlling interviews, not being bounced around. Now she felt panic taking over. They knew. Knew what she had come to tell them. Knew everything. She gripped the arms of her chair very hard, feeling it was her only physical hold on reality, trying to regain control of a reeling mind as she watched her fingers whiten with the pressure.

'He's told you, then. I've come too late.'

Suddenly she was furious, not with the people who were putting her through this ordeal here, but with the man who had taunted her at the inquest and now betrayed her.

Peach's mind was working fast as he watched her suffer. She could not mean Horace Tattersall. According to the old man's account, he had not been seen as he watched her drive her car into the grounds of Wycherly Croft on that fatal night.

'We know about your movements last Saturday night, yes, Mrs Harris. You were seen entering Verna Hume's house. You were also seen leaving it. At around nine forty-five. You don't deny that?'

She shook her head, feeling the blood rush again into her face. 'Hugh told me he wouldn't tell you. Just wanted me to know I'd been seen, he said. The bastard.' The word spat like poison from her lips, retaining its force even for this pair who were used to much fouler words, because somehow they knew that she was a woman not given to such invective.

The detectives, shaken for a moment by this new piece of information, but determined not to show it, did not even look at each other. They watched the woman opposite them as she glared at her shoes, trying hard to regain some sort of control of her senses, wondering now why she was here, since they seemed to know all that she had come to tell them. Lucy Blake said softly, 'When did Hugh Pearson tell you that he knew this, Mrs Harris? After the inquest?'

She nodded miserably. They seemed to know everything, these two. She should never have tried to deceive them. 'He saw me driving into the cul-de-sac, he said. Waited until I drove out again and

321

followed me home.'

That explained why Horace Tattersall hadn't seen his car. If Hugh Pearson was speaking the truth, he had seen her drive in off the main road and had waited at the end of the cul-de-sac until she returned. Peach said, 'Why did you go to that house at that hour? We'll have the truth this time, please.' Always hit a man when he was down, it was the only safe time. That was one of Percy's maxims. Even if this time it was a woman: equality demanded it.

She looked up at them, for the first time in minutes, realising now that she could scarcely expect them to believe what she had to tell them. 'I went to have one last go at her about the business. I thought if I got to her in her own home, I might get her to reconsider.'

Peach looked at her as if she were a specimen under a microscope. 'And why at that time?'

She looked at him wide-eyed. Whether in anger or surprise he was not sure. Perhaps neither, for when she replied she sounded unexpectedly embarrassed, when he had thought she was well beyond that. 'I suppose I thought that after she'd seen Hugh, she might be more approachable.

Well, all right: I mean after she'd had sex. I knew it excited her. Especially with Hugh. I thought she might be more generous, if I got to her not long after he'd left, while she was still feeling satisfied. That's why I went at that time. I knew Hugh should have been there at nine. If his car had still been there, I wouldn't have gone into the house until he left.'

'How did you get in?'

'I had a key, from the days when Verna and I started the business. We used to plan things at her house, before we had proper premises of our own.' She paused for a moment, thinking of the time when the world was at their feet and it seemed a more exciting and less dangerous place. 'When she didn't answer the door I used my key.'

She glared at them defiantly, waiting for them to challenge her, expecting them to say her story was as lame as it sounded now in her own ears. Instead, Peach merely said, 'And was she more sympathetic?'

Abruptly, Barbara was exhausted. Either this man knew what she was going to tell him and was merely teasing her cruelly, like a cat with a mouse, or he was never going to believe her. It was hopeless, and

323

her limbs felt a sudden, overwhelming lassitude. 'Verna was dead. She was lying on her bed with her eyes open. I didn't touch anything.' She spoke in a hopeless monotone.

'Not even the body?'

'No. I could see that she was dead. I left immediately. I ran out of the house. It suddenly hit me that whoever had killed Verna might still be in the place.'

There was a long pause, while they weighed this and waited to see if she would give them any more. Then Lucy Blake said, 'And this is what you came here to tell us?'

'Yes. I don't suppose you'll believe me, but I didn't know you knew already that I'd been there that night.'

Peach said, 'You made a mistake when we interviewed you, Mrs Harris. You revealed then that you knew Verna Hume had died on Saturday night, though you tried to shrug it off.' Then, because he didn't want a spat between two of his suspects in this case, Percy reluctantly broke one of his rules and volunteered a morsel of information. 'For what it's worth, Mr Pearson didn't tell us about your visit to the Hume house. Though it was of course

324

his duty to do so. Our information came from another source entirely.'

She stared at them wildly for a moment, trying to digest the implications of what Peach had said. Then she shook her head and dropped it forward listlessly, so that the grey roots at the base of that long crown of chestnut hair were for the first time visible. Lucy Blake found it one of those searing moments of pathos which strike us when we are least ready for them. She said, 'We shall ask you to sign an amended statement in due course, Mrs Harris.'

Barbara Harris looked at her in surprise; she had almost forgotten her presence in her contest with Peach. She said wearily, 'Can I go now?'

Later, much later, DS Blake sipped her half of bitter, while Percy contemplated his pint with a steady satisfaction before he touched it. The Bull's Head was almost empty in the early evening.

Lucy said, 'She thought she was coming to make a great confession, when we knew already that she'd been to that house on Saturday.'

'Deflated her a bit, that!' said Percy with

satisfaction. He took an investigative pull at his pint.

'Do you believe that she found Verna Hume already dead when she got there?'

'Worthy of further investigation, that is. But it's the one new fact that we learned from her visit that is of most interest to me. If Hugh Pearson saw her coming out of the avenue as he says, he was in the vicinity himself that night. But he didn't tell us that, did he?' Percy seemed to find his fellow golfer's omission extremely satisfying.

He allowed himself another long, leisurely swallow, set the glass down and looked at it appreciatively as he wiped his moustache with the back of his hand. 'Naughty lad, our Mr Pearson!'

Twenty-Five

The police force is a large organisation, with more personnel than even the largest of British companies. Yet its organisation is often unwieldy and improvised, owing more to historical development than to any plan based on existing situations and resources. Management structures and practices should reflect the best industrial models.

Where other forces pigeonholed Whitehall guidelines, Brunton led the way. Imitate industry, they said: right. Everything stopped for golf. Well, almost everything. Not every officer played the game, even in these egalitarian days. So on the police society golf day, well-meaning non-golfers like DI Bancroft and DS Blake could surely be left to keep the villains in check and the public in order for a day.

The only snag for Percy Peach was that he had been drawn with Tommy Bloody Tucker. He didn't believe the groups had come out of the hat that way, but he couldn't prove otherwise, and long experience of the Crown Prosecution Service had taught him that there was no use in argument without evidence.

He consoled himself that there were two other blokes in their team of four who seemed sound men, suitably hostile to incompetent superintendents. And he was out of Brunton, enjoying a bright morning by the sea on a beautiful links course; Southport and Ainsdale was certainly that.

The course was rather too good for Chief Superintendent Thomas Bulstrode Tucker, but that also had its consolations.

The first hole at S and A, as all good golfers affectionately call the course, is a long par three, nestling agreeably among the dunes and surrounded by bunkers. Superintendent Tucker regarded it with awe while the team waited to tee off and gave it as his opinion that the hole looked bloody impossible.

It was one of his better judgements of the year, as far as his own play went.

Tucker pulled his tee shot low and left into wild country. He was prepared to abandon it, but Percy found it among brambles and brushwood, in a lie which put his superior in severe danger of a hernia as he played his second. And his third. And his fourth. 'Bad luck, sir!' said Percy as a red-faced Tucker gingerly extracted his ball from the brambles with a bleeding hand.

Peach's own ball, helped by an appealing bounce from the hump on the right of the target, was on the front of the green. He holed out in three, to congratulations from the other two members of their team. Tucker mumbled a ritual approval while glaring a real and massive resentment.

The hole set the pattern for the rest of the round. Peach, favoured by a few helpful bounces which seemed wholly appropriate on such a beautiful morning, played well. Tucker having begun abysmally, got worse. Percy enjoyed his day more and more.

And, incredibly, the team prospered, even carrying such a passenger as Tommy Bloody Tucker—the superintendent spent enough time in willows and heather, far away from his three companions, for the sergeant and the young constable who were the other members of the team to be made well aware of Percy's opinion of his chief. The competition involved taking the best scores from any two of the four on each hole. Though they were invariably discarding Tucker's score, the others combined well enough to produce two good scores at each hole, and the team prospered.

Because of his high handicap, Tucker had shots allotted to him at every hole, which enabled Percy to keep him playing from some impossible situations: Tucker almost broke his wrist against a tree on the right of the sixth; on the short thirteenth, he had to play his ball from the water hazard behind the green.

'It's only just under the surface—worth a try, sir, with your extra shot. Just make sure you don't ground the club!' said Percy cheerfully.

Tucker stepped gingerly into the edge of the dark pond and stared at his battered ball with a hopeless malevolence through the water. Moments later, he emerged with his bright red trousers irretrievably besmirched to the knees with thick and evil-smelling black mud.

'Bad luck, sir,' said Percy sympathetically. 'A valiant try. I think your third effort skidded across into the bunker.'

The two other members of the team turned studiously towards the distant sea and the empty sky before they smiled.

It was at the celebrated sixteenth hole, a taxing par five known as the Gumbleys, that Tucker's humiliation was completed. With a good drive here along the valley fairway, the second shot can be played over an eighty-foot-high hill of dunes to a fairway and green that are completely invisible. The superintendent hit one of his two decent drives of the day; his malodorous two-tone trousers moved down the fairway with something approaching a swagger.

Percy knocked his second over the top of the hill with a five-wood, then insisted on climbing to the top of the bank to assist his chief. 'I can't see my ball,' he bawled back to the distant figure below him. 'This is where the team needs you, sir!' Tucker had twice asked Percy to call him Tom on the golf course, but Peach seemed unable to rid himself of his working habits. It helped to brand Tucker as a pompous twit who stood, even here, upon the trappings of rank, as people looked down at his sweating figure from adjoining tees.

Percy held a club imperiously aloft to give Tucker a line on the blind shot. The unfortunate man addressed his ball with a vein throbbing ominously in his forehead, took his club back with studied slowness, then lurched into a dramatic heave, which sent his ball low and irretrievably left. Percy, watching from the ridge with massive resignation, shouted, 'Lost in the hawthorns, I'm afraid, sir. Better play another.'

Tucker slashed his second ball on to the railway line and out of bounds. 'Never mind, sir. Difficult game at times!' yelled

Percy from his vantage point. From the second tee above the fairway, one of Tucker's contemporaries, now a chief constable and thus entitled to do such things, afforded the superintendent's efforts a round of applause and a raucous ironic cheer, so that Tommy had to grimace a smile as he trudged after the rest of his team.

Peach's ball was mysteriously safe after all, on the edge of the fairway. He made a par without difficulty. The young constable made a birdie four. He had proved as skilled as Percy had suspected he would be; to escape from work with a rank as low as that, you had to be pretty good. Well, they were imitating the practices of British industry, weren't they?

Twenty minutes later the four were back in the clubhouse. Percy left immediately to get back to the Hume murder case. His evening game at the North Lancs and this half day at Southport and Ainsdale were his only time off in a week of twelve-hour days. Leisure well earned and well spent, he thought.

Four hours after Percy's team had completed its round, when all competitors were back in the clubhouse, T.B. Tucker,

Chief Superintendent in charge of the Brunton CID section, allowed himself to be pushed forward to claim the trophy his team had won. His public skills were as polished as his golfing ones had been coarse. He thanked the S and A for their excellent course, and made a speech calling attention to the skills of his three companions in victory. His audience thought how appealingly modest he was.

In other parts of Lancashire, his staff were busily at work. He might by the end of the week be able to announce and claim credit for another sort of victory. Chief Superintendent Tucker would no doubt be appealingly modest about his own part in it.

In returning to the real world, Peach drove only as far as Preston. There he picked up DS Blake as arranged, and drove along the other side of the Ribble's wide estuary to Lytham St Annes.

The Osbornes were expecting them—Lucy had phoned to arrange this meeting in the morning. The pair looked their age as they stood together at the big window at the front of their bungalow and watched Percy's blue Mondeo turn into their drive.

Both had very white, anxious faces. They did not touch each other, but stood very close, as if each craved comfort from the other. Lucy had a sudden premonition that what came out of this meeting might divide rather than unite a couple who seemed so devoted to each other.

The four sat down in the neat lounge with its worn but comfortable furniture. 'Time for some straight talking,' said Percy Peach with relish.

The Osbornes glanced at each other, wondering how long they would be proof against such directness. Peach sat on the edge of his armchair, as impassive as a squat, perfectly modelled Buddha, his fringe of black hair neat beneath his small, delicate ears, his dark eyes giving the impression of seeing and recording more than was merely present in front of them. It was Alice Osborne who said tentatively, 'What exactly was it you wanted to know, Inspector?'

Her voice went up at the end of the sentence with her Geordie inflection. Peach gave her what he thought of as his encouraging smile. To the nervous elderly woman opposite him, it seemed to be how a shark might grin before a meal.

'You could start by telling us why you went to the murder victim's house at dead of night, Mrs Osborne.'

'I told you. I was looking for something.'

'I might buy that. But it wasn't photographs, as you admitted eventually when we questioned you about it at the station and it wasn't jewellery either, was it? Though you tried to sell us that idea as well. So just what were you looking for?'

She looked up into her husband's troubled face. He said quietly, 'It's all right, lass. You tell them. It can't hurt me.' He was as gentle, as persuasive, as if she had been a sick child.

And he succeeded, in reassuring her. She looked back at Peach and found that he had lost some of his terrors. She said slowly, 'I wasn't looking for anything in particular. I was searching for something that might connect Derek with this awful business, that's all. It wasn't until I got there that I realised how hopeless it was. Poking round in those big rooms with a torch, not knowing what I was looking for.'

There was a kind of heroism in the visit though, however mistaken it might have been. To go to a large empty house where a murder had taken place at dead of night and begin a systematic search would have required nerve in a young lawbreaker, let alone a frail old woman who had never broken the law in her life, thought Lucy. Unless, of course, she had ruthlessly smothered her stepdaughter in the same place three days earlier; DS Blake made the automatic CID reservation not to judge things by appearances.

Lucy said, 'Tell us now exactly why you went there, Alice. As Derek says, it will be much the best thing to do.'

'I was looking for something—anything —which might have connected Derek with Verna's death. She had some kind of hold over him, you see. I knew that. She may have been a bonny lass, but there was something wicked about her. Whenever she came here, she upset him, even though she was his daughter. At first, I thought it was just that she resented me taking the place of her mother by being married to him. I knew she hadn't liked that.'

'It wasn't that,' said Derek, almost as if he was talking to himself.

'No. I don't suppose I really thought it was, by the time she died. But I didn't know what it was, this hold she had

336

over him. Derek still hasn't told me.' She looked up at him, more in hope than resentment. He shook his troubled face from side to side, as slowly as if the movement gave him physical pain.

Peach said enigmatically, 'Anything there which linked your husband or anyone else with the crime was removed long before you went to the house, Mrs Osborne. That's what we put scene-of-crime teams into places for.' She looked up at him expectantly, but he wasn't going to tell her whether they had found anything in that house which linked Derek Osborne with the killing.

'No. I was a silly old bat, wasn't I? Thinking I could get my man off the hook, simply by going into the place and finding something like that.'

Her old, lined face gave a small, sad smile. It was left to Lucy to voice the chilling thought which had driven her into her bizarre course of action. 'You thought Derek had killed his daughter, didn't you, Alice? That's why you wanted to find out what hold Verna had over him. You thought it would link him with her death.'

The old grey head nodded. Confession

was proving a huge relief, when all she had anticipated was an ordeal. 'It seems awful that I could even consider Derek killing his own bairn. But you didn't know Verna.'

'No. We've got to know quite a lot about her, though, since her death. There are other people with reasons to hate her, you know, as well as your Derek.' Lucy wondered how much older than her own mother this frail, defeated yet courageous woman might be. Perhaps to children their parents were always old; to others, Agnes Blake must seem a vigorous and resourceful woman.

Alice Osborne's head now jerked up in alarm. 'I don't believe Derek killed her any more, you know. That was just a day or two of madness after her death, when we were all in shock. You mustn't take any notice of an old fool like me.'

'Not such an old fool, Mrs Osborne,' said Peach, not unkindly. 'You were right to think that the daughter had been exploiting some hold she had over the father. Wasn't she, Mr Osborne?'

The sudden switch of his focus caught Derek Osborne off guard. He recoiled six inches on his chair, almost as if he had been physically struck. For a moment, he

338

looked as if he would deny the allegation. Then he said, in a voice so low that even in that quiet room it barely carried, 'I don't want to talk about that. I can't.'

He put his hand on top of his wife's smaller one as they sat together on the sofa, but it was he, not she, who needed support now. A seagull, swooping so low over the garden that it barely cleared the line of well-worn washing, screamed harshly, its call unnaturally loud in the silence.

'You'll have to talk, Mr Osborne. We can do this here or at the station. It's your choice.' It was a line he had delivered truculently a thousand times before, but never had he been so quiet in his insistence. He sounded almost regretful.

Derek Osborne said, 'Not here, anyway. I can't do it here.' He stood up and went into the hall. For an absurd moment Lucy feared that he might run away, that they and he might have the indignity of a chase across these neat suburban gardens which the old man could never win. Then he reappeared wearing an overcoat which was of good quality but at least twenty years old. 'I'm ready,' he said. Then he went over to where Alice still sat on the worn sofa and said, 'I'm sorry, lass. I can't explain this. I love you.'

Without waiting for any reaction, he turned and led the way to the front door. Lucy wondered for a moment if he thought this would be his last exchange with his wife in this place, if he expected to be arrested and detained. But when he was sitting in Peach's Mondeo, he said, 'There's no need to go to any police station. Just take me somewhere away from Alice and I'll talk.' He waved at his white-faced wife as the car drew away from the bungalow; neither of them even attempted a farewell smile.

Peach glanced sideways at the taut figure. 'All right, Derek. We'll go wherever you say.'

Five minutes later they were sitting on a bench on Lytham Green, within a hundred yards of the defunct and sail-less white windmill which appears on all the postcards and has given that mile of smooth green seaside turf its definition, for locals and visitors alike. There was a brisk but not unpleasant breeze, sweeping in the scent of seaweed from the edge of the estuary fifty feet below them. Percy gazed across the water towards the course at

Southport, where Tommy Bloody Tucker was at that moment receiving the trophy they had won; it was scarcely eight miles away across the water, though nearer to forty by road. Already his enjoyments of the morning seemed to belong to a different world.

There were not many people about late on this midweek afternoon, so that the three could sit on a bench and speak with total privacy. The two younger figures without coats and the frail older man huddled in his overcoat looked for all the world like day trippers enjoying the sun and the sea air. For thirty seconds or so, they watched a boat on the horizon, making its slow, almost imperceptible way towards the docks at Liverpool.

Then Peach said, 'We can shorten this, perhaps. You should know that we are aware that you were making regular payments into your daughter's bank account, Derek. Payments of two hundred and fifty pounds a month. Except for the last one: that had just been increased to three hundred pounds. My guess is that this was to be the new regular sum.'

He spoke softly, almost regretfully, not at all in his usual ebullient manner. Perhaps it was just another tactic, thought Lucy. Perhaps he had decided that he was going to get more out of the troubled man beside him by persuasion than confrontation.

If it was no more than that, it at least showed insight, for Derek Osborne responded in the way most helpful to them. He said, as though they already knew everything he had to tell them, 'Verna didn't need the money, you know. It meant very little to her, but it was crippling me. I think that was what pleased her. She enjoyed hurting people. Perhaps me most of all.'

Peach said gently, 'We know that your daughter wasn't much liked by anyone. I'm sorry. Perhaps she was most dangerous to those who thought they loved her.'

Osborne looked sharply sideways at him, but Peach continued to gaze out at the swirling waters of the Ribble estuary. After a few seconds, the dead woman's father said, 'You're right. She had a hold over me. Maybe you already know—you seem to know everything else. When she was seventeen, some years after her mother had died, I went to bed with her one night.'

Lucy Blake stared resolutely out over the waters, denying herself the gasp of astonishment the old man's last words had almost provoked in her, feeling that the slightest movement from her might break the spell and stop Derek Osborne from talking. Nevertheless, the elderly man suddenly leant forward and sideways, looking right into her face, forcing her to look at his tortured, deeply lined features. 'You don't want to be hearing this, young lady.'

Lucy managed a small smile. 'I've heard much worse in this job, Mr Osborne, believe me. Many times.'

'Really? I suppose you see the worst of the world, all the time.' Then, as if he had only so much consideration to expend on others, he was back with his own agony, turning directly away from her, directing his statements to Peach, as if by shutting Lucy out of his vision he could close her ears to this. 'It was a moment of madness, and she led me on. I suppose all men say that.'

Percy, careless now of what Lucy might feel, anxious only to have the information out of Osborne, said, 'Men do say that, in all sorts of situations. But that doesn't mean that it can't be true, in a few of them at least.'

Osborne nodded abstractedly, so that they were not even sure if he had heard and registered this encouragement. 'I suppose it wasn't all that much, really, not in your terms. We kissed and cuddled, with no clothes on. There was no penetration. Not that that made any difference. Verna spoke as if I'd fucked her stupid for months on end.' The bitterness and frustration came bursting forth in the sudden obscenity from this quiet man.

'And your daughter used this incident to blackmail you. Right up to the time of her death?'

Osborne nodded wearily. 'From the time I married Alice onwards. I'd have told her to get lost if it had been anyone else she was threatening to tell. Even Sue—her sister knew well enough what Verna was like, how she liked to slash at anyone else's happiness. But I couldn't let her hurt Alice and me, could I?'

'No, Derek, perhaps you couldn't.' Peach was silent for a moment. Blackmail was the worst crime of all in his book, apart from murder, he supposed. 'But your daughter won't be worrying you any more.

344

Or extracting any more money from you. Did you kill her?'

Osborne, exhausted now, but full of the relief that the shame he had hugged to himself for so many years was out at last, allowed himself a mirthless smile. 'No. Alice thought I had done, I think. For a day or two.'

'Yes. But even then, she was anxious to protect you. It couldn't have been easy to go to that house at night as she did, even though it didn't help.'

'Will she need to know this?' Suddenly the exhausted face filled with a new alarm.

Peach said, 'Not from us, provided that what you have both told us is true. But these things tend to come out. If they do, it would be much better if she found the facts out from you. She's going to want to know what you've told us, you know, when you get back. Do you really want to feed her more lies?'

He gave a long sigh, which seemed to be dragged from the roots of his being. 'No. I don't suppose I do.'

'It won't be easy. But explain the circumstances. A lonely man and a pretty daughter up to mischief. I think she'll understand, knowing both you and

Verna. And you and Alice are a bit too old to have secrets from each other, don't you think?' He watched the old man weighing his arguments, seeing the logic, trying hard to accept that he must do what he had paid to avoid doing for years, what he had thought he had escaped with Verna Hume's death. Percy said gently, 'My colleague was right, you know. We see much worse, almost every day. It wasn't anything so very terrible. If you explain it properly, Alice will accept it, I'm sure.'

They dropped him off at the bungalow a few minutes later. Lucy looked back through the rear window of the car and watched him walk slowly, very slowly, up the short drive of the neat little bungalow, between the bright red rows of salvias he had planted out only that morning to complete his garden display. As Peach's Mondeo turned the bend at the end of the avenue, the door opened and Osborne turned towards the dark rectangle and the peace he had to make.

They were through Preston and two thirds of the way back to Brunton when Peach turned the car off the road and into the almost empty car park of a Little Chef cafe. He did not get out. Having made this first move and stopped the car, he was lost for words.

Eventually he said, ridiculously but with considerable relish, 'Tommy Bloody Tucker was bloody awful at golf this morning!'

Lucy felt as if she had been brought to a playreading and given the wrong script. 'And how were you?'

'Quite good, actually ... It seems a long time ago now.'

'Yes. You were very good with those two this afternoon.'

'Felt like a social worker with old Derek there at the end, though. I'm not much good at the caring policeman act, am I?'

'On the contrary, you were very good indeed, I thought. And it wasn't just an act was it?'

Suddenly, clumsily, they were embracing. Neither knew afterwards who had made the first move. She held him hard, feeling his broad shoulders gradually relax, caressing his lips gently with her tongue, feeling a moustache for the first time in her life tickling her upper lip. She had never fancied men with moustaches.

He let her go eventually, nuzzling her ear with his nose for a few seconds to postpone the moment when he would have to look into her face. 'You smell nice,' he muttered into the forest of clean, soft hair.

She giggled a little, breaking the spell, looking into his face, finding it full of a comical surprise she had never seen in it before. 'I think I might like a coffee now,' she said.

Later that night, Lucy rang her mother as she had promised to do. The job was going all right, she said. She thought they might be near to an arrest in the Hume murder case, if what her DI said was right.

'I hope he treats you properly, that man,' said her mother: it was one of her ritual statements of worry.

'He treats me very well, Mum. He's a gentleman, is Percy Peach.'

Parents couldn't expect to know every development in their children's lives, she thought later. And in Derek Osborne's phrase, at least there had been no penetration.

Twenty-Six

Margaret Ashton was a nice woman. Thirty-five years of age, happily married and with a picture of her husband and two lively children on the sideboard. Tall, dark-haired, intelligent, and loyal to her friends.

But she was no match for Percy Peach.

She had been determined to stand by her friend Sue Thompson. If that meant supporting Sue's story that she had been at the cinema on that Saturday night, then so be it. She knew perfectly well that a decent lass like Sue, the very best kind of single parent, could never have murdered her sister; it was surely quite impossible for anyone who loved Toby as much as Sue did to have killed anyone. Because she was such a nice woman, Margaret didn't see the *non sequitur* in that argument.

It was no contest, really. With a short statement of what a murder inquiry involved and a smiling explanation of the fate awaiting accessories after the fact,

349

Percy Peach broke her resolution to assist her friend into small pieces and cast them upon the winds of a brisk morning.

No, she hadn't actually been to the Rialto cinema with Sue on that fateful Saturday evening. No, she had no idea where she had really been in those hours when the baby-sitter had been with Toby. Yes, she realised that the bounds of friendship should have stopped well short of lying on her friend's behalf. Yes, she did see now that conspiring to deceive the police in the course of their inquiries was a very serious offence. She was really very sorry that she had even considered wasting police time like this. And she did hope tremendously that there wouldn't be any repercussions from conduct that she now realised had been very foolish indeed.

'That remains to be seen, Mrs Ashton,' said Peach as he swept imperiously out of her neat little house.

'Quarter to ten already,' said Percy, as he turned the Mondeo into the small estate where Sue Thompson had her council house. 'Doesn't time fly when you're enjoying yourself.'

Lucy Blake reflected that he had not

350

even mentioned the previous e~
the things they had done. ~0
unexpectedly that she was p~
that. She didn't want anything ~
their working relationship and wha~
was learning from it. Besides, she wouldn't
have known what to say if Percy had raised
the matter of where their private life went
from here.

Sue Thompson looked very white beneath her yellow hair. Lucy, who was
fair-skinned herself and sensitive to these
things, thought how unfair it was for
some people that their colouring should
be so suggestive of their feelings and
their health. A woman with darker skin,
a Barbara Harris for example, would have
been able to dissemble far more easily than
this vulnerable creature. Lucy decided that
almost all men were more difficult to size
up than women like this.

Despite her drawn face and pale, tight
lips, Sue Thompson tried to take the
initiative, to begin with a little show
of aggression which might keep them at
bay. 'I rang the people at work to tell
them I couldn't get in until later, as you
suggested. But they weren't pleased, and I
can't blame them—Fridays are busy days.

351

It's really very inconvenient.'

Percy grinned the mirthless smirk which said that he didn't take this seriously and wasn't going to apologise. He had on a black polo-necked shirt with sleeves which stretched tight over his muscular arms; it seemed to have been chosen to match his jet-black moustache and the neat fringe of hair round his bald dome. To Sue, he looked more than ever like the medieval torturer she remembered in drawings depicting the questioning of Guy Fawkes.

He said, 'We could have questioned you at work. But that would have been much worse for you, I think. Had you told us the truth when we saw you on Wednesday after the inquest, this meeting wouldn't have been necessary at all.'

'I don't know what you mean. I told you: I was at the cinema last Saturday night. The Rialto. With Margaret Ashton.'

She had gone straight to the single lie in her evidence, they noticed, pinpointing it for them. Her words had carried less conviction with each phrase she had spoken. Perversely, Lucy found herself reacting in the woman's favour: at least she was transparent now in her deceit, as a practised dissembler might not have been.

Peach said, 'Obviously Mrs Ashton has not phoned you in the last twenty minutes. I've come from there, you see. She wasn't able to support your story, when she knew what was involved.'

All Sue Thompson's flimsy bravado dropped away. She sat down heavily on the single fireside chair in the small lounge, whose only abnormal furnishing was the collection of colourful toys in the wire basket beneath the window. 'I shouldn't have asked her,' was all she said; her shoulders drooped heavily, making her seem squat and shapeless in the chair, as she had not been when she was standing.

'No. And she shouldn't have agreed. She realises that now.' A trace of Peach's satisfaction came out in the last phrase. 'So where were you on Saturday night, Mrs Thompson? No more lies, please: you've already wasted quite enough police time.'

When she eventually replied, Sue's voice was flat, defeated, exhausted, the voice of a woman who could no longer conjecture where this might be leading her, and perhaps no longer cared. 'I went to see Verna. At her house. Because I knew Martin was away in Oxford, you see. I suppose you'll want to know the time. It was about eight o'clock.' She delivered the facts she had tried so hard to conceal all at once, like pieces of garbage she was anxious to bin and be rid of.

She stopped there, as if she had told them all they needed to know and cast away her last defences. Lucy Blake said softly, 'And you wore jeans and a green anorak. Your visit was witnessed, you see, Sue. You were observed both entering and leaving the house.'

A grim, hopeless smile at her own naivety, at the idea that she should have even thought that she could deceive the police machine with her feeble lies and her flimsy attempt at an alibi crossed her face. 'I went to plead with Verna. To ask her not to make it difficult for Martin to divorce her and come to me. I should have known better.'

'She refused?'

'No, she didn't. But she laughed at me. She said that she'd finished with him, and I was welcome to what was left. She said she'd already told Martin he could have his divorce, but it would cost him. He'd have to pay to get rid of her. Then—then she was awful about

Martin and what he did in bed. Said she supposed it might be all right for a cabbage like me.'

Her voice should have been shrill with emotion and resentment. But it remained flat and defeated, though her cheeks were suddenly wet with tears. Lucy prompted, fearful of the reply she might hear, 'And did you kill her, Sue?'

The moist blue eyes looked up at them, for the first time in minutes. But Sue Thompson made no attempt to defend herself. She sounded almost surprised as she said, 'No. I stopped up my ears at the things she was saying about Martin and me. She was screaming at me, like a witch. Then she looked at the clock and told me to get out. Said she had a real man coming to see her. A man who knew what a bed was for. A man who knew how to please a woman.'

'So you left. At about quarter past eight, would you say?' Lucy quoted Horace Tattersall's timing: he had thought she had been in the house for about fifteen minutes.

'I don't know. Probably. I was too upset to notice the time. I just wanted to get away, as far from her as possible.'

Peach came in again, turning the screw of the rack he had left untouched for a good five minutes. 'So you've now confessed to a heated argument with the deceased on the night of her death. But you're telling us that your sister was alive when you left.'

'Yes.' Listless still, as if she no longer cared whether she was believed or not, as if events must now take their course without any further attempt at interference from her.

Lucy Blake felt that she carried some of the other woman's heavy, defeated emotion back into the car with her. She was grateful to Percy for dissipating it as they drove out of the winding avenues of the council estate. 'A quiet Saturday night, and people in and out of that respectable bloody house like a dockside brothel!' He sighed. 'Thank heavens for nosy old buggers like Horace Tattersall.'

The sun was high as the morning advanced towards noon; only a few weeks to the longest day of the year. Percy whistled softly at the wheel as they drove through the highest part of the town, along a ridge where the few mill chimneys which had not been demolished lay like smokeless skeletons below them. The air was clear and the sun was warming even the brisk breeze which swept across this elevated road.

'You're cheerful,' said DS Blake.

'I usually am, when we get near to an arrest. It's the thief-taker in me. Except that this is more than a thief. Besides, I shall be able to play golf this weekend, if we've solved this one.' He whistled again the finale from Haydn's trumpet concerto, which he had heard that morning on Classic FM and could not get out of his mind. Being quite new to the game of golf, though he had been a league cricketer of note for fifteen years, experience had not yet taught him the golfing axiom that when you arrive expecting to play well, you invariably play badly.

Lucy thought furiously, wondering if she had missed some vital, obvious fact in all this. She said a little desperately, 'They all seem to be telling the truth to me. Perhaps I believe people too easily to be a CID sergeant.'

'Possibly.' Percy smiled happily. 'Most people do tell the truth to the police, most of the time. Trouble is, it's the lies that are the interesting part, usually, so you have to spot them.'

'What about Sue Thompson. Was she telling us the truth?'

Peach pursed his lips. 'I should think so, wouldn't you? She didn't strike me as being a good liar. But then the best ones never do.' He turned the car into the private parking beside the Georgian building which housed the head office of Pearson Electronics. 'Hugh Pearson thinks he's a good liar. But he isn't, is he? Bet you wouldn't trust him, even when he was telling you the truth.' He threw open the driver's door and sniffed the day appreciatively as he stepped out. 'Let's get him hopping about a bit, shall we?'

Hugh Pearson made a great play of telling his secretary that he was not to be disturbed during their visit. 'If there are any calls, I'm in a meeting. And you'd better get on to Charles Yates: tell him I'll ring him back as soon as I'm through with this.'

He took them into his spacious private office and waved a hand expansively at the armchairs opposite his desk. 'I hope this won't take long. Naturally I'm anxious to be of every assistance to our gallant defenders of law and order—especially when they arrive in so comely a form.' He afforded Lucy one of his most appreciative smiles as his eyes ran swiftly over the nyloned knees below him. 'But you do come upon me in the middle of a very busy day, and I can't pretend it's entirely convenient.'

Peach waited patiently until the words dried up and the blue eyes transferred themselves reluctantly from DS's thighs to DI's face. Then he accorded Pearson his own pre-prandial smile, which had been compared to a hungry Dobermann's recognition of its dinner. 'Shouldn't tell us porkies, lad. Then we wouldn't need to interrupt the smooth running of the emporium.' He looked round the room, taking in the drinks cabinet and the expensively framed prints on the wall, deliberately keeping his eyes off the face of the man at the wide mahogany desk.

Pearson found this quite unnerving. It was difficult to bluster when a man didn't look at you, but he had a try. 'Now look here, Inspector, I've changed my schedule to accommodate you, and if the best you can do is to come in here accusing me of lying, then I'm afraid I shall feel compelled to take things up with your superiors. I'm sure Superintendent Tucker wouldn't be pleased to hear that you'd been making wild—'

'Superintendent Tucker would be most interested in the full details of your relationship with Verna Hume! Which we haven't yet explored.' Peach's black eyes fixed on him suddenly, then seemed to bore into his face as the colour left it. His words flew like stones across the wide, low-ceilinged room. Lucy had the strangest feeling that Percy was defending her honour against this vain and shallow man, that his anger this time was real, not feigned. She thrust aside this surely ridiculous idea.

Hugh Pearson was shaken, but he was not so naive as to pinpoint the area of his lying for them, as Sue Thompson had done with her denials. He said, 'I told you we were lovers. That we had been for months. What more do you want? The details of the positions we adopted? The number of times we did it with her on top? How often she—'

'If we thought these things were relevant, we should certainly ask you about them. In the meantime, you might tell us why you chose to conceal the fact that you had arranged to meet Verna Hume on the night of her death.'

Pearson's eyes widened, staring like a transfixed rabbit's at Peach's stoat's smile. But the next blow came from another source. DS Blake's voice came soft and cool. 'We have the dead woman's diary, Mr Pearson. Your name is the only entry under last Saturday's space. It has the time 9 p.m. beside it.'

'Which is very near the time she died,' said Peach triumphantly, as if he was slipping the last piece into an agreeably taxing jigsaw. 'Both the forensic evidence and our own inquiries over the last few days now indicate that.' He appeared to find that thought infinitely satisfying as he watched the man before him quite literally squirming in his executive chair.

As Hugh Pearson transferred his weight from buttock to buttock and back again, the leather seemed to be getting uncomfortably hot beneath him. 'I didn't go there. Not on Saturday night. All right, I should have done, but I didn't.'

'And you expect us to believe that?' Peach's tone echoed just how ridiculous that notion was.

'It's true. Honestly, it's true. Look,

Inspector, I can see now that I've been a fool.'

'Really, sir?' Peach's long-suffering face said that such an obvious fact should have been apparent to the man long ago. 'Would you care to tell us where you were at nine o'clock on Saturday night, then?'

'I—I didn't go to see Verna. I wasn't at the house on Saturday night.'

'I see. And yet you claim to have been able to see Mrs Harris leaving the place. To be more specific, you say that you saw her driving away from a house in which lay a body which was still not yet cold. Because she found in Wycherly Croft a woman who had been killed within the previous hour.' No harm in accepting Barbara Harris's version of events, thought Percy, if it put this smug bastard on the line. Wet lettuces, his mother used to call people like Pearson; but language had gone downhill since then.

'I've been a fool. Nothing more than that.' There was rising panic in Pearson's insistence which Peach sniffed appreciatively.

'You've got some convincing to do, lad. Can't expect us simply to believe you, you know. Especially when you've lied to us before.' Peach seemed to find that reflection splendidly gratifying. He gave Pearson his most relaxed smile, like a dog surveying a bone which it knows is coming its way any minute now.

'I didn't go to Verna's house on Saturday night.'

'So you say. Yet the evidence of your appointment is there in the murder victim's diary. It was only when we presented you with that fact that you even admitted you'd planned to be at Wycherley Croft.' Peach pursed his lips and whistled soundlessly through them. 'And then Mrs Harris says you've admitted to her that you were in the vicinity at the time of the death. Looks bad, to suspicious CID officers like us, that does, Mr Pearson.'

Pearson looked desperately at the woman he had hoped to charm, but found no solace there. Lucy Blake, taking her cue from Percy, did not look at their panicking victim, but shook her head in sad agreement with her chief. She pretended to consult her notes. 'Nine o'clock, it says in Verna Hume's diary,' she confirmed, as if she felt the case was about to be wrapped up.

'All right! I should have gone there, but I

didn't.' Pearson was shouting now, heedless of what his curious staff might hear on the other side of the heavy mahogany door. 'I wanted to tell Verna I was going to finish our affair. It was all getting too heavy for me. She was talking about marriage, about divorcing her husband to be with me, but I wasn't ready for that.'

'So why didn't you simply tell her that?' Peach made it sound the easiest thing in the world.

'I wanted to. I'd tried to hint that I wasn't into the affair as seriously as she thought. But she wasn't an easy woman to talk to.' To Pearson, who always talked among his drinking companions as if he could handle any woman, the first admission he had made in his life that he had actually been afraid of one was peculiarly difficult. 'I planned to tell her on Saturday night. I—I sat in my car for an hour at the end of her road, rehearsing what I would say, what I would do when she turned on me.'

Peach glared at him, daring him to say more. 'And that's today's story, is it?'

'It's the truth.'

'Hmm. No witnesses, I notice.' He

brightened, as though an acceptable solution had just struck him. 'What about a lovers' quarrel between the two of you, with her screaming and you trying to shut her up, pushing a pillow over her face to stop her shouting, holding it there. You might even get away with manslaughter, with a good brief.'

'No! I didn't go into that house at all. I've told you the truth.' But Pearson was defeated now, scarcely expecting to be believed. He said desperately, 'It was while I was sitting at the corner of the main road, trying to pluck up the courage to confront Verna, that I saw Barbara Harris drive into the cul-de-sac, and come out again a few minutes later. I guessed she'd been to Wycherley Croft.'

'What time did you get there?'

'I was supposed to meet Verna at nine, as you say. But I was late. It must have been after half past when I got to the end of the road: more like quarter to ten, I should think. I'd been driving around trying to plan what I was going to say to her.'

'Did you see anyone else you knew turn into that road?'

'No. It was nearly dark. I only recognised

Barbara Harris because I knew her car; I'd picked Verna up from Osborne Employment a few times. I thought it was her, so I watched for her coming out again.'

It was probably true, Peach decided reluctantly. And if it was true, Pearson would not have been parked there when their killer drove in to Wycherley Croft on that fateful evening. 'Don't leave the area without letting us know your movements,' he snapped irritably as he rose.

Then, abruptly, they were gone, leaving a severely shaken businessman combing his tousled fair hair and wondering how much of his discomfiture would be apparent to his staff when he felt ready to move among them again.

Peach drove slowly, revolving events in his mind, wondering how much resistance their murderer would offer, reviewing the evidence they could offer the Crown Prosecution Service if a vehement denial was the response.

There had been silence for a full five minutes when Lucy Blake said, 'She isn't much of a loss to the world, this Verna Blake. But I know it's not our job to worry about things like that.'

'And thank God it's not,' said Percy

firmly. 'This job's difficult enough as it is.'

He might have been more severe upon her for such unprofessional thoughts, he supposed. But they made her sound very young and innocent, the way he might once have been himself, though he could not remember it. Made you blinkered, sometimes, this job did: you had to be, if you were going to collar the villains. He would have preferred a different murderer himself. But crime wasn't tidy, and it was just as well you didn't have a choice, sometimes. Certainly just as well for that conceited young wanker they'd just left.

And there was always the excitement that came from closing the net on a killer.

Twenty-Seven

It was not a theatre day for Richard Johnson. Good word, theatre, he thought. He never went in there to perform as a surgeon without the nervous excitement which all actors are said to feel in the wings while they waited to go on stage. Once there, he lost his tension in the supreme concentration which was necessary for success. But he was always aware that he was the star, the central figure around which the drama of life and death revolved in that quiet, enclosed, sterile room called the theatre.

It was the place where he was most at home, most sure that he was thoroughly in control of both himself and events around him. But the rest of the hospital was good too. He felt a surge of contented confidence as he drove between the high Victorian pillars which were almost all that remained of the original building. He was lucky, he thought, as he parked the big BMW in his designated space: not many people actually enjoyed going to work as he did, or experienced that little surge of satisfaction he felt as he moved from private into public life.

He conducted his morning ward round in his usual self-assured manner. He was brisk, more so than the other consultants, yet his patients never felt that this was an empty exercise, or that he did not have time for them. There was no small talk, but he knew each individual by name;

knew the details of their cases and what he was trying to achieve with them; knew their worries about what was going to happen next.

He offered comfort, but no false comfort. When he agreed with the ward sister that a mother of two young children might go home, he shared her joy in the reunification of the family. Without any affectation, he went behind the screens and held the wasted hand of the man who was transferring to a hospice for his final days, sharing his serenity, envying his courage, thanking him for the little, unsuccessful time they had spent together, finally silent because his charge wanted to be quiet for these last few moments they would spend together.

The old man looked at the edge of his cold, wasted paw, almost invisible between the surgeon's dark, strong, yet delicate hands. He said, 'I didn't want a darkie to treat me when I came in here, you know, lad. It seems daft now, right daft. But it shows you can still learn something, even right at the end.'

Richard Johnson smiled down at him. He did not speak. Watching the little cameo, the sister decided that knowing when to be silent was one of his greatest strengths in his exchanges with patients. After a little while, the consultant rose.

'Goodbye, Walter,' he said to the old man. 'You're going to the best place, you know. I'd like to go there myself, when the time comes.'

Although he was used to death, the bright weather outside seemed inappropriate to him as he went out into the broad corridor which linked the wards. Life went on, as everyone knew, but weather like this seemed to mock those who had to leave it. Death should come dressed in nature's wilder garb, with thunder and lightning and storm, as Shakespeare dressed it. Or was that just abnormal death, like Verna's?

When he went into his secretary's room, she was standing, looking at a picture on the wall. He scarcely ever saw her like this. Almost always, she was at her desk, with the wordprocessor whispering in front of her and the filing cabinet within reach on her right-hand side. She was clearly upset.

'Those detectives are here again. I put them in your consulting room.'

She should have worn a black cap, he thought, for she made it sound like a sentence of death.

He found them standing by the window, looking across the canal at the old industrial town with its grubby nineteenth-century bricks and its terraces of workers' houses snaking away over the hills. It was not until they were all seated that Peach said, 'Have you spoken to your wife, Mr Johnson? Since we visited her yesterday, I mean?'

'I didn't even know you'd been to see her,' said Johnson. And in that moment, he knew he was lost. It was over. He didn't know how he could ever have thought he might get away with it.

Peach, as quiet and to the point as Johnson had been himself with patients a little while earlier said, 'She wasn't able to support your story. About your movements on Saturday night, I mean.'

He nodded, accepting, feeling his world tumble about him, envying that old man he had just left who was about to die. When he did not speak, Lucy Blake prompted, 'It *was* a story, wasn't it, Mr Johnson?'

He didn't answer her directly. He said with infinite sadness. 'So Carmen didn't help me, in the end.'

Peach said, with a touch of his normal harshness, 'She couldn't, could she? You

371

were asking her to lie, to shield a murderer. We should have arrested you eventually, without her help, and then she'd have been an accessory after the fact. And where would your children have been then?'

Johnson nodded, speaking as if in a dream. 'The children always meant most to her. But that's fair enough. I didn't deserve to be put before them.'

Peach cautioned him then, in a measured voice, speaking the ritual of arrest which was so familiar to him, so strange to the dark-suited man before him. Johnson listened like one in a dream to the warning that anything he now said might be given in evidence. At first they were not sure that he had registered the notion that it might prejudice his defence if he did not mention when questioned something which he might later rely on in court; then he swatted the air near his temple as though a troublesome fly was plaguing him.

'If Carmen isn't supporting me, I'm finished,' he said. He sat down at the desk he would use no longer, and for a moment it seemed he might cry. But then he put his elbows upon the desk and set both hands precisely at the edges of his forehead, as if it was important now that his head should have support. 'She should have told me, that's all. That would have been a kind of loyalty.'

Peach, scenting a descent into the examination of a marriage, said briskly, 'You went out earlier than you said on Saturday night, didn't you? And you went to Wycherly Court before you went to the hospital.'

Richard Johnson nodded slowly, then spoke as if even now he could not quite comprehend his actions. 'I went to see Verna. To tell her I was serious, as she had pretended to be when we—when we first got involved.' He glanced quickly at Lucy, and she realised that he had almost said, 'When we first went to bed together.' Such old-fashioned consideration came oddly from a murderer, she thought.

Peach said insistently, 'And you argued. And the argument ended up with your killing her.'

'Yes. I couldn't believe what had happened at first. I still find it difficult to believe it now, though of course I must.'

That was the line for him to take in court, thought Peach. Crime of passion. British judges weren't yet as sympathetic

373

to the idea as the French, but they were moving that way. Johnson would no doubt have the best brief for the job: Percy used that thought to harden his line. 'You didn't get what you wanted. So you suffocated her. Your mistress became a victim.'

Johnson, as a scientist, accepted each unwelcome statement with a tiny nod, as a fact he could not dispute. 'She told me I meant nothing to her. Never had done. It had been a fling with a black prick, she said, nothing more.' This time he was too involved with the pain of his recollection to consider DS Blake's reaction. 'She told me to go home to my dull wife and tell her that Verna Hume had bigger fish to fry.'

Peach, trying to take the emotion from a confession he needed, said quietly, 'This exchange was taking place at about quarter past nine, I suppose.'

For a moment, Johnson looked at him as if he could not comprehend the question, as if time was irrelevant in this maelstrom of lust and hatred. Then he actually smiled; perhaps in bitter resignation, perhaps in recognition of the farce that lay at the heart of his tragedy. 'Yes. She said that I was ridiculous: that the idea that she might have lived with me was even more ridiculous. Perhaps I looked amazed: I don't know. I don't remember saying anything. Then she told me to get out, because the man she was going to marry was coming to the house tonight—he was already overdue. He was going to take her in this very bed, she said. I should go home to my wife and think about them coming together. It might get me going.'

The surgeon was suddenly very still, repeating the phrases like one under hypnosis, as if it was important to get them exactly right, until they could see the scene in that bedroom, where the corpse had lain undiscovered for another day and more.

Peach said quietly, 'And that was when you killed her.'

The even, trance-like tones resumed. 'I found myself with the pillow over her face. Anything to stop that awful mocking voice; anything to cover that harridan face that I had thought I loved. I've no idea how long I held it there. I don't think I even thought of killing her. I just wanted to make sure that when I took the pillow away there would be no more words, no more of that mouth twisted in such contempt for me. But I knew she was dead when I left, of course. I am a doctor, you know.' He smiled again; this time there was no doubt that he was appreciating the irony of that fact. 'I had written Verna a rather foolish letter declaring my love for her. She waved it in my face while she taunted me. I took it away with me.'

'And you went directly from Wycherly Croft to the hospital.'

'Yes. I was coming here anyway, to check on my patient. It was only when I got here that I thought I might be able to establish an alibi.' He stopped and looked around the bright room, as if he were coming out of his self-imposed trance. 'I can think here, you see. I've been all right at work this week, even after that dreadful night. Even when I felt you getting closer to me.'

He was like Othello, thought Lucy. That other man who had killed a wife in her bed had been perfectly at ease in public office, master of all he ruled, yet totally lost in the intimacies of his private life. She bent to the shoulder bag she had set beside her chair, producing the handcuffs she had brought for this arrest.

Richard Johnson looked at them; they were the first intimation of the horrors which lay ahead of him. 'Is that really necessary? I still have a reputation in this hospital. I have done quite well here, I think.'

Or as Othello said, 'I have done the state some service', thought Lucy. She looked at Peach, who gave her the slightest of nods. Thankfully, she returned the bracelets to her bag.

Three minutes later, she sat with Johnson in the back of the police car. He looked not at her but at the grimy streets of the town he had served so well, at the people he passed, who would be reading the sensational tabloid accounts of his fall the next morning.

Back in the office beside his consulting room, his secretary, her experienced, efficient face streaming with tears, was ringing round to cancel his list of appointments for the afternoon. After each call, she strove to compose herself for the next one, muttering over and over again the same phrase.

'Such a waste,' she said. 'Such an awful, awful waste.'

This Large Print Book for the Partially sighted, who cannot read normal print, is published under the auspices of

THE ULVERSCROFT FOUNDATION

THE ULVERSCROFT FOUNDATION

. . . we hope that you have enjoyed this Large Print Book. Please think for a moment about those people who have worse eyesight problems than you . . . and are unable to even read or enjoy Large Print, without great difficulty.

You can help them by sending a donation, large or small to:

The Ulverscroft Foundation, 1, The Green, Bradgate Road, Anstey, Leicestershire, LE7 7FU, England.

or request a copy of our brochure for more details.

The Foundation will use all your help to assist those people who are handicapped by various sight problems and need special attention.

Thank you very much for your help.

Other MAGNA Mystery Titles In Large Print